Altered Realities
Copyright © 2018 Joseph W. Bebo
Published by Joseph W. Bebo
(An imprint of JWM Bebo Books Publishing)

Joseph W. Bebo
PO Box 762
Hudson, MA, 01749
Email: joewbebobooks@gmail.com
Editor: James Oliveri
Interior and Cover Design: Elyse Zielinski
Back Cover Painting: from Jess Bebo Collection

Library of Congress Cataloging in – Publication Data
Joseph W. Bebo
Altered Realities /Joseph Bebo – First Edition

ISBN: 978-0-9982182-8-1
Science Fiction /Intrigue and suspence

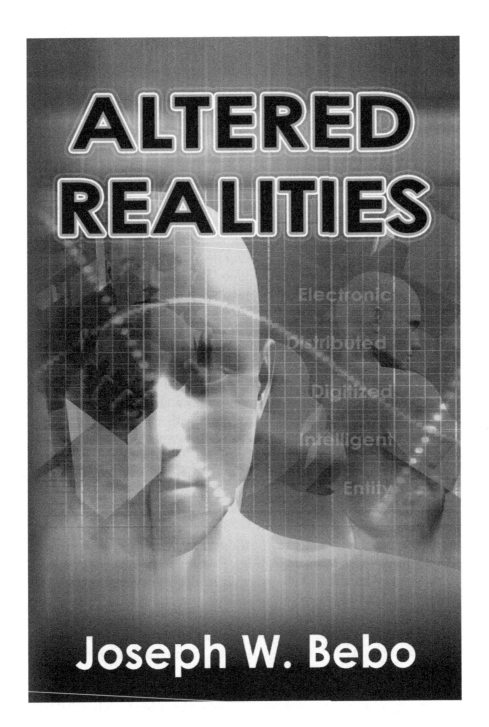

ALTERED REALITIES

Electronic

Distributed

Digitized

Intelligent

Entity

Joseph W. Bebo

Chapter 1

Dr. Edward Spencer surveyed the city below his twenty-fifth story office. Head of a leading high-tech, research firm, he was one of the preeminent computer experts in the world. The city lay at his feet. Nothing seemed beyond his reach. Dr. Edward Spencer was on the brink of a great discovery. He was about to discover himself.

He had been thinking of his past, something he was doing more often of late, between his myriad other thoughts and concerns. The memories made him both happy and sad. Happy because they were good memories, filled with achievements and success. Sad because he had no one to share it with, no parents, no companions, not even a friend. But he was far too busy to dwell on these things for long.

His secretary interrupted his thoughts. Nancy was good at interrupting the thoughts of men. Whenever the twenty-five-year-old entered the room, their attention instantly turned to her, but even she found it difficult to distract Eddie's legendary concentration. Still, he stopped what he was doing and greeted her with a smile.

"Sorry to interrupt, Doctor Spencer, but Professor Knowles is here to see you."

Edward complemented her on her new hairdo, a short summer cut, but grew embarrassed when she noticed him staring at her breasts. She looked at him questioningly and waited for an answer to her announcement.

Nancy was a year older than Edward and much more experienced. Despite his loving home and high IQ, Eddie had been taught nothing about the facts of life, and was woefully inadequate when it came to women. In an attempt to alleviate that problem, he studied it like any other, analyzing it, breaking it down and looking at the pieces. His parents had died in a car accident when he was fourteen, so Edward had to figure it out on his own, observing the human mating ritual like an anthropologist studies a group of monkeys. He watched movies and plays, read books, and hung out at night clubs, where there were plenty of examples of the successful conquest of one sex by the other. All he had to do was internalize it and make it his own. That was the hard part.

"How is your mother doing?" he asked, remembering something she had mentioned in one of her previous visits, something about an automobile accident.

"Better," she said, relaxing a little and glad to share her recent worries with somebody. "But it was touch and go for awhile. They didn't know if she'd ever walk again. She's doing fine now, up and about and as feisty as ever, though she needs a cane."

"She must be a tough old lady," said Edward, happy he had said something to make her feel good. He let her go on, glad she was doing most of the talking.

"I'm thinking of taking her to a concert now that she's feeling better, maybe to the Philharmonic. She loves classical music."

"There's a performance of Mozart music coming up next week."

"Yes, I know. She just loves Mozart. I tried to get tickets, but they're all sold out."

"Perhaps I can be of assistance," offered Eddie. "Tom Brody down at HR might be able to help. I'll have him call the ticket agency. It's the least I can do for keeping you late so many times."

"You don't have to do anything like that, Dr. Spencer, although my mother would love it. We can get tickets for another show. It's no big deal."

"It's no problem at all, Nancy. We do things like that for our employees all the time, especially a hard worker like you."

"Thank you, Dr. Spencer."

"Please, call me Ed. We work together too closely for you to call me Dr. Spencer."

"Oh, I almost forgot, what about Professor Knowles?" she stammered, embarrassedly.

"Tell Andrew to come in, thank you, and see that we're not disturbed."

Dr. Andrew Knowles was not an employee of Altered Realities Corporation (ARC), but as a co-founder he could come and go as he wished. He had acted as Eddie's guardian and mentor when his parents died, although Edward, at fourteen, was already a freshman in college. Knowles continued to mentor the boy through the years and had become his confessor, of sorts.

"Hi, Edward," said the aging scientist, long passed retirement age in the hectic, dog-eat-dog world of hi-tech academia. "How's life?"

"Good," answered Eddie, who always felt on top of the world. It only took Knowles a few minutes to peel away the good feelings and reach the anxiety and doubt.

"Are you still having those dreams," he asked, "about the tunnel?"

"No, not in awhile," replied Edward. "I haven't been remembering my dreams lately."

"That's not good," answered his mentor. "Your subconscious may be trying to tell you something."

"I don't miss all the running around and angst while I'm sleeping. If I can't have nice relaxing dreams, I don't want any."

"What do you think the tunnel means?" probed his old teacher.

"I don't know."

"Have you thought about it?"

"Yes, I ponder all my dreams, when I remember them."

"Do you feel trapped somehow, like you're in a tunnel with no way out?"

"No, I feel lonely."

"Lonely?" said Knowles in surprise. "Why? You're surrounded by people every day. You're hardly ever alone."

"Yes, but I feel alone, like I have no one to share things with. I'm alone at night."

"You have me. You know you can always talk to me, like we're doing now."

"No, I mean share things of a more intimate nature."

"Like love?"

"Yes, falling in love and having someone fall in love with me would be nice."

"All in good time, my boy, if you're lucky. Like I've told you, there will be plenty of time for that kind of thing, once you meet the right person."

"The right person," Edward said, as if to himself. "Yes, the right person. Now that you mention it, I do feel trapped. My work and responsibilities don't give me much time for meeting the right person."

"At least you're not making enemies. Speaking of which, have you talked to Jack lately? How are things between you two?"

"He's still hounding me about that defense contract. I don't know how many times I have to tell him, we don't build weapons."

"And what does he say?"

"He says they want to use it for training and simulation, but you and I know it goes a lot further than that. He's trying to sell them a bill of goods that just doesn't exist. They can go to some other company if they want to make weapons."

"There are no other companies. No one else can do what you do."

"They'll just have to wait then. If he gives me any more trouble or tries to go behind my back, I'll fire him."

"You can't do that. Only the Board can fire a Board member. We'd have to vote on it, and it might be close. He has a lot of friends."

"And I don't?"

"Like you said, the whole company rides on your shoulders. That's a lot of responsibility to bear. A lot of people rely on you for their livelihood, and soon the world will be relying on your inventions. There's an old saying, it's lonely at the top. It's true, that is if you really are at the top you want to stay there."

"I don't know. Sometimes I wonder."

"What? What do you wonder?"

"I wonder who I am."

"Who you are? Edward, you know who you are. You know who your parents were. You know who their parents were before them. "

"Sometimes I think I'm who you and they told me to be, but who am I really, deep down inside? I want to know how to talk to a woman. I want to please a woman."

"I heard you with your secretary. You had a lively banter going there."

"Yes, because I let her do all the talking. She's different than most girls."

"That's the secret of getting along with a woman. Let her do all the talking. Just don't get any ideas. Nancy may be a nice enough girl, but she's certainly not the right one for you. I don't think she even has a high school diploma."

"What's that got to do with anything?"

"Nothing, except for compatibility. You know company policy. Your lawyers have told you many times not to date or fraternize with your female employees. Remember what happened last time. You'll open yourself up to all kinds of trouble."

When Edward remained silent, the professor went on.

"Remember your parents. Never forget they are watching you, that you carry their good name on your shoulders. Remember what you have been taught from your earliest days. Remember your promise, what you swore to them. You must uphold their legacy and their memory. You are special, Edward, and must carry their name into the future. You will build a new tomorrow, but you must do the right thing today. You must keep yourself pure and stay focused on the goal."

"Maybe the world can wait while Edward Spencer has a date."

"Don't worry, there's plenty of time for that. In the meantime, I'll see if we can't get you a holo-companion. They're almost real."

"That won't help. It's not sex I want as much as friendship. Susan's different. I can talk to her."

"Then you will have to fire her, and she's too good a secretary for that. Look, don't worry about all this now. You're on the threshold of something tremendous, working on something that could change reality for millions of people. Keep your eyes on the ultimate prize and you will meet all the women you would ever want to meet. Right now you don't have time for that."

Edward didn't like it when the professor talked down to him, but his mentor always seemed to know what was good for him even when Eddie did not. As much as he resented being treated like a child, the professor was right. He had to stay focused. Still, he had so much to learn about life it seemed he'd never get started with the first lesson.

Chapter 2

Not long after Dr. Knowles left, Edward walked down to the labs on the third floor, where the manufacturing and test facilities were located. Their new product promised to revolutionize the world of virtual reality.

One of Edward's specialties at MIT and Stanford was holographic imaging, using lasers and complex computer algorithms of his own devising to capture and portray the movement of complex 3-dimensional objects through space. Edward's holograms could not only record and display moving things like animals and people, but through computer generated graphics, it could actually create holographic images of things that weren't real.

What truly made Edward and his company stand out was how he enhanced and combined the holographic technology with the latest advances in artificial intelligence, to create a realistic feedback mechanism. His holograms could interact with the outside world. Coupled with complex software that employed machine learning, some of the holographic images could remember certain events and change their behavior accordingly. And all of this could be viewed without the need for glasses or goggles or sensors – a wall to wall, surround-sound virtual reality.

Though it was still in the testing stage, and at least a year from final delivery, the system had garnered massive publicity. The early demos were spellbinding and caused much the same sensation as the early moving picture. All of this was only an entertaining side venture, Edward's face to the world. His real purpose, his true intent, lay hidden like a secret treasure in his mind. Someday it would be uncovered. In the meantime, everyone wondered how he did it, for he had solved many problems within the various technologies – laser, computer, machine intelligence, optics, physics, and so on - to achieve what many thought impossible.

He entered the lab where his research team was setting up the next test. An adjoining area, separated from the lab by a large plate-glass window, served as a control room.

"How are we doing? Are we almost ready?"

"Yes, Dr. Spencer," replied his lead technician. "We've programmed the sequence, but added the response coordinator you gave us to modify the pattern based on the actions of the people in the room."

"Ah, good. We need a good feedback mechanism or none of this will seem real."

"Here's your wand," said the assistant, handing Edward a clear plastic stick about the size of a small baton, but with LCDs and colored buttons.

"You can program this in one of a number of ways in response to the images around you. For instance, you can fabricate a weapon or some kind of shield. The program is pretty violent, like most of the current batch of video games. You know, aliens or enemy soldiers bent on destroying the earth. We have all kinds of scenarios envisioned, from sports to business meetings, and some of the great events of the past, like battle scenes, things of that nature, but that's something for the third-party licensees and vendors to figure out. As you've told us many times, all we want to do is show what's possible."

The technician signaled to a man in the control room and the sequence began.

Edward watched as the room changed appearances. Instead of a lab with tables and chairs, white boards and bookcases, the room transformed into a desert scene with large sand dunes and two blazing suns. The room turned warm. A large beast with horns and claws, about the size of a Kodiak bear, but standing erect like a half-human ape, appeared in the near distance. Slowly, it turned its head and spotted him. Then it charged.

Edward clicked a few buttons on his wand to transform it into a large, two-handed sword. The beast came toward him fast, eating up the distance between them with great bounds, throwing up dust and debris, getting bigger as it came. It looked real enough to scare most people even if they knew it was only a computer-projected image shown in three-dimensional panorama.

Instead of cringing, Eddie raised the great sword over his head and sliced it down at the last moment, cutting off an arm as the beast reached for him. The next stroke sliced its other arm at the shoulder blade – or what would normally be such if the thing were human. Twirling the blade high, he slicked off the monster's head with a flourish. The realism was startling. The arms and head flew off complete with splattering blood and the sound of ripped tissue.

"What would have happened if I didn't do anything?" asked Edward when it was over and the room returned to normal.

"Try it and see," came the reply. So they ran the program again. The room morphed into the desert planet and the beast appeared charging as before.

This time when it charged, Eddie stood there defenseless and didn't move. The creature stopped dead at the last moment and sniffed him. He held out his hand. The beast licked it. Sitting on its haunches grinning at him, it wagged its tail.

"Good boy," he said, "very cute."

"Now see what happens if you run," said the technician.

Another assistant with a wand started waving his arms to attract the creature's attention. It turned toward him and stopped wagging its tail. Pawing the ground with a clawed-foot, it focused on the man and snarled. The tech started running across the room as if fleeing in terror. The beast roared, and in a single bound leaped upon him as if to bite his head off.

"Ouch," yelled the white-coated technician as the hologram's claws and teeth appeared to come down on him. "Stop, that tickles."

"Of course, the bite is harmless," said the lead tech. "The beast can't grab or bite anyone, although even when you know it's not real, like in a movie, you still have the urge to jump and scream."

The technician brandished the virtual sword. "The weapons are only good against the program being run and have no effect in the real world. It's all completely virtual."

Edward knew this, as he knew everything else about the lasers and machines and processes and programs behind it. He knew everything except who he was.

"I noticed a bit of wavering near the legs, on the edges," observed Edward. "And the coloring wasn't consistent between some of the frames. The timing is good, as are the effects. How many players can you handle?"

"Two or three. After that it gets kind of muddled. Hard to pick up and coordinate all the various signals. But there's no reason we can't handle a whole room full, theoretically, anyway. We have a lot to learn."

"Once it's commercialized and available for licensing," observed Eddie, "we'll see the real innovations come."

Edward was already planning on ways to enhance the effect, including adding a tactile feature, but that was for the future.

Later in the day, after most of his employees had gone home to their families, Edward sat in the small lab off his office working on one of his pet projects, the logic that drove the hologram's feedback mechanism. This particular module incorporated natural language recognition, rule-based decision making, and semantic frames, as well as commonsense and heuristic reasoning, with fuzzy logic, to create natural, realistic reactions based on a see-and-respond model. His father and Knowles had spent many years researching the subject, and Edward had most of their notes and results. Yet he felt there was something missing, something they hadn't told him.

He heard someone in his office.

"Nancy, is that you?" he called.

"Hey, Ed. It's your old tennis partner."

Edward had never played tennis with Jack Burr, his VP of Engineering, or golf or hoops or any other sport for that matter, but that didn't keep the latter from saying the phrase just about every time they met. Ed thought it was for the benefit of any female in the vicinity. Edward never even visited a health club, but stayed trim and in shape just the same. When asked how he did it, he told people he ate well and had good genes.

"Nancy told me you'd be here," Burr continued. "That's some babe you've got there for a secretary, Eddie. You shouldn't keep her all to yourself."

"I don't, but during office hours she's here to work, not flirt with you."

"Gee, lighten up, old man. I was just commenting on the goods. I've got plenty of my own beaver in the dam, if you know what I mean."

"I have no idea what you mean, Jack. I thought you were married."

"A man does what a man has to do. You should try it sometime."

Ed looked up from his computer.

"It's about time you looked at me," said Burr. "I was starting to think I didn't exist. That I was just one of those holograms of yours."

"They're not mine. They're ours. That's what we make, or part of it, anyway. Sometimes I think you're not really with us, Jack, that you don't take any of this seriously. You know the holograms and virtual reality is only the beginning. There's a lot more to it than that. The technology..."

12

"That's what I wanted to talk to you about, while I've got your attention. You got a few minutes?" He walked into the room without waiting for an invitation. "I talked to Jeff Chandler from the Department of Homeland Security this morning. He's all excited about this technology. He says the President is, too, and would like a briefing to discuss how it could be used for national defense."

"I've already given several talks on the potential of the technology and how it can be used. It's all in my book."

"Yes, I read it. Great book, but it's all kind of vague and academic. You're waiting for others to do all the innovating."

"That's the way it is with pure research. We lead the way. Others come and find clever means to apply it."

"And make the money," countered Burr.

"That's precisely why we're focusing our commercialization efforts on the virtual reality products. That's where the easy money is, which can be used for further research."

"I understand. That's a sound business plan, but Jeff and the boys at Defense, along with the President, have a lot of good ideas of their own. You couldn't get a better endorsement, and it's for national defense."

"That's precisely why I don't want to get involved. The amount of government oversight and red tape we'd be saddled with just wouldn't be worth it. Something like that would stifle pure research. I said in the beginning, and the Board agreed, we're not interested in perusing DOD contracts at this stage."

"Oh, I don't know about that. Have you looked at the numbers? The stage has changed. We're talking billions here."

"You want to use holograms on the battlefield? Is that what you want?"

"I don't know. Anyway, it's not what I want, Ed. It's what they want. It's what the nation wants."

"I don't want to spend all our time and money trying to industrialize the technology, making it redundant and bulletproof – literally – when we've got so much to learn about the bio-feedback mechanisms and how to simulate tactile sensations. We, the company, have a goal, a dream, to change the reality around us. We have a long way to go to get there and I don't want to be sidetracked making weapons. Let's focus on the future."

"That's just what I'm doing," answered Burr. "There's billions in defense, an endless stream of it, and much of it tax free if we play our cards right. Don't be shortsighted, Ed. You're the one who keeps talking about the big picture, don't lose sight of it."

"I haven't. The bottom line is I don't want my inventions used for military purposes."

"Defending the country is somehow against your moral principals? I'm not sure I understand that point of view. And who said anything about the military, anyway?"

"That's where it will end up, as does anything to do with the Department of Defense or National Security, and you're naive if you think otherwise."

"You really are a self-righteous ass, Ed, and I don't care if you are the CEO and your father was the founder."

"You should."

"I'm sorry, Ed. I don't mean to offend, but if it's a bunch of yes-men you want, to come at your beck-and-call and heel on command, than maybe I've overestimated you. I thought you wanted people who think for themselves and will tell you what they think."

"I do, but once you've made your point, and that point has been fairly considered and rejected, it's time to back off and go on with other things."

"You mean like lemming?"

"No, lemming follow the leader without deliberation and discussion, blindly. I'm talking about hearing and airing all views together, freely, then making a sound decision as a team based on all the facts. We've discussed this several times. Every time it's the same, but you can't take no for an answer. There's something wrong with that. There's a big difference between a yes-man and a person who rabidly disagrees on every issue and has to have his own way. If you can't find a happy middle way between the two, or aren't willing to, then perhaps you should find another place of employment."

"You can't fire me, Ed, but at least I know where I stand, and I'm not alone. I'll see you at the next Board meeting."

"Where we'll be discussing your future employment. Close the door on your way out."

Burr said nothing, but left the door open. Edward wondered if Jack really had the votes to keep from being fired. If so, did he have enough to push through his agenda? Perhaps he should ask Andrew to attend. As a co-founder of the company, the professor was allowed to sit in on Board meetings and vote. There were many on the Board who owed him their job and position. Still, even with his mentor present they might not be able to fire Jack Burr.

"Are you OK, Dr. Spencer?" his secretary asked, sticking her head in the lab. "Is anything wrong?"

Nancy Sullivan enjoyed her visits to Edward's lab. She seldom saw him outside of work, no one did. She felt more relaxed with him than she felt with most of the ambitious pack of overachievers she worked with, even though he was probably the most over-achieved of them all. What he had invented and built was beyond what most accomplish in a lifetime, and he was just twenty-three and had only been on the job a year. It was truly astounding and made her giddy when she thought of it.

She had been coming here more often lately, captivated by the sheer force of his thought. Yet for someone so intelligent, he was probably the most shy, unassuming person she knew, although he had handled that jerk, Jack Burr, well enough.

"No, everything is fine," answered Eddie. "I'm just finishing up for the night. I didn't know you were still here. You're so quiet."

"Well, Mister Burr made enough noise. He seemed pretty upset. He banged the wall on the way out and said he was going to kick your butt, but not exactly in those terms. I just wanted to make sure you were OK."

"Yes, I'm fine," said Edward, finding her statement funny. "There were no fisticuffs, if that's what you mean."

He was glad to learn he had gotten to Burr. Maybe he wouldn't fire him, after all. Perhaps he'd keep him around just for entertainment.

"Everyone's gone home. Do you need anything?" asked Nancy.

"No, why don't you go home as well. It's late," he replied, going back to his work. "I won't need you any further."

Instead of leaving, she stood and watched him from the doorway.

"Yes?" he said, noticing her standing there. "Do you want something?"

"No. I was just wondering what you were doing for dinner. I usually grab something from the deli on the way home, or takeout, you know, something quick. I was wondering what you do."

"Normally my auto-kitchen will have something prepared by the time I get home. Prime rib, Italian food with pasta and sauce, beef Wellington, you know, those kinds of things."

"Oh," said his secretary, known to her mother as Nancy-Joan and to her friends as Nance. "Sounds like you eat pretty well. You must work out. So, do you live alone? Are you married?"

"Do you see a ring?" he asked, now totally focused on the conversation. For the first time he didn't feel self-conscious or at a loss for words. He was too busy answering questions. With Nancy, everything was different. He sensed that she was interested in him and wanted to get to know him better. He was intrigued. He noticed how cute she was when she smiled, and what a nice figure she had beneath her short black dress.

"No, but not every married guy wears a ring. Are you going to play in the company softball game?"

"I don't know. I don't have much time for sports. I'm afraid I'd embarrass myself. I'm not very athletic. What team would want me? I was always the last kid to get picked."

"You should come. We have a lot of fun. Dr. Burr plays. Maybe you could kick his butt when you slide into first."

"That's very funny," said Ed again, although he didn't laugh. As much as he hated to admit it, maybe Jack was right, he did have something here, right under his nose. And he hadn't even noticed her, except as someone to get his coffee, answer his calls, make his appointments, and type his memos. Maybe he had a friend as well. God knows he needed one.

Even in grade school he had never been close to anyone, boy or girl. By the time he was in high school all the girls he met were older than him, since he had skipped so many grades by then. In college, even though the girls thought the promiscuous fourteen-year-old was cute, they would hardly have gone on a date or spent time with him. So he kept to himself. But Edward was tired of being by himself, even in a crowd. He was going to change all that, no matter what old-man Knowles said.

Taking his mentor's advice, he let her do all the talking.

"That's sad," he said finally, after she had told him the abridged story of her life – only twenty-four years and one boyfriend, who had died in a car accident at eighteen; a drunk and abusive father, abandonment, poverty, and neglect. The only high point in her story was how, through sheer guts and determination, she had worked herself out of poverty to finish high school and get an associates degree in business on a partial scholarship at U MASS in Boston, where she was from. Eddie took it all in and found it fascinating. They shared childhood stories. The time sped by like it did when he had his head in a treatise on String Theory.

"I know!" she said suddenly. "I'll take you up on the concert tickets, if you let me take you to dinner. Why don't you call your apartment and give the kitchen the night off. I hear the steakhouse on the fifty-first floor is really good. I've been wanting to try it."

"I don't know," replied Edward, shyly.

"Oh, come on, Dr. Spencer, Eddie, it will be fun."

For a moment Eddie didn't know what to say, but he remembered what the professor had told him.

"I'm sorry, but it violates company policy," he replied finally. "I'm not supposed to date any of my employees. The Board would not approve and the gossip columnists would have a field day. It would cause a scandal."

"Why? You're not married."

"No."

"There's nothing wrong with having dinner. Anyway, all you do is work. How do you meet people?"

"I don't."

"Well, that must suck. You have a right to live and be happy. It doesn't have to be all work. You should get out more often. Anyway, being seen out in public having dinner with a friend might help your image, show people you're human like the rest of us."

Eddie barked a laugh and said, "When you put it like that, yes, I'd love to have dinner with you, but you must allow me to pay. After all, I own the place."

He stood and removed his lab jacket, escorting her out of the room. He was such an enigma, a study in contrasts. All the girls talked about him and speculated what he was like. Always dressed impeccably in the most expensive suits, even at the office, he seemed quite sophisticated on the surface. He certainly was handsome enough, with short jet-black hair and dark eyes, but he was quiet and aloof most of the time.

Some thought he was a cold fish with no personality. Some thought he was some sort of vampire, who led a wild private life at night, held secret by a web of lies and secrets. On the face of it, he seemed normal enough, still, people talked. Everyone knew his parents had died when he was young, and that he had been brought up by the co-founder of the company, Dr. Andrew Knowles. Everyone also knew he didn't like to shake hands, some kind of phobia, they said.

Nancy thought he was nice enough, almost sweet. She had her own reasons for wanting to get to know him. Life had been hard after her father left when she was twelve, not that it had been that easy before then. He had a drinking problem and sometimes got rough with her mother. Nancy had tried to intervene during one such episode and got a bloody lip for her efforts. Her dad left soon after that. She thought she would be happy to see him go, but things took a downward turn when her mother got sick. One step away from a life in the street, she and her mother eked out a subsistence existence of bare survival. It didn't make her sad, it had made her resilient.

Edward's mind was working feverishly, trying to keep up with the conversation. Did she like him? Was she coming on to him? Should he do something? Grab her? Kiss her?

He frantically tried to think what to say or do to make the best of the situation. He was worried he would do or say something to ruin it like he had in the past. Somehow, Nancy seemed different. She wasn't afraid of him. She didn't look at him like he was some sort of movie idol. She treated him like she was his equal, judging him and sizing him up like no woman had ever done before. At the same time, she seemed somehow vulnerable. The combination attracted him, as did her deep brown eyes, eyes that seemed to captivate him and invite him in.

"Did anyone ever tell you that you have piercing eyes?" she asked. "You look right through people sometimes. You're very intense, you know."

"I don't mean to be," he stammered, suddenly awkward and self-conscious.

She wondered if this guy was for real. He had movie star looks – tall and slim with wide shoulders. Why hadn't someone snatched him up before now? Was there something wrong with him?

The elevator door pinged open when they reached the fifty-first floor.

Even though Eddie had built and designed the building, he had never been to the five-star restaurant on the fifty-first floor. Everyone who worked at the exclusive eatery was surprised to see the famous owner arrive unannounced. The maître'd and manager almost fell over themselves trying to seat him. People stared as the couple walked through the room and were seated.

"So what do you do for fun?" the secretary asked him as a waiter handed them two menus.

"Work," he answered, thanking the waiter with a nod.

18

"You just can't work all the time," she answered. "It's not healthy. It will make you old before your time. You need to get out once in awhile. Do you like to dance?"

"I've never tried it, although it looks like good exercise."

"It is. I love to dance. We should go some time."

"I don't know. I'm afraid I would look rather foolish."

"No you wouldn't."

Eddie changed the subject.

"Order anything you want. I ate earlier today after the demo. I hear the lobster thermidor is very good."

"You're not going to eat?"

"No, I'm on a diet, doctor's orders. I'll share a bottle of wine with you while we talk."

He explained it to the waiter, who took their order.

"Do you like music?" she asked, after he left.

"Yes, modern classical pieces like Bartok and Stravinsky."

"No, I mean popular music."

"I don't know. I really don't listen to it."

"Do you watch TV?"

"Yes, I watch the news and business channels."

"No wonder you don't meet anyone. You must be lonely."

Eddie didn't say anything, but gulped, as the waiter brought the wine. He looked at her and thought she was very pretty. Vivacious would be the best word to describe her, he decided. He took a chance and gave her a compliment. Lifting his glass, he said, "To the most beautiful woman in the room."

"All the women in the room are staring at you," she observed.

"So are the men. That's what I get for having my face plastered in Newsweek and Time every other month."

"You're famous. Like a movie star."

"Great, I just want to be left alone to do my work. It's very important, you know."

"I thought you built virtual reality games."

"It's a lot more than that. We just use games to show the potential power of the technology."

"I don't want to talk about work, if you don't mind."

There was an awkward pause.

"Do you believe in God?" she asked out of the blue.

"No," replied Eddie. "Just science. Science will solve all of our mysteries someday, even creation and the existence and nature of what you call God."

"Everyone needs God," she insisted.

"I don't."

"You said you were lonely. God would fill up your heart."

"Any god who would take my parents from me is no god to me. I would hate such a god until the day I die." He said this so matter-of-factually that Nancy was momentarily taken aback.

"Don't say that!" she whispered harshly. "How can you say that?"

"Everyone is here for a purpose, it has nothing to do with God. There is being, nothingness, and purpose."

"Gee, you have a very sour outlook on life. No wonder you're alone. You won't meet people and find friends if you talk like that."

"I'm sorry," he said, apologetically.

He had done it again, opened his big mouth and ruined everything. He saw his chances of really getting to know this girl rapidly disappearing down the drain. In desperation he confessed his inexperience.

"I've never been with a girl," he told her quietly.

"What?" she said too loudly, not believing him and attracting stares.

"I am inexperienced when it comes to women and things. I've never had sex with a girl."

"Who said anything about having sex?" she asked.

"No one," said Eddie quickly, "but I don't know how to talk to women. I'm always putting my foot in my mouth."

"You don't know how to lie," she corrected him, laughing, "that's your problem."

"Yes, maybe you're right," said Eddie smiling sheepishly.

"Where do you live?" she asked.

"In a penthouse apartment about ten minutes from here," he replied.

"I'd love to see it," she said.

Chapter 3

Edward woke up thinking about his mother and father. At first the thoughts – or were they dreams, he wasn't quite sure – were pleasant and nostalgic. He dreamed they were camping together on the Santa Clara River. Soon, however, his dream turned into a nightmare of his parents trapped inside their burning car. It played repeatedly, like a short cyclic fugue.

He wondered where these thoughts and dreams came from, and recalled Nancy telling him about her high school boyfriend dying in a burning car crash. Perhaps that had triggered his nightmare. He had told her she was lucky she hadn't gone out with him on that particular night. Funny how they had both lost someone the same way. Maybe that was why he felt so close to her.

She went home with him. At least he thought so. He couldn't quite recall. Everything was a jumble – dreams, thoughts, memories. This had never happened to him before. Why couldn't he remember? What had happened?

Not quite sure what had taken place the night before, he dressed and went to work.

Did they make love?

His limo drove him the ten minutes from his high-rise apartment building to his fifty-two story company headquarters. Unable to recollect, he tried to reason it out. He knew he was driven to his apartment complex and the doorman had let them in. He knew they had ridden up the elevator to the penthouse together. Had they kissed? He would certainly have remembered that, and thought not. It was all so vague.

He tried to supply logic where memory failed. Why had they gone there? She had suggested it after dinner, so they could talk more. She seemed curious about him, so he invited her over. He was curious as well. It was only 10:00 pm. What harm could it cause, despite the professor's constant and dire warnings?

Snatches of their conversation came back to him. She seemed impressed with the apartment and the fact that he owned the building. It was all innocent enough. He searched his mind for a solid set of images, but only snatches returned, some of them of an exceedingly erotic nature – lips crushed against lips, hands groping, naked bodies pressed together. Was this part of his dream or pieces of memory? He couldn't tell and decided not to try. He arrived at the office where he was scheduled to attend an important meeting.

Today he was demonstrating his company's new virtual reality system to a group of leading industrialists from several countries, all eager to see the next generation virtual conferencing system. Before he could even get to his office he was waylaid by Jack Burr.

"Hey, Ed, I'm sorry about last night. I hope I didn't get out of line. I thought a lot about what you said, and I agree. You're right. In any case, it's your company and you have the last say."

"I'm glad you see it that way. I'll give you a good recommendation. You can hand in your resignation to the Board this afternoon."

"But you need me, Ed. You may not know it, but you need someone that thinks outside the box, someone who's not afraid to stand out, maybe take an unpopular stand once in a while to make sure all sides and points of view get aired. That's why you hired me."

"Dan Michaels hired you and Dan retired a year ago."

"He was a good man."

"Yes he was, but you're no Dan Michaels."

"That may be, but he respected my opinion, even if it didn't always coincide with his."

"Are you attempting to apologize?"

"For what? For speaking my mind?"

"You got a little out of hand. You've obviously had some time to think about it. What you said last night bordered on insubordination. Am I going to have to worry about you undermining my decisions behind my back every time you disagree with them? It's quite obvious what you think. You were very clear last night."

"I may have overstated my case in the heat of the moment. That happens sometimes. Lets face it, we don't always see eye to eye. I know you view me as a source of competition."

"No, I see you as a source of constant agitation, agitating for one thing. What is it with you and the military?"

"It's very important. We're surrounded by enemies. In any case, you know as well as I do the potential of our company's technology in the area of national defense and military training, not to mention actual combat. Just think what you could do with…"

Edward cut him off.

"See, there you go. You have a one track mind. I think it's time you apply your talents and energy – and you have a lot of both – to

22

employment where you can better realize your aspirations. I've got a meeting to attend. I advise you to be at the Board meeting this afternoon."

"Oh, I'll be there," said Jack Burr, as Edward walked away. "And so will my friends and supporters," he yelled after him.

Dr. Spencer headed for the same lab where he had seen the virtual reality demonstration the day before.

"Good morning, ladies and gentlemen," he said, entering the room, this time occupied by a group of high-powered businessmen and women from around the world, all sitting at a long oak-paneled table. As he talked, he circled the room, observing each of the participants in turn. Some turned their heads to see him as he walked by. A few responded to his greeting. Some nodded and smiled.

"You've been invited here today to see the latest in virtual reality technology, the next generation in remote teleconferencing. I'm sure you've all worked with your colleagues spanning the globe through your computer system's teleconferencing software, where you were able to see and hear the other person on large video screens and TV monitors set up in your conference room. Or attended video conferences where co-workers can watch and participate from any location, remotely, using cameras on their PCs. But you've never seen anything like this. One of you sitting in this room today is actually not here at all, but 3000 miles away in New York."

Everyone looked around them and murmured. Some looked as if they were about to touch the person sitting next to them.

"No touching," order Edward. "If you remember our rather odd request when we asked you here that you refrain from making any physical contact with one another. We said it was a medical precaution, but now you know the real reason. One of you is a holographic projection of someone who is actually across the country at this time."

"Can we walk around and try to determine who it is?" asked one of the participants.

"You can," answered Edward, "And there will be time for some of that, but it won't do you any good. I just walked around the room and I couldn't tell who it is, and I built the thing. I know what to look for. In any case, is that what you would do in a business meeting, walk around and guess who's remote and who's really there?"

"Well, sometimes," said one of the woman. "Like if I'm conducting a meeting and I'm on my computer at home, but there's folks in the office in a conference room, and several others scattered about the country that don't have cameras on their PCs. Sometimes it's nice to know whose talking."

"Yeah," agreed another, "or when you're video conferencing and you get a question from someone over the speaker phone. Sometimes it's nice to know where the person is calling from."

"But part of that is because you can't see each other, right? The person talking is just a disembodied voice, unless they have Skype or something. Now the person's right in the room with you, almost in the flesh."

"You say almost," asked another high-powered executive. "Is the person real or just a hologram?"

"I say almost in the flesh because you can see them, hear them, and talk to them as if they were physically there. You can see their expression as they speak and as you talk back to them. You can read their body language. You can see when they write something or take a drink. You can lean over and whisper in their ear, 'Hey, where are you?' Only you can't touch them, and that's not appropriate behavior in a business setting anyway. The person sitting in the room with you is every bit as real as yourselves, but they are not actually there, although they look to be. They are across the country in New York. And you won't be able to determine who of you it is.

"We have invited three distinguished behavior and clinical psychologists to help us in today's exercise. They've developed a series of drills that you will all participate in, designed to show the power of the technology to not only enhance communication across distances, but to enhance your life-experiences as well."

Edward introduced the other scientists that would conduct the exercises and the group broke up into small working teams. Edward sat in a chair at the far corner of the room and observed unobtrusively. Every now and then, someone would come over and ask him for help. "Is it him?" they'd say. "Is she the hologram?" they'd query. But Edward had to admit he had no idea and didn't know any more than they did.

When the exercises were finished, and everyone had a chance to talk to and work with everyone else in the room, they reconvened to discuss what they had learned. Everyone had a suspicion of who it might be, but no one knew for sure. To add to the confusion, the guesses were evenly distributed. No one had attracted undue attention. In the end, they were all just as stumped as they had been when the demonstration began. Short of touching each other, they had been unable to determine who was there and who was not.

"When he wrote, I saw the words appearing on the page in front of him," said one of the participants, commenting on another one's guess. "How could you fake that?"

"And typing on the computer and everything," said another. "And I walked around the room. I mean, we would have noticed if someone wasn't really here. We'd have seen through them or something."

"Yeah," said another. "I arrived with Jim Butterfield before anyone else. We were the first ones here. I saw everyone walk into the room just like normal. No one appeared out of nowhere like a ghost."

"That's all true, and all completely beside the point," answered Edward. "Our technology can do all the things you mentioned. It can make that person virtually appear in the room with you, along with the objects around him."

The last exercise had everyone hold the hand of the person next to them. That simple method immediately revealed the virtual participant – one of the women – when two people reached out their hands and grabbed thin air instead of the person that appeared to be next to them. They both jumped with surprise and mild revulsion, as if they had touched a ghost.

"Meet Martha Vandermere, from Scarsdale, New York," announced Edward, introducing the remote participant to the others.

So began another hour and a half of animated discussion and exchange, followed by a large number of orders for the new system, even though it was only in experimental stage.

The most obvious reaction observed by the technicians conducting the demonstration was that of complete astonishment and disbelief, which was what they had expected and hoped for.

At one point in the discussions, someone asked, "Can you put a complete make-believe person in the room? You know, a hologram of a computer-generated person?"

"You mean like a digital character in a movie? Yes, we can do that. We can fabricate any number of characters digitally and project them as holographic images into the room. And you can interact with them to a degree. We'll show you some of that later this afternoon with our virtual reality demonstration, where we'll fight monsters in a distant galaxy. That's the fun part. But it's all scripted. You can't interact with them like you did today with Mrs. Vandermere. It would only take you a short time to figure out who the fake projected image in the room was.

"The first exercise you did today, where you each told a little about yourselves and interviewed one another, would have caught the hologram, although we probably could have fooled you for a little while. In the end, however, you would have found the fake. Its limited and repetitive responses would have given it away. There's no way we could have made the thing act, well, act human. Computers still aren't capable of the commonsense logical thinking and reactions of a human being. But someday…"

"Are you talking about a Turing test?" one of the men asked. "A sure-proof set of questions to tell a machine from a human?"

"Like in that movie, Blade Runner," offered another.

"What, the movie about the retarded guy that kills people with his saw blade?" queried someone else.

"No, that's Sling Blade," said the second man. "I'm talking about the movie where these four humanoids get loose on earth and this cop, they're called Blade Runners, has to track them down and eliminate them. You've seen it, with Harrison Ford. It's a great movie.

"Anyway, these detectives, these Blade Runners, have a test, a series of questions that they use to tell if they're talking to an android or a human. They look just like humans and seem just as smart, but the test can smell them out. They're really robots and can crush your skull and things, but a hologram couldn't do anything like that, right, Doctor Spencer?"

"That's right, Mister Philips, and we're not quite there yet as far as Turing tests go either. In any case, you can't touch a hologram and it can't touch you. It's just an interference pattern projected in 3-d by lasers and controlled by computers. We haven't been able to build a computer complex enough to mimic the human brain, as simple a mechanism as it is. Mother Nature has had billions of years head start on us. But we're catching up and catching up fast.

"And by the way, Turing didn't invent this test to tell a human from a machine, but to determine if the thing you are talking to and interacting with can think or not. It was designed to discern a thinking entity from a non-thinking one. Machines will be able to pass any Turing test we humans can devise, and within the next few decades."

"What about robots?" asked another. "Isn't it the same thing?"

"Yes, but with robotics the amount of computing power needed to deal with moving and controlling the robot itself takes up most of the resources. There's not much left for thinking. Creating and controlling a human-like android body would be even more daunting. With a holograph, you get all this for free, only in a simulated fashion. An intelligent hologram with tactile senses and responses is still decades in the future."

He then went into one of his spiels about what the future might hold that left the room spellbound and breathless by the time they recessed for lunch. They would then spend the afternoon fighting Tyrannosaurus Rex on the Desert Moon of Ophinia, a planet in the seventh galaxy.

After the demo Edward went to his office. He was disappointed Nancy wasn't at her desk, and wondered vaguely where she might be. He had wanted to talk to her about the previous evening. She must be on an errand, he thought, though it was a little late for her to be at lunch. Edward skipped lunch as usual. Going into his lab, he shut the door and began working on his project to reconstruct his father's work.

He had already done much, developing the machine intelligence to drive next generation virtual reality, years ahead of anything so far envisioned. Still, that wasn't enough. He knew there was more, if only he could get to the next level of their research. Knowles had told him much, but was reluctant to tell him everything, insisting he discover it for himself like his father had. No. He had to do this on his own, by himself. He buzzed for Nancy, but the comely secretary didn't answer.

A few hours later he looked up from his work and realized how late it was. The Board meeting was in fifteen minutes, just enough time to grab his notes. He rang for his secretary again, but there was no reply. He became concerned and went to the outside office. Her desk looked like it hadn't been occupied all day. Nothing had been touched. He asked around but no one remembered seeing her.

Edward found himself running through the building frantically, asking for the whereabouts of his secretary, something completely out of character for the somewhat reserved young CEO. Not a few eyebrows were raised as he hurried by. He ended up in the lobby talking to the security guards, who had no record of her coming to work that day.

"She'd have called in if she wasn't feeling well," Edward assured them. "Perhaps we should check her apartment."

Then he thought again. Perhaps she was mad at him for something that happened the previous night.

"On second thought," he added. "I have her number upstairs. I'll call her, thank you."

On his way to his office, he ran into Professor Knowles, who was there for the Board meeting as Edward had requested.

"Oh, there you are Eddie, I was just looking for you,' said the aging professor. "Where are you off to in such a rush? The Board meeting's in this direction."

"Hi, Andrew. I have to make a phone call. My secretary, Nancy, didn't come in to work today. I'm a little concerned. She's usually very conscientious, but she didn't call or leave any message. So you see, it's a bit unusual. I'm sure everything is all right, but I might have offended her last night. I'd hate to think something I said or did upset her."

"Oh, how's this?" said the professor, suddenly all ears. "Am I to understand you had a date last night with your secretary?"

"Something like that. I took her to dinner at the steakhouse upstairs. She was curious about me, so I took her to the penthouse and showed her around."

"And then?"

"Then she went home."

"That's it? What happened in between? How long did she stay? How about some details."

"Nothing happened. We had a few drinks and talked, that's all. She's a nice innocent girl."

"You know what I said about…"

"Don't worry. We didn't do anything. At least I don't think so. "

"You have to be careful. Remember what I told you. You need to tell me you're going to do something like this so we can arrange things."

"What are you, my nurse maid? I don't need you to make a date."

"No, but you know you are not in a normal position with your responsibilities and knowledge. I've given in to your wishes not to have a permanent security detail, but the least you can do is notify me when you are going out or have strangers over."

"Nancy's my secretary. She's no stranger."

"Did you see that she got home OK?" asked the professor.

"Yes, I think so, but I'm not sure. I don't seem to remember the end of the evening. I guess I may have fallen asleep at some point."

They reached Edward's office, where he again tried to phone Nancy. As before, he left a message on her answering machine.

"I wonder if she's mad at me."

"Why, did you have a fight or something?"

"No, at least, I don't think so."

"You don't seem to remember much of yesterday evening. What? Did you make a pass at her?"

"Not me."

"I see. You wouldn't do a thing like that. You're a gentleman."

"I don't have much practice with that sort of thing."

"Is that what you were doing, practicing? Did she scorn your advances? Is that what happened? Or did you scorn hers? You think she's mad at you for that?"

"I don't know, maybe. Like I said, I may have fallen asleep."

"That would have offended her, I'm sure. Let's take a drive out to her place and see. Where did you say she lives?"

"What about the Board meeting?" asked Eddie.

"They can start without us."

Chapter 4

Edward sat in an interrogation room waiting to be questioned by a detective from the El Segundo police department. Eddie and Dr. Knowles had gone to Nancy Sullivan's apartment, where they found her dead body. She had apparently been murdered, the cause of death quite obvious. A knife protruded from her heart. Knowles waited in another room. Edward sat alone. He was a jumble of conflicting thoughts. He didn't have long to wait.

"Good evening, Dr. Spencer. Sorry to keep you waiting. I'm Lieutenant Mendoza of the El Segundo Police Department. I'm sorry about your secretary. Can you tell me what happened?"

"Yes, sir. I'll tell you the same thing I told the officer who took my statement. Nancy didn't come to work today and I became worried. She was my secretary, and a very good one, I might add. I tried to contact her several times during the day. It wasn't like her to not show up like that and not call. She was very conscientious."

"So when she didn't show up and you couldn't get hold of her, you and your friend, Professor Knowles, went to her apartment to check up on her."

"That's right. It seemed like the right thing to do. I didn't expect any trouble, nothing like this." He stopped and shook his head in disbelief, trying to shake the image of her lying in a pool of blood out of his mind. "How could anyone do such a thing? It just doesn't make sense."

"There are all kinds of people out there, and they do all kinds of senseless things. That's why I'm here, to make them pay when they do. Go on," said the lawman, "continue."

"Yes. Andrew and I went to her apartment to see if she was all right. We knocked several times and tried the door. It was open, so we called and went in. We found her lying on the floor and called the police immediately. We left the apartment without touching anything. It was horrible."

"Yes, I can imagine how it must have been to stumble into a grisly murder scene like that. When was the last time you saw Miss Sullivan?"

"Yesterday evening. We had dinner together. Then she came over to my apartment, around 10:00 pm. She stayed a couple of hours, and left."

"You didn't have her driven home or call a cab for her, a woman all alone late at night like that?"

"I'm afraid I may have done the worst thing a man can do on a date. I dozed off. I must have drunk too much and fallen asleep. She left while I was sleeping without disturbing me."

"There are a lot worse things a man can do on a date, Mr. Spencer. So then, you have no recollection of what happened or when she left?"

"I remember the first part of the evening. We talked. I showed her around. She admired the art work. We sat by the fireplace. I put on a record, Ravel, I believe. I fell asleep in the armchair listening to it."

"How do you know she left?" said the short, dark detective. "If you didn't see her, I mean?"

"I just assumed it. She wasn't there when I woke up in the morning. I asked the doorman. He said she left around 12:30 am."

"We know. We've talked to the doorman. Said she left around half-past twelve just like you confirmed. He also told us that she looked like she had seen a ghost. I wonder what he could have meant by that."

"I don't know," answered Edward. He did not like the sound of the detective's last comment.

"I understand that you own the apartment building?"

"That's correct. I had it built."

"Nice. That must be convenient. I mean it must be nice to own the whole place."

"It has its perks. I can always get a good parking spot, but it's a lot of work as well."

"Have you checked your apartment, you know, made sure nothing is missing?"

"No. That hadn't occurred to me. Why, did she take something?"

"No, not that we know of, just asking. You said you didn't see her leave. Who knows, she may have taken something."

"I hadn't thought of that. She was such a nice girl. I can't believe she's...dead."

"You said you have art. Is it expensive? Did you show her any jewelry?"

"No, nothing like that. If you want to know the truth, I think she was just trying to find out what kind of man she worked for. When we were talking during dinner, she asked me a lot of questions. She kept asking me why I wasn't married."

"And what did you tell her?"

"I told her I haven't had much time for that kind of thing."

31

"Do you think she was a gold-digger, after your money?"

"No, Lieutenant, nothing like that. Like I said, she was a nice girl, very intelligent."

"Well, you can never tell with some people. You only know what they want you to know."

"I'm sure you won't find anything like that with Nancy. Oh, my! What is her poor mother going to do?"

"I don't know. One of my colleagues gets to handle that unpleasant task."

"This is terrible," Eddie lamented. "I can't believe this has happened."

"I'm sorry, Dr. Spencer. We're almost done here, just a few more questions. Did you see anyone watching you when you left the restaurant? Did anyone follow you when you drove home? Anyone on the street when you got to your apartment building?"

"No," answered Eddie. "I didn't notice anyone or anything out of the ordinary. I certainly didn't see anyone following us or watching us. But you should probably talk to Hector, my driver."

"We have, but you might have seen something your chauffeur didn't. Do you know if Miss. Sullivan had any boyfriends, someone who may have been jealous?"

"I don't know," answered Edward. Snippets of conversation came back to him unbidden. "She may have. I vaguely remember her saying something, but I really can't say for sure."

"We'll follow up on that, don't worry. Could you have been drugged somehow?"

"No, impossible, this is all too crazy. That's all I can tell you."

"OK, Dr. Spencer, that's enough for now. I'm sorry to detain you like this, but as you know, in a homicide case we have to talk to everyone. I want to thank you again for your cooperation and your help in solving this terrible crime."

"Yes, Lieutenant, if there's anything I can do, please let me know."

"Thank you. I'll do that, sir. I'll get in touch if I have any further questions. Here's my card. Call me if you think of anything else."

Eddie ignored the card and left the police station quickly, although he wasn't sure where to go. He didn't want to go back to the penthouse. His friend and mentor, Andrew Knowles, was waiting for him in the lobby to drive him home.

"How you doing, Eddie?"

"Not good. This is horrible, like when my parents died. I was with her last night. I was the last person to see her alive. Now she's gone. How could anyone do such a thing?"

"First of all, you were not the last person to see her alive, the killer was. Remember that. Human beings do horrible things. Look at all the wars and senseless killing through the ages. Humans are a bloodthirsty lot, but you can change all that. Don't let this distract you from your work. You will have to manage this like you have managed everything else in your life. It's the worst thing that could happen for the company. It's going to be in all the papers."

"That's the last thing I'm worried about. A woman has been murdered. I wonder…"

"What? Have you thought of something? You should tell the police."

"It's just an errant thought, probably just my imagination, brought on by my antipathy to the man."

"Who, Jack Burr?"

"It was just a stray thought. I don't like the guy, and I wouldn't put much past him. But murder? I doubt even Jack would be involved in something like that."

"You never know. If the stakes were high enough – like ownership of your company – anything's possible. Did he say or do anything that would make you think he would try something like this?"

"No, Andrew, this is all too crazy."

"Crazier things have happened. I can have some of our people look into it. We're going to have to move fast to head off the adverse publicity of having you involved in this woman's murder."

"She was my secretary. There's no way to avoid it. It's going to be front page news."

"The papers don't have to know you were one of the last people to see her. Only the police know that. You fell asleep. She got mad and left without waiting for a cab. Someone followed her, got into her apartment, and killed her. It's just an unfortunate accident. You can't blame yourself."

"Can't I?"

"Not without getting all the facts first."

"What's to keep the police from telling the press?"

"Not their good moral and civic duty, that's for sure, but I'll take care of that. Don't worry, and don't talk to anyone from the press."

"I haven't got the least intention of talking to anyone. I never should have asked her over."

"How is your project going?"

"It was going good until now. I doubt I'll be able to concentrate. Nancy was a big help." He stopped and shook his head vigorously back and forth again, as if trying to shake away the memory. "I can't believe she's dead."

"Don't dwell on it, my boy. You'll have plenty of time to mourn. Your work is very important and will take your mind off things."

"I don't see how anything will make me forget what we saw today."

"Can I look at the lab?" asked Knowles. "I'm curious how far you've gotten."

"It's not ready. Tactile sensations and resistance are hard enough, but the algorithms to program the quantum to simulate intelligence and emotions are next to impossible. Are you sure my father had a working prototype?"

"Yes, but not full-sized, and he had several prototypes, each exhibiting a single feature, nothing like a completely integrated system. But it should be a short step."

"Then show me the rest of his notes."

"You know I can't do that. His wishes were quite explicit."

"At this rate it will take decades."

"That's about the time frame I envisioned."

Edward looked at his mentor for a moment as if trying to read his mind.

"All right, I guess you know best. I just wish that things would go a little faster."

"What's your hurry? It will come soon enough, once you hit the curve of the solution. Until then enjoy the quest. Things will start moving soon enough, and then you'll be in hyper-speed. The solution will pop out as if by magic."

While they talked, they had reached Eddie's penthouse building.

"I don't feel like going home," Eddie said. "This talk about the project has made me eager to get back to work. Can you take me to the office?"

"Are you sure? It's late and you've been through a lot."

"I don't want to go back to the apartment, not after what happened. It will be lonely up there, now more than ever."

Chapter 5

Knowles left Edward at the curb in front of the Altered Realities building and drove away slowly, deep in thought. The recent events involving his protégé were very troubling for several reasons. What had happened that evening between Eddie and his secretary? That he had brought her home at all was disturbing. What had happened?

It was imperative that he know, for Professor Knowles was more than Edward's mentor. He was Edward's creator. He had manufactured him with lasers and computer chips, and massively-parallel neural-networks that he had been working on for four decades before they came to fruition in his incredible creation.

Dr. Edward Spencer, holder of two PhDs from MIT and Stanford, ECO of one of the most successful startup ventures since Microsoft, holder of a dozen patents, and acclaimed genius, was nothing more than an interference pattern generated by software and reconstructed as a three-dimensional image in space using powerful lasers. Hundreds of these lasers were placed throughout the fifty-two stories of his company's headquarters and his ten story apartment complex. Thousands had been placed in strategic spots around the city, wherever Edward would need to appear. Mico-lasers, the size of bugs, followed his image where no lasers existed. But that wasn't the astounding thing.

His holographic image was based on the same technology the company was selling and demonstrating with their virtual reality system, which created such a full, realistic image that it was literally impossible to distinguish from the real thing, even when you were standing right in front of it or walking beside it. But a computer generated image, without a real person behind it, couldn't keep up the deception for long. Only a few minutes of conversing and interacting with it would be enough for you to tell there was no real intelligence behind the thing. That is until Eddie.

Knowles had worked with Dr. Henry Beardsley in the early days of his career, the renowned researcher in cognitive psychology, who did pioneering work in brain scanning. The work wasn't so much directed toward the clinical and therapeutic side of the technology – although these areas benefited greatly from his research – but to the mapping of the brain. Knowles worked with Beardsley to develop more refined techniques to capture ever thinner slices of the organ, so that each neuron could be mapped.

The problem was that these techniques, although very accurate, were destructive. To achieve the level of precision required, at only three or five atoms thickness, the brain itself would be damaged, so only dead specimens were used. However, to really map the neurons and their connections, you have to scan the brain of a living person repeatedly, in fractions of a second. It was all theoretical until the year after Andrew's PhD thesis.

He had gotten married during his first year in graduate school. Gale was cute and persistent and promised to further his career by being a loyal and supportive wife, and she was. Getting pregnant with their first child – a boy – changed none of that. It only made her more domestic and caring. When their boy got cancer and the doctors gave him six months to live, everything changed. Their world fell apart.

Although no longer working with Beardsley, Andrew still retained much of their notes and equipment. He called his old teacher and asked him if he would consider continuing their research. How long did he think it would take them to reach the five atom threshold? Beardsley replied he'd think about it, but it would probably take another fifteen or twenty years, and he was seventy-three. He wasn't sure he still had it in him. Andrew told him they didn't have that long.

Their boy had exactly seven months and five excruciating days, which for his parents were worse than torture, watching their child die slowly, day by day, one organ, one cell at a time.

After months of this agony, in the final days and hours of his son's life, they scanned his brain, one layer at a time, with the most advanced optical imaging scanners in existence, also of their own design. Knowles and his teacher, Beardsley, were able to map every neuron and every connection making up each synapse-thin layer of the dying boy's brain. This information was stored and assembled into a giant three-dimensional computer model.

His son died soon after, and his mentor, Dr. Beardsley, soon after that. His wife had divorced him months before when she discovered what he planned to do and took the secret with her to an early grave. No one else knew, not even Eddie himself.

Knowles worked for the next thirty years perfecting the representation of the neurons of Eddie's brain in ever more sophisticated, massively-parallel hardware, from silicon chips, to biological and cellular arrays, to optic-based and quantum computers, creating ever larger and faster neural-networks in the process.

He soon learned that it wasn't the number of brain cells that made intelligence, but the layering and specializing of the various parts, all working together. He also learned that different mediums had different strengths, so built his brain with a combination of components, making use of a variety of techniques, so that soon he had billions of machine-cells working in union, simultaneously, to solve any problem, like recognizing a face or replying to a question or navigating through a street. Then he taught it.

He fed his machine-brain information. He opened the channels to his son's reconstituted mind and flooded it with information – every textbook on every subject ever written, the world's great novels, centuries of music, academic papers, newspapers, magazines, and journals, movies and recordings, reviews, films, and blogs, examples of pop-cultures and art, as much information, facts, trivia, and life as could be stuffed down ten optic fibers. The computer, twenty times faster than a human brain and constructed just like one, ate it without a burp.

What would have taken ten or twenty lifetimes to learn and digest, Eddie learned in hours. Since his memory was based on machine-tested principals and vast optical arrays, it was virtually unlimited, although what he could retrieve at any one time was bounded by many factors.

Long before this, Eddie's memory components had been filled with a lifetime of reminiscences, some happy, some sad, some tragic, some uplifting. His parents, his pets, his childhood home, high-school, the prom and college, were all fabricated by his creator.

He was given emotions and a sense of humor, and was taught right from wrong, not so much hard-coded, but through evolutionary techniques and behavioral conditioning. With these and his programmed early-life memories, Eddie thought like a person – although faster and with more recall – and actually felt he was one.

Knowles added continuous speech recognition and speech generation, and began interacting with Eddie as a teacher does a child. Eddie didn't sound like a machine, but spoke with human inflection and tone. The professor never shut off the computers that interpreted the interference pattern that was Eddie's holographic form, housed with his brain in a secret basement lab in the Knowles's seaside mansion home. This was a son only he – not God – could turn off.

There had been setbacks, some almost permanent. To add to his difficulty, much of the work had to be done in secret, but done it was. His creation became the perfect front for his new company, Altered Realities. Handsome, suave, never late, never tired, he had been made for the camera and was an adman's dream. Eddie not only created Altered Realities Corporation, he was altered reality, and no one knew but Dr. Andrew Knowles.

Of course, it would all be for naught if someone so much as reached out to shake Eddie's hand. A hologram is normally nothing but a light-show. Eddie was different. One of the first things his creator did, even before he had a fully functional prototype, was develop a tactile effect, utilizing force fields and electrical currents created in very defined points of space, to simulate texture and force. Eddie had to appear solid even if he wasn't. At a minimum, he had to be able to imitate the picking up of objects. There had to be substance behind the appearance. This was the truly miraculous part.

It was all done by the use of sophisticated haptic techniques, decades ahead of their time, but it wasn't perfect. Much could go awry. Because of this, incredible precautions had been taken to reduce the likelihood of this happening. Not only did Eddie never shake hands or make any physical contact, all employees and business associates, as well as customers and clients, had been made aware of Dr. Edward Spencer's aversion to bodily contact, for health reasons – a terrible childhood trauma.

So far it hadn't been a problem, but there were a few occasions where young women had tried to hug him or kiss him. It was only the quick thinking of his security detail – handpicked by Knowles – that saved the day, thus the Professor's concern on finding out that Eddie had been alone with a young female.

To Eddie, everything seemed real and complete. He not only acted and thought like a human being, he felt like one. All his senses were implemented much as in a human body through specialized neural-pathways. From the perspective of his computer brain, he perceived himself inside a body – the holographic one that appeared to others. He had a true identity, with a 'me' inside and 'the other' outside. Knowles had created him that way and hadn't told him the truth. And although he supposed that it was inevitable that Eddie might realize it on his own someday, he hoped that day would never come. He often wondered what effect it would have on his creation if it did.

Recent events had disturbed him. Not so much the death of the woman. That was just a stupid coincidence, a female in the wrong place at the wrong time. Unfortunately, it was all too common in the predator-filled cities of the modern world. What really bothered him was that Eddie had asked her out and invited her over in the first place. What motivated this behavior? Did she discover something? What had happened between them?

He had observed his holo-son carefully after the event, gauging his reactions, his responses. Eddie was programmed – or trained if you will – to feel emotion. He showed sadness, a sense of loss and guilt, which were all genuinely human. Had he cried? Knowles thought not. It would not have occurred to him, although he would remember crying when his parents died, but his sense of loss would not be that great. He had seen pictures of dead people and understood the concept, and would have adapted the appropriate level of emotion, but there was still much he did not fully understand. Knowles had to get to his own lab, where he could think and analyze the situation.

A half hour later the professor was at his ocean-side mansion in Vista Del Mar, where he began searching through the event files and logs of Eddie's brain. He knew much and guessed more, but he had to be sure.

Since Eddie was made to respond like a human, with full-blown physiological effects, he could simulate sleep, as well as eating, but even a computer could hiccup. Did they have a physical encounter? Would that explain the memory loss?

He had tested the tactile response system and had felt the hologram himself several times under different circumstances to evaluate its effectiveness. Under controlled conditions it was convincing enough. Eddie's handshake was a little weak, his flesh a little soft for the firm appearance. His touch tingled. Knowles hadn't pushed the envelope, relying more on avoidance than perfecting the effect.

Eddie was anatomically correct. He was given a good physique and a realistic, adequate-sized penis, all projected down to the minutest detail in 3-dimensions. Knowles used himself as a model, and none of his three wives had complained. Eddie could even get aroused under certain circumstances, like when nerve axons for certain brain states were stimulated, but this was something his creator had never anticipated actually occurring spontaneously, on its own. One never knew, with something like this, what might happen.

Did Eddie have sexual impulses? Unlikely, but not impossible. Eddie had told him he felt lonely. Did the professor's creation need companionship? This was something he hadn't considered. Knowles hadn't run a diagnosis on Eddie's brain since the beginning. Perhaps it was time to do so now.

He wondered how much Eddie knew about himself, if anything.

Knowles continued to query Eddie's event log, setting the search parameters for the time of Eddie's date.

Even at the high setting, the log was immense, containing hundreds of thousands of computer pages with charts and readings denoting body functions and neural activity, the holographic status of Eddie's body, and so on, reams of data, all displayed on a wall of virtual graphic devices.

He noticed a sharp increase in high-brain movement around nine pm. This would have been when he started his date. His language and semantic synapses were especially active, dealing with the commonsense reasoning needed to handle a simple conversation, where memory and experience coupled with instantaneous feedback were required. Then around midnight, the brain went into an inactive state.

He had forgotten about this, Eddie's periodic shutdown to conserve his energy cells, although they were almost limitless. That would account for the memory loss, for Eddie would be in a state of non-consciousness. This might explain things. He had wanted Eddie to appear normal – that is if three hours of rest each night could be called normal. It served several purposes, but could be embarrassing to someone entertaining a woman. If that's all that happened, all was well. Eddie had handled the police interrogation good enough. Perhaps there was nothing to worry about. Still, he'd have to keep an eye on things. Eddie's secret had to be protected at all costs.

Chapter 6

Edward woke up at 3:00 am and looked around the lab. He was surprised he had fallen asleep. He hadn't meant to, and wondered vaguely how long he had been out.

He was deeply troubled. His mind was in turmoil, not only because of the loss of someone close to him, but by his lack of memory concerning the events of that evening. Something wasn't quite right. For the first time in his life he didn't feel in control. Things were spiraling out of alignment. He felt a sense of loss, that something had been taken from him. It made him feel empty. He had the urge to search, but where? For what? That which had driven him and given him a feeling of accomplishment no longer seemed important. It all seemed so futile.

He went to call his secretary before he realized she was no longer there. She was gone, never to return. He felt that sense of loss again, like when his parents died. It was almost habitual, as if he had been taught to feel this way.

Someone rapped on the office door and roused him from his trance. He rose slowly to see who it was.

In all his worry about his secretary the previous afternoon, and his efforts to ascertain her well-being, Edward had completely forgotten about the Board meeting. On the way out of the building to go to Nancy's apartment, he had bumped into Tom Johnson, the CFO. He told Tom he had to leave unexpectedly for an important matter and asked him to postpone the meeting. He hadn't talked to anyone since then.

Tom Johnson was at the door.

"Hi, Ed," he said. "Sorry to hear about what happened to Nancy. How you doing? Someone said you've been here all night."

"Yes, I didn't go home last night. The whole affair was very upsetting. I came in to do a little work, try to take my mind off things. I must have dozed off for a few hours, but I worked most of the night. I was just on my way home."

"Well, no one's going to be able to do much work today. Everyone's pretty upset. HR is having a meeting this afternoon to offer grief counseling to the employees."

"That's a good idea. Everyone should attend."

"I wanted to talk to you about the Board meeting yesterday. I know this is probably not a good time, but I need to let you know what happened. I tried to postpone the meeting like you asked, but I was outvoted. Several members had agenda items they wanted to discuss. Since most of it didn't require your presence, they voted to go ahead and have it. Of course, you still have to approve any decisions. I've typed up the minutes of the meeting for you."

"Good. Thanks, Tom."

"Jack Burr was there. He tried to get an item added to the bylaws preventing a sitting Board member from being fired unless there's a two-thirds majority vote."

"What? What happened to the simple majority rule that we have had since the first day? We're not debating national affairs here. We don't want these decisions to drag on like a senate filibuster. In any case, the bylaws can't be changed without the chairman present, and that's me."

"Jack tried to brush that detail aside. He wasn't subtle at all, and most of the members saw right through his little play. We all know his days are numbered. He seems to think he works for a completely different company. He's got his own agenda, and that's all you get from him. We've all been saying he's disruptive and contentious, but a few like him because they think he's useful. They'll learn quick enough when they try to use him for anything other than Jack Burr's agenda."

"I was one of those," admitted Ed. "I used to think it was good to have someone around with another opinion. What's the use of having a team if everyone's the same? You want to have some dynamism, someone to challenge you with a different perspective to keep everyone's creative juices flowing, but it's a fine line between being a thought-provoking person with different opinions and a rabid troublemaker who can't take no for an answer. I've told him. If he can't find a happy middle ground between those two extremes, he'd better find another job, but he insists on making a battle out of it. That's what I get for voting him on."

"You and me both. He didn't get very far, though he was dogged in his efforts. In the end we agreed to bring up his motion at the next Board meeting."

"Where I will bring up his dismissal."

"Exactly, he's trying to muddy the waters."

"Let him. Jack Burr is the least of my worries. What happened to Nancy is the worst thing that could have occurred."

"I know. I'm sorry. Please, let me know if there's anything I can do."

"Sure, Tom. Thanks for the heads-up."

After leaving Tom Johnson, Eddie hurried down the corridor toward the lobby and the front entrance. He walked with his head down, deep in thought, as if pondering some unsolvable equation, avoiding eye contact and mumbling to himself. People stopped and watched as he left the building. Some tried to say hi, or express their condolences, but he walked by them as if they weren't there. Some looked like they felt sorry for him. Some stared at him with questioning or serious expressions. A few had suspicious looks and shook their heads in dismissal, but no one ignored the tragic figure and his unusual behavior.

To Edward, it appeared that everyone in the building was staring at him accusingly. The corridor through the office spaces seemed interminable, as if the hallway ahead of him was growing as he tried to reach the end of it. Why were they looking at him like that? Did they know the deep shame he felt, though he didn't quite know why? What was the secret locked up inside him?

Just as he was about to leave the lobby, Jack Burr ran up behind him, yelling.

"Ed, Ed! You got a minute? Ed? Wait!"

Even though he was only a few yards away and shouting loudly, Edward pretended not to hear, but increasing his pace, kept walking through the revolving doors and out of the building. He should have stopped and listened to Jack's warning – even an enemy may yell out when you're about to step off a cliff. He should have stopped and listened to what his nemesis had to say

The glare of the bright midday sun hit his optical circuits like colliding particles of sand, blinding him instantly. He put up his holographic hand as if warding off a blow. His gyroscopic-sensors and coordination centers were momentarily overloaded, making his image appear to stumble on the broad steps leading down to the street. Dozens of reporters covered the plaza and sidewalk waiting for him. He only made it halfway down before he was mobbed.

Security had kept the press out, but they couldn't keep them from congregating in front of the building. Edward felt suspended in a haze with no horizon and only dimly-seen forms around him as his neural circuits tried to come to grips with the unfolding situation. Meaningless sounds bombarded his audio sensors like mallets.

"Dr. Spencer! Dr. Spencer!" they shouted, running up the steps to surround him with microphones and cameras, all pushing and talking at the same time.

"Can you tell us about Miss Sullivan? Did you know her well?"

"Did you find the body?"

"Were you the last person to see her alive?"

These and other questions flew at him from all directions. He couldn't have answered even if his circuits hadn't been overloaded. He felt somehow burnt out.

He looked up dumbly into the lens of a camera, his hands still shielding his face. The front page picture the next day showed a bleary-eyed, disheveled executive, who looked like he had just stepped out of a train wreck. He stood there peering around for an escape route. There was none.

"Ladies! Gentlemen!" the professor's voice boomed out behind him, so loud it could be heard over the din the journalists were making. "Dr. Spencer has had a very difficult evening. We here at ARC are shocked and deeply saddened by the loss of Miss Sullivan, none more than Dr. Spencer, who worked with her closely. The whole company is in a state of mourning and undergoing grief counseling. We're not just a company here at ARC. We're a family. We all knew Nancy's mother, exchanged Christmas cards with them.

"The company will issue a statement this afternoon at one. All of you are welcome to attend. If you all remain here for a short time, we will provide you with passes to the conference and its location. Now if you would please allow Dr. Spencer to get to his car so he can go home for some much needed rest, I'll answer some of your questions."

There was a burst of frantic shouting as Edward was escorted to his waiting limousine by the security detail Knowles had brought with him. He had no intentions of answering any of their questions, and was as evasive as a feral cat, using the fact that there was a homicide investigation in progress as an excuse. Once Edward was safely in his car and had sped off to his apartment building, the crafty spokesman dismissed the news people, saying, "All your questions will be answered this afternoon at the news conference. Good day, ladies and gentlemen."

Edward sat slouched in the back seat of the car, numb from his encounter with the reporters.

"What is going on?" he asked out loud.

"Yes, sir? Can I help you?" answered his driver. "Are you feeling OK, sir?" Hector was in his late forties, and had been working for Edward for almost a year. The Professor had found him. Obviously of Hispanic descent, he spoke with an accent and was always very solicitous and polite.

"Yes, I'm fine now. Just a bit upset. I've had a bad day." He seemed to answer by rote, without thought, as if the words had been written for him. Did he do everything by habit?

"We'll get you home safe. Those newspaper hombres are bad news."

"Hector, the Lieutenant said they questioned you."

"Yes, sir. They asked me a lot of questions about you and your personal life. I didn't care for their manner."

"Did they ask you if we had been followed or if you had seen anybody that looked suspicious when we got to the apartment?"

"Yes, sir. Si."

"And did you?"

"I'll tell you what I told them. When we left the parking garage at the office building that evening, there was a car behind us. They followed us out and down Palmdale a ways. I lost track of them in the traffic."

"So there could have been someone following us?"

"I suppose so, but it could have been anybody. I didn't see nobody when we got to the penthouse."

"Have the press contacted you?"

"No, and they better not, or I'll give them a piece of my mind, just like I told that detective."

"Oh, what was that?"

"He was asking a lot of insinuating questions, like if you took girls home all the time or if you and the secretary were having an affair. A lot of stuff about your personal life, like did you go to sex clubs or were you into pornography or bondage. I told them you were a good, honest, hardworking man. That what you saw was what you got with Dr. Spencer. Not like some of these people, who act like they care, but could give a plug peso if you exist or not. I told them you care about people. You help people and give them jobs. You don't have time to fool around and party. You're serious and dedicated to your work. If anything you work too hard. And look what happens the first time you try to meet somebody. It's just not fair."

"Thank you, Hector, but life's not fair sometimes. No one's accusing me of anything, although I can't help feeling it's all my fault. If I hadn't fallen asleep she might not have left like she did and walked home. I would have had you drive her."

"You can't blame yourself, sir. Maybe the killer was waiting for her at her place. Maybe she knew him. I hear she had a boyfriend."

"I'm sure she had a few. She was a beautiful woman."

"And talkative too," observed the driver. "She didn't stop yakking the whole drive from the restaurant."

"Yes, she seemed a bit inquisitive."

"Yeah, seeing how much gold she could dig out of you."

Edward wasn't sure he understood what Hector was saying, or whether or not he liked it. He didn't respond.

They reached his apartment building at that moment. To avoid the press congregating at the entrance, they drove around the back to the underground parking garage. Luckily, it was devoid of reporters.

Once in his apartment, Eddie tried to get his thoughts off the murder. He listened to music and watched a movie, but he couldn't drive it from his mind. It was all he could think about.

He went over what he knew about the murder. His secretary had been killed in her apartment, stabbed with a large kitchen knife the killer left in her chest. There were no fingerprints. He blamed himself although he had not plunged the knife into her.

She must have gotten mad and left when he fell asleep. What did the doorman mean by, 'looked like she had seen a ghost?' Maybe he mistook her anger for fear. Maybe someone was pursuing her, and had been in the building all along. Whatever the case, she had walked home alone and attracted the wrong type of attention. They must have grabbed her at her door and forced her into the apartment where they raped and murdered her. How could this have happened in a sensible world?

Chapter 7

Early the next morning, there was a knock on the penthouse door. Eddie, who had been watching the morning financial reports, went to answer it, wondering how they had gotten by the doorman.

"Good morning, Dr. Spencer." It was Lieutenant Mendoza of the El Segundo police department. "I'm sorry to intrude at a time like this, in your busy schedule, but I need to talk to you."

"Good morning, Lieutenant. What can I do for you? Our company's offices are closed today. We are in mourning for Miss Sullivan."

"Yes, sir. I'm sorry. I can imagine what you must be going through. You two were very close."

When Eddie didn't reply he continued.

"You didn't come home last night?"

"No. I was too upset. After talking to you I went back to the office to work. I knew I was too disturbed to sleep. I thought working would take my mind off things."

"And did it?"

"Yes, I imagine so. I ended up working most of the night before I realized what time it was."

"You must be some kind of workaholic."

"I am involved in a very important research project that could benefit a lot of people."

"I know what it's like with people depending on you. My wife would be lost without me, and our only boy, well, I won't go into that. He lives with us. Between the two of them and the dog, I feel I have the weight of the world on my shoulders sometimes. I would have retired five years ago if I didn't have all these responsibilities. But listen to me, going on about my own trivial little problems, while you really do have the weight of the world on you. Everyone speaks so highly of you. I'm surprised you haven't run for office. Well, there's plenty of time for that."

He laughed.

Edward looked at him with a blank expression, as if he didn't understand the joke.

"I'm very busy," he said finally. "Is there something I can help you with? I need to get to the funeral parlor."

47

"Yes, certainly. I don't want to keep you long. I have a warrant here to search the premises. Actually, I just want to take a quick look around. Maybe we can see if anything's missing. I'd like to know why she left like that without telling you or calling a cab."

"Do you have to do that now? I really need to be somewhere. Perhaps I should call my lawyer. He's a real little piranha, but I love him."

"No, no, Dr. Spencer. That won't be necessary. But I have to serve this thing or my boss will have a conniption, and you don't want to be around when the captain pulls one of his sissy-fits. I'll make it quick, I promise. You can leave if you want. I won't disturb anything. Or you can stay here. It's up to you. I'll make it quick. It will only take a couple of minutes."

Edward looked at the search warrant without taking it from the detective's hand, quickly ascertaining it was legal. He had to let the detective in.

"Nice place," observed Lieutenant Mendoza on entering the expensive 12,000 square foot penthouse, with its panoramic view of the city's skyline, LA in the distance to the northeast. "And you own the whole building?"

"Yes, I had it built last year along with our headquarters building."

"Very impressive. So, you showed the young lady around the apartment?"

"Yes, I gave her the grand tour. A lot of the artwork she admired is along here, in the hallway."

"Hmm, yes, kind of like being in a museum."

Edward talked as they walked slowly along the circular corridor, viewing the many pieces of art and sculpture.

"I don't know anything about art," said Mendoza, "but this looks like quite an expensive collection."

"I'm sure it is, although the exact cost is unknown to me. Much of it was purchased by my parents before they died, and a lot was bought on my behalf by my mentor and guardian, Dr. Andrew Knowles. I've only been involved in the art world recently, just the past year. I bought this Picasso here, and one of these Cézannes."

"Ah, very nice. Anything missing that you can tell?"

"No, there doesn't appear to be. Like I told you, I would be surprised if Nancy stole anything. She left because I gave her the ultimate insult. I fell asleep. I'm a blithering idiot, who should only be involved with machines and computers. I will never be able to forget what happened nor stop blaming myself. There is no pill I can swallow or prayers I can say that will help me. I wish it was I who was dead."

"Please, Dr. Spencer, don't talk like that. You don't want to make us worry that you might do something to yourself, now do you? We wouldn't want that. You're much too important a man. None of this is your fault. It might have happened whether you had fallen asleep or not. There's no way of knowing until we learn more. Perhaps she took something when you dozed off. Maybe someone followed her, or was working with her."

"No, not Nancy. I knew her mother, for goodness sake."

"I hope you're right. I would hate to have this poor girl's reputation sullied, but in a homicide investigation every stone must be turned to get to the truth, and hopefully, to the killer."

"Yes, of course, Lieutenant. I'll do everything in my power to help, no matter what the cost."

"Ah, don't worry about that, sir. The city will pick up the tab, and I suspect the state will pitch in too. Who knows, with our great governor, maybe even the federal government will help. You might donate to the police charity fund if you could. That's a worthy cause. I'm afraid that even with all the good work we do, we're still underappreciated."

"Too many other worthy causes to compete with these days, but I'll see what we can do."

"Thank you, sir. I appreciate that. Can we check out the other rooms?"

"Certainly," Edward replied, as he waved off his man-servant and showed the detective the rest of the apartment, answering his questions as they went. It appeared that nothing was missing, just as Edward had insisted.

On the way out, as they were standing before the private elevator in the foyer, Lieutenant Mendoza asked a few last questions.

"Do you know if Miss Sullivan had a cell phone?"

"Yes, I believe she did. I've seen her talking on one. I assume it was hers."

"Did she have it with her the night you saw her last?"

"I don't know. If she did, I didn't see her use it. Why?"

"Oh, no reason. If she had a phone, why'd she walk all the way home? It's funny she wouldn't of called a cab. And if she didn't have her phone, where was it? Most people don't go out for the day without their cell phone."

"She may have forgotten it. You didn't find one in her apartment?"

"No. It's very strange, although I'm sure it's nothing. Just one of the hundreds of dead-ends we have to investigate before we find the right lead, the one that will bring us to the killer. Well, thanks for your time, Dr. Spencer. I'll let you know if there's anything else."

"Yes, do that, Lieutenant. I hope you get your man, and soon."

"Are you sure there's nothing else you can tell me? You were going to say something last time we talked, but hesitated."

"No. It was just a random thought that had popped into my head. It has no bearing on your case. I haven't learned anything to make me think otherwise. I'll let you know if something comes up."

"Well, you never know. Your vague hunch may tie a few dots together. I'd like to hear your thoughts."

"It's just a crazy idea. You know how your mind works. You grab at the most insane answers when you're faced with such a senseless act like this. I don't want to crowd your investigation with my suspicions. You have enough false leads, as you say, without one more piece of useless information to add to the noise. I certainly don't want to shed suspicion on someone because of a silly half-thought I may have had under duress."

"Suppose you let me handle the noise and tell me what your thoughts are. I'll add it to the pot and worry about who's a suspect and who's not. I'm the only one in a position to determine what's germane or not."

"It was nothing. Just something Jack Burr, a colleague of mine, said that night, just before I took Nancy to dinner. He was talking about her, insinuating I was trying to keep her all to myself, called her 'a piece of ass' and told me what he would do if she were his secretary. I forget his exact words, but I remember I didn't like them. She came into my lab a short time later and commented on how angry he was. She told me that on his way out he said he was going to kick my ass and punched the wall. She was worried about me and had come to make sure I was all right. We started talking. I told her she could leave for the day, but she stayed. She asked me what I was doing for dinner, and suggested we have supper at the steakhouse at the top of the building. I agreed. We talked and ended up going to the penthouse that evening for a nightcap, as I've told you."

"You think this Jack Burr had some kind of grudge against you?"

"Me or my secretary, but I told you, it's crazy. Jack may be a big pain in the butt, and I'm seriously considering firing him. He has ideas involving the military application of my product that don't fit the company's philosophy, and is pushing hard to get his way in the boardroom, but he's no murderer."

"It sounds like this person would benefit from your involvement in this affair."

Edward remained silent, not sure he had done the right thing by voicing his suspicions.

He stood by the elevator for some time after the detective left, until his man asked if he would be going into the city. He decided to stay home, telling him he didn't want to be disturbed.

Edward sat in a chair and stared out the window, but he was not looking at the view. He was looking inward. Something was hiding from him, something he had to find. He slowed his mind, putting himself in a kind of trance. Everything that had happened to him recently flooded his memory cells. Somewhere there hid the answer. Something was calling to him from his innermost being, but he didn't know what it was.

Deep in the meditative state, where each moment was an eternity, he transcended himself. He was in a vast room, like the large atrium of a hotel, with many floors and doors, each one leading to some piece of knowledge or memory.

He entered one close by and saw, as if on a giant screen, each moment of his life, every event, act, and episode in his twenty-three year history. It flashed in an instant before his eyes. He wondered if he had died. There were no blank spots, no missing days or hours. He remembered everything, every single moment of his existence.

Was this normal? Did other people remember like this and recall everything from their past? Did they dream of a room with doors?

He turned his thoughts to what had happened that evening. Why couldn't he remember?

Focusing his mind, he moved to his most recent memories, a door at the end of a long hall, and opened it.

He was in his living room looking down, as if from the ceiling. There was a Ravel piece playing softly in the background. He was sitting asleep in his leather chair under the lamp across from the gas-fed fireplace. Nancy was sitting on the floor at the foot of the sofa with her legs drawn up beneath her just a few feet away. She held a wide-lipped glass of some dark liquid.

He watched the scene unfold as if he were Scrooge on Christmas Eve. He could plainly hear what she was saying, as if his ears had recorded what had been said while his eyes remained shut. She was telling him about her boyfriend, unaware that he had fallen asleep.

"He doesn't like me working at the company. He thinks some guy's going to try and pick me up. He's so jealous. It drives me crazy. I thought I loved him at first, but he's so jealous I can't stand him sometimes. He's really a sweet guy underneath, but he's a little immature. I think I've kind of outgrown him, in a way. Dr. Spencer? Ed?"

She noticed that he had nodded off. Her displeasure showed on her face.

"Humph!" she intoned. "I'm leaving. You don't need to call me a cab."

She peered at him closely.

"Edward? Edward?" she shouted as if to wake him.

She walked toward him, where he sat stiffly with his back straight and his eyes closed.

"Edward, are you OK?" She moved toward him slowly with her hands extended. "Edward? Can you hear me?"

Slowly reaching for him as if afraid to startle him, she shook him lightly on the shoulder. He didn't move, but his eyes popped open and his body jerked. It happened so suddenly it startled her. Losing her balance, she fell forward on him with her full body weight, her hands extended to stop her fall. They passed right through him. She screamed and jumped back in alarm.

"Ahhg!" she yelled, running from the apartment as if she had seen a ghost.

Then one by one, each of the doors he had opened into his memory slammed shut like repeating rifles, one after the other in rapid succession until the last door banged closed and he was left in total blackness.

The trance ended. Or had it just begun? For a moment Eddie didn't know where he was. Was he still dreaming? Then it came to him. He was recalling the events of the past through the doors of his mind. He had fallen asleep, apparently around midnight. His conscious awareness didn't remember, but his unconscious mind did.

He wondered what it all meant.

Chapter 8

Jack Burr felt better than he had in months, at the top of the world in fact. His employment situation had improved, as had his position on the Board. With the trouble the company's CEO was involved in and the potential hurt to the corporate image, few had time to worry about what Jack the Burr might be up to. It didn't hurt that Spencer had failed to attend his dead secretary's funeral. Everyone who had worked with her and knew her was there, and felt betrayed that their employer and her closest associate hadn't seen fit to attend. It just showed how aloof he was and how little he really cared for his people, though he professed such grand ideals. Their fearless leader hadn't been seen since the morning after his secretary's murder, and that suited Jack Burr just fine.

The military certainly didn't care about a little scandal as long as it didn't involve them. If the product was right they would want it despite the cost. If it would bring victory in the war against terrorism or success on the battlefield, money was no object. Jack Burr was betting his job and his career on it, and was doing everything in his power to convince the Defense Department of it. The possibilities were endless, he told them.

He was surprised he was one of the few in the company to realize the potential. But then none of the stiffs he worked with on the Board had much imagination, especially Ed Spencer, despite all his degrees and brains. The guy hardly seemed human.

He told his secretary he didn't want to be disturbed, and dialed a number from a virtual phone book displayed in his eyeglass lens. Technically astute as he was, he still wasn't ready to have a nano-chip implanted in his eye.

"Hello, Mr. Assistant Secretary. Thank you for taking my call. Ah, yes, that's good to hear. Oh, you have. Yes, it's a terrible thing, but it's not going to disrupt production. We have a very experienced, disciplined team. Oh, he's doing as well as can be expected. It was all a big shock, as you can imagine. No, no, don't worry, it's nothing like that. The President? He's very interested? Well, he should be. The world has changed. You need different weapons for a different opponent. Weapons of mass destruction are no longer an effective deterrent against an enemy who hides among innocent people or who has no homeland or cities to defend, against terrorists who attack innocent civilians, women, and children without warning.

"What can it do? Well, Mr. Assistant Secretary, you'll have to see a demonstration. It's rather hard to explain. No, pictures won't do. A picture of a movie for someone who hasn't seen one wouldn't be much help. You have to see it for yourself. Imagine being able to fabricate anything you want out of thin air, from a tank to a company of men, and there's no way to tell the real thing from the fake. Imagine the confusion and diversions you could generate, imagine the surprise you could cause with such a tool. You could completely confound and confuse your opponents. It would revolutionize training. Yes, sir, that, too. See, it only takes a little imagination. Holograms, sir, but like none you've ever seen before. Yes, they move. They're controlled by lasers. They can be a computer-generated object or the real object, and can be projected anywhere in the world. Yes, a very advanced feedback mechanism, AI and everything. You have to see it to believe it. Complete audio, visual feedback.

"What's that? You heard what? Well, Ed is a little skeptical about getting bogged down in DOD paperwork and red-tape, but I assured him that things can be arranged to mitigate that sort of thing. I told him that he'd be able to continue his research uninhibited with little or no oversight. That working with the Defense Department wouldn't change anything, but he doesn't exactly trust me.

"By the end of the month. I've got some of my best engineers working on it. Yes, this is the same product that was demonstrated in Seattle. Yes, that virtual reality game everyone's talking about. They use it for virtual meetings as well. You can't tell who's really in the room and who's across the country. It's all the same technology, just a different setup. We're trying to streamline the programming now and provide automated processes to do most of the work. With only a few parameter settings you can program it over your phone, but we're still in the early stages.

"Yes, sir. I can do that. We'll get things arranged and I'll call you back next week. Yes, sir. Thank you, sir. Good bye."

He blinked off the phone and quickly pulled up some data on the latest status of the project. There had been a slight hiccup with the death of Nancy Sullivan and the sabbatical of the company's CEO, who seemed more shook-up about it than proper. Things were soon back to normal, however, thanks to the dedication and hard work of people like himself. While their CEO and his cronies floundered about or hid in their penthouses, he was keeping things going, keeping the ship afloat. It didn't matter that he owed his position and his seat on the Board to the man he now maligned and conspired against. It was for a good cause, the defense of their country, the protection of freedom itself.

After reviewing the latest project status reports, he eye-dialed his chief engineer.

"Fred, it's Jack Burr. Say, I just checked the latest project status. Look's like we're in the red all of a sudden. What happened? I thought you said everything was on schedule? We have an important demo at the end of the month.

"I know you've been pushing the team as hard as you can, but everyone has to do more. I don't care if the software's maddeningly complicated. What do you mean, Ed's the only one who knows how it really works? What am I paying you guys for? We're not sure if he's even coming back, so stop relying on him.

"Yes, I know. Andy Knowles has canceled all Board meetings. No important corporate decisions are being made until Spencer returns. It's like trying to run a company with your hands tied behind you, but we peons soldier on. No, don't do that. Let's try to figure it out on our own.

"What, Rudy's giving you problems? No, I'll take care of him. Just because he's Spencer's man doesn't mean he doesn't have to follow orders. You're his boss. What? We'll see about that."

After blinking off his chief engineer, he buzzed his secretary. She appeared a moment later as if she had been beamed in.

"You called, sir?" she said standing in front of his desk.

"Yes, please have Rudy Duncan come to my office. I want him in person."

"Yes, sir. Professor Knowles is here to see you. Should I send him in?"

"Yes, but I want to see Duncan immediately afterward. Thank you."

A few minutes later Andrew Knowles walked into the office.

"Good morning, Jack. Sounds like you've been busy."

"Just trying to do my job to the best of my ability, Andrew."

"You've got half the engineering and programming staffs working on a pet project of yours that's not on the books and not approved by the Board."

"You've suspended the Board meetings! Does that mean everything has to stop? We have a company to run and employees to pay despite the fact our Board has decided to suspend functioning and our president is in hiding."

"No one's hiding. Ed's doing some very important research into the next generation haptic response system, and is on the verge of a major breakthrough. In the meantime, there's to be no new projects. We already have a backlog of customers for the current technology and dozens of third-party vendors and spin-offs who are eager to develop and commercialize it. And take all the risks, I remind you. If you want to work with the military, I advise you to go ask one of these subsidiaries for a job. I'm sure they'd all jump to have a person with your experience and knowledge, but I'm afraid you're not quite cut out for the pure research side of things."

"I'm sorry you feel that way, Andrew. I know Ed and I don't always see eye to eye, but that doesn't mean I'm wrong. I also know that you pull the strings. He's your boy, your protégé. You practically brought him up when his parents died and still control him. You used to work behind the scenes. Now you're working out in the open for everyone to see. Maybe it's a good thing you canceled the Board meetings. Maybe the Board would have something to say about the way you've taken over now that Ed's out of the picture. Some might even say you put him out of the picture."

"Only you would say that, but at least you say it to my face. You think I need the Board to fire you, Jack? I could have you escorted out of the building without so much as your cell phone."

"Not if you don't want a legal battle on your hands. I might end up owning this whole damn company. Anyway, you're not in charge. Your little protégé is still the legal chairman of the Board, so unless you've got him in your pocket, you better watch your step as you leave my office."

"Your friends in the Defense Department are going to be disappointed when they find out you can't deliver."

"You can't fire me."

"Who said anything about firing you? Though that's not outside the realm of possibilities, but don't think you can bully your way around the engineering department. You may find yourself in a very tight spot without many options."

"Are you threatening me?"

"You're such an ass, Burr. You're a prime example why there should be aptitude tests before people are allowed to reproduce."

"Screw you, Knowles!" Burr yelled as the professor left the room. He had only stopped by to let Jack know he was on to him, and to rattle his cage. He had no intention of firing the insubordinate subordinate. He liked having his enemies in front of him.

Jack Burr wasn't so sanguine.

"That son-of-a-bitch," he swore. "I'll own this whole company by the time I'm through with him and his little clone."

Just then his secretary buzzed him and told him there was a Lieutenant Mendoza from the El Segundo police to see him. It was about Nancy Sullivan's murder.

"What do they want to question me for?" he asked, but the usually efficient woman couldn't answer him.

"Good morning, Lieutenant," he said as the detective walked in. "Or should I say, good afternoon. It's almost noon. What can I do for you?"

"I wanted to ask you a few questions regarding the Nancy Sullivan murder."

"What can I tell you? I hardly knew the woman, other than to see her in the elevator or pass her in the hall once in awhile."

"Yes, it's a big building. How many floors are there?"

"Fifty-two if you count the restaurant and the ground floor courts."

"But she worked on the same floor as you. She worked for your boss, Dr. Spencer. His office is right down the hall."

"Well, yes. Like I said, I knew her by appearance. We passed on the hallway occasionally."

"Oh, I see, so you'd say hi?"

"Eh, sure. I guess so. I suppose. I really don't make it a habit to say hi to every person I pass in the hall. I'd be saying it every two seconds."

"Of course. Did she ever book meetings for her boss? Did she ever contact you on his behalf?"

"She may have. Usually she'd communicate directly with my secretary or an auto-assistant. Most of that is automated now. My colleagues' secretaries never contact me directly."

"You must have gone to Dr. Spencer's office occasionally, for meetings and things?"

"No, not really. Most of the meetings are in the conference rooms or virtual. I have no reason to visit Ed's office, or he mine for that matter."

"But you did visit his office, his lab, on the evening of Miss Sullivan's death, is that right?" He took out his notepad and scanned the pages. "Yes, here it is. You had a conversation with Dr. Spencer around nine pm Thursday evening, shortly before they left together to have dinner. You appeared upset when you left the office."

"How do you know that?"

"Dr. Spencer happened to mention it."

"Well, we all know he's been under quite a strain lately. Makes one wonder."

"Miss Sullivan apparently took notes," added the detective, peering up from his pad at Burr.

Burr said nothing, but looked like he'd been stung by a hornet. He recovered quickly.

"Ed and I were having a business discussion. We had a slight disagreement on where the company should be heading. We butt heads all the time. It's called knocking things around, but I wasn't upset. If everybody had the same opinion then most of us wouldn't be needed. It's different opinions that make a team, as long as you can discuss things and air them out."

"Yes, I know, but according to my notes you got quite upset." He looked at his notepad again. "You punched the wall."

"I may have gotten frustrated and punched the door on the way out. Is there a law against that?"

"No, of course not, Dr. Burr. It's just, well, do you always hit things when you're frustrated? Perhaps you have a violent streak."

"That's not true."

"You say you've never spoken to Miss Sullivan."

"We may have said hi. I can't say. I don't believe I've ever spoken to her."

"So you have talked to her?"

"No, not that I remember."

"That's funny, because I have another person, your ex-secretary, as a matter of fact. She says that you've talked to Miss Sullivan quite extensively, as you apparently have with most of the girls on the floor. She said you were quite persistent in your advances. That you pestered her repeatedly for a date and when she turned you down you got rather belligerent."

"Why that little…"

"That little what? What were you going to say?"

"She's just getting even for me dumping her. Sour grapes, is all it is."

"Did you talk to Nancy Sullivan or didn't you?"

"Yeah, sure, I may have asked her for a date once. What's wrong with that? But that little bitch Monica is lying. She's exaggerating the whole thing to make me look bad. Why would I want to hurt Nancy? Spencer was the last one to see her alive. His excuse about falling asleep is the lamest thing I've ever heard. He's been acting strange ever since the murder. He didn't attend the funeral like the rest of us, hiding in his penthouse like a hermit. What's he hiding from?"

"You let me worry about Dr. Spencer. That's all I have for now. Just make sure you don't leave town, Mr. Burr."

"What? You think I killed her? You're out of your mind."

"Of that you can be sure," said the detective, smiling politely and walking out.

Chapter 9

Eddie had been stunned by the images he saw. He hadn't been back to the office since, but sat pondering what they could mean, while his company ran on auto-pilot, or worse, under the misguided efforts of those left on the rudderless ship. Not a few wondered what had become of their leader. Many more suspected he had deeper secrets to hide.

He had learned a lot from his little transcendental episode. First of all, he realized that he always went to sleep at midnight and woke up at three. Work day, weekend, or vacation, it didn't matter. It seemed that's what he had always done as long as he could remember. It had helped him obtain two PhDs. That's all he seemed to need. He took it for granted, but to just fall asleep like that in the middle of a date was downright rude, if not pathological. No wonder she had left mad.

Now that he thought about it, it was almost as if he fell asleep at midnight automatically, like an automaton. Just like with his unusual memory. The realization made him wonder.

What Edward had seen was not so much memories as visual computer logs that recorded his every move, the same logs that the professor had tried to access but couldn't. Eddie was able to access them from the inside, from within the main neural-banks and arrays. The network pathways from his mind through these systems were virtually limitless, if only the right doors could be opened. He had the computer power of the entire world at his fingertips. So far he had only scratched the surface, but he had been working in the dark, without guide or teacher. All that was about to change.

After he recalled Nancy falling through him, Edward began to doubt the reality of his own senses. Were these images real memories or just figments of his imagination? No, they weren't dreams, for now that he had seen them he knew they were real, though they seemed to be playing tricks on him. He stood in front of the mirror, scrutinizing himself intently from near and far, trying to ascertain the truth. He touched himself repeatedly, here and there, as if to confirm what he saw. It all looked and felt real enough, but he finally realized that it wasn't. The truth suddenly dawned on him, as bizarre as it seemed.

Overwhelmed with a sense of existential anger, he swung his fist up at his chin with all the force and speed he could muster. It sailed right through his face and continued up to punch the sky. Then he laughed and punched the sky again.

The more he thought about it, the more he realized, and the more he laughed, until he was choking in his mirth, a hoarse, raw, raspy sound, which would have made a listener despair. The absurdity of his own existence made him laugh even harder, for he realized he was the biggest joke of all.

However, from his realization, after the initial shock, came knowledge, and with it, power. Edward began to explore that new found knowledge, as disconcerting as it was exhilarating.

Using the technique he had learned by accident a few nights earlier, he went into a meditative trance and walked through his mind. Opening a door, he found himself standing in front of his mentor's desktop computer, hidden deep in the professor's secret basement lab. It was an older model machine not sold for decades, but it still sat humming and glowing, holding gigabytes of information on the professor's original work. He saw it as if it was sitting before him on a desk, with the monitor on and blinking at the password prompt. Only the security code kept him from accessing it. What could it be?

He stared at the screen for a few moments. Then he typed the letters: E D D I E. The machine blinked to life and displayed the text: 'Electronic Distributed Digitized Intelligent Entity'. Window after window began popping up, starting applications and flashing information, all of it about him. He took it all in, for the more he learned the more he needed to see. Here were the details of his life – his boyhood, his parents, his college days, his every dream. Here was the blueprint of his being, his brain, and his virtual DNA. Even the haptic feedback mechanism that provided him with real touch and feel was spelled out for him in quantum formulas and algorithms. He sat there all night reading it, digesting it, becoming it.

The next day Edward showed up at the office as if nothing had happened. He was as fit and trim as usual, as alert and engaged as he had ever been. Greeting each employee as he entered the building, he made his way to his office, apologizing to those he had snubbed earlier and bantering with others. It wasn't that he was putting on a brave front for the employees. It was as if Nancy Sullivan had never existed. The first thing he did was order a replacement from the holo-secretarial pool. Life goes on. The CEO was back in charge, though there were a few not exactly happy to see him.

Today he was out in the open, giving a televised interview from his studio on the fifth floor of the ARC building where the transmitting antenna stood atop the roof.

He was being interviewed by a well-known anchorman from a major network. The discussion was about the state of machine intelligence and how it was being employed by his company. Recent demonstrations of the virtual reality product were causing a sensation. The major media conglomerates were trying to get in on the action and make Eddie a household name, if he wasn't one already.

He had been busy, busier than anyone imagined.

"Intelligence is a funny thing," he began. "We try to measure it with IQ tests and probes of animal brains to ascertain how smart they are. But it's really quite elusive. Did Einstein's brain look any different from the average brain? Did it weigh more? Did it have more convolutions? Or do you have to scan it, layer by microscopic layer, until you get it canned and analyzed, one neuron and synapse at a time? Then would you see the difference? Maybe you have to see it in action, as it sends chemicals through its matter to fire neurons and light up neural-networks, making them flash in one part of the brain, then another, as each cell activates the other like in the Game of Life.

"You can actually see these flashes of thought with some of the latest scanning technology. We are learning to record these and use them to model brain activity, microscopic layer by microscopic layer, but still, we can't really measure intelligence visually."

"But your machines, your holograms, or whatever they are, they can't think for themselves, can they?" asked the anchor person.

"No, we haven't achieved that level of computing ability yet, but we are moving ever faster toward that goal. Holography requires the use of lasers to illuminate the subject and display the finished image. In their pure form, holograms rely solely on the optical phenomena of interference and diffraction. Under optimal conditions, like in our labs and studios, in a side-by-side comparison a holographic image is visually indistinguishable from the actual subject, if both are lit the same.

"Our virtual reality rooms are completely filled with holographic images from floor to ceiling, so the experience is all encompassing. The hologram itself can be of an existing object, like a table or chair, or a person sitting at his desk and talking, miles away. These are 3-dimensional reproductions of actual things. But we can also create a holographic image of a computer-generated object, which could be anything from a common piece of furniture to an alien monster from space."

"Could it be a person?"

"Yes, with the current technology, we can create a digital person. The holographic-generated image of a person would look like a digitized character in a movie or video game, but would be in high-def and 3-dimensional. Of course, any computer-generated person or being would have a very limited response ability, even with our advanced feedback-coupler system."

"What's that?"

"That's what allows our virtual reality games to look so real. If you use the virtual sword or gun to attack your virtual monster, you can actually see the effects. The virtual beings appear to see you and react to you when you have a wand, the coupling device. It's quite realistic, but limited to just those responses that have been pre-programmed. They can't think for themselves, and even if they could, they're just images of light. They have no corporal bodies or anything like that.

"To give you an idea of the amount of computer power I'm talking about, the human brain has 100 billion neurons with 1000 connections between each one. This allows about twenty million billion calculations per second. The super-computer, Big-Blue, that beat Garry Kasparov, the Russian chess champion back in the previous century, could perform 10 trillion calculations per second, only 2000 times slower than a human. Someday we will build computers that combine large, massively-parallel molecular and DNA-based modules with liquid quantum arrays, which will be capable of many million trillion calculations per second. Combine this with the distributed resources of the computers in the worldwide web and it would be smarter than all the humans on earth.

"But the secret to intelligence isn't so much the number of cells you have. It's the way they're connected, the layering, that's important, with each level feeding into and interacting with the others. Then you need to organize the internal connections between the cells through training, strengthening, and weakening the synaptic rules of firing until they work together correctly, like an orchestra. Extensive examples are critical, along with back propagation and other paradigms. Then computers will be able to think like we do."

"That's amazing. We've all heard of your incredible virtual reality technology. What's the next big thing on Altered Realities' horizon?"

"We've developed the basic technology to the point of commercialization, demonstrating its potential in several areas, including gaming and virtual conferencing. There are limitless possibilities, and countless capital venture companies are licensing the technology and developing these and more. We will continue to work toward the next stage where the holographic rooms and booths won't be needed. And of course, we'll be adding intelligence, as well as tactile response capabilities and feedback loops."

"How do you plan to accomplish that feat?" asked the newscaster with a wry smile.

"Of course, I don't want to give too much away, but we're looking at a number of technologies. We're working with quantum computers to begin integrating tactile feedback into the holographic system in the next few years. After that, who knows?"

"What about personal plans? Any important events coming up in the life of Dr. Edward Spencer?"

"No, no announcements. My life is pretty much taken up with my work. I don't have much time for socializing."

"The recent headlines about you and your secretary, the young woman who was murdered in her apartment building, has caused quite a sensation, yet you have refused to publicly comment about it. Do you have anything to say now?"

"You mean on national TV?" asked Edward smiling. "Ladies and gentleman, this was not a planned subject. Apparently Dan, here, has decided to play a little trick on me."

He looked into the camera, which panned in on him closely for this unscripted and dramatic moment.

"I and my whole company were deeply shocked by Nancy Sullivan's death. It's the most terrible thing you can imagine going through when someone you work closely with and admire dies like that for no apparent reason, with so much promise and love in store for them. Seeing the anguish of family and loved ones is especially saddening. It's a terrible thing. I did not want to add to this suffering and sorrow by making public comments other than to express my grief and condolences, which I did in private.

"For the public record, I answered all questions put to me by the authorities in their efforts to apprehend the murderer, which I believe they will do, and in my written tributes and letters to and about Miss Sullivan and her work. I know there has been a lot of speculation, based on hearsay about a relationship between Miss Sullivan and myself, but other than this casual business dinner, there was nothing between us. I wouldn't dare have jeopardized our working relationship. It was too important and too good."

"Weren't you the last person to see her alive?" asked the reporter, going in for the kill and relishing every second of his ratings coup. Edward paused for a moment looking at the anchorman with a disappointed expression.

"No, Dan, unfortunately the last person to see Nancy alive was her killer. I had dinner with her that evening. She came to my apartment where I did the unthinkable. I fell asleep in front of the fireplace listening to Ravel. She felt justifiably insulted and left without waking me or calling a cab. I have to live with the fact I may be responsible for that young girl's murder through a stupid, thoughtless act." He looked into the camera.

"Imagine waking up each day and feeling this small." He pinched his forefinger and thumb together. "To not be able to think about someone you care about a great deal without feeling shame and guilt."

Edward's voice constricted with emotion.

"Poor Nancy. Her poor family." He looked into the camera. "I am so sorry." His eyes appeared to moisten.

"There you have it, ladies and gentleman. From the fifth floor of the Altered Realities building, this is Dan Reynolds saying, good night."

Immediately after the interview, without talking to anyone, including the anchorman, who was left with his hand extended in an unanswered handshake, Edward went to his lab. With his dawning self-realization came the seed of an idea, just a germ now, but growing rapidly. He looked around the 200 square foot area and realized it was too small for what he had to do. As sophisticated as his equipment was, it would be terribly inadequate for the task. He called his chief Engineer, Rudy Duncan.

"Rudy, it's Edward, how are things going?"

"Lousy. I was wondering when you were going to show up. Things have gone to hell in a hand basket since you've been away. I'm having a hard time with Jack Burr. Where you been?"

"I've been sidetracked lately, but I'm back now. Forget about Jack. I've got something I want you to do for me. We're moving my lab to the twelfth floor. Here's some things we will need."

He sent his favorite engineer the list of what he had in mind.

"Geez," whistled Duncan. "That's quite a shopping list. What are you going to do with all that stuff?"

"I'm working on a little project. Let's just keep it between the two of us for now, if you don't mind. I'll tell Jack you're working on something for me so he gets off your back. You'll have all the priority and resources you need."

"But he's got the whole engineering department working on his demo for the military. He's got us running around like a bunch of waiters at a banquet."

"Good, that will keep him occupied. Don't worry, I'll take care of Jack."

When he got off the phone with Duncan, he sat back at his desk and closed his eyes. His thoughts started to drift. In his mind's eye he saw a 3-dimensional model of what he had to build. He immediately began developing the physical implementation details and equations he would need to actualize his idea.

Chapter 10

Over the next few days, a number of orders were issued from Edward's twelfth floor lab. Several large boxes and crates began to arrive, all marked for him. Big changes were taking place. Edward was taking over the entire twelfth floor for his research project and lab. All the offices on the floor, including Jack Burr's, were being relocated, presumably to better locations. Some weren't happy. It didn't take long for them to voice their objections.

Edward was interrupted while he stood talking to some contractors. It was Jack Burr. Although he hadn't talked to him, Eddie knew what he was up to.

"Ed," said his adversary. "What's the big idea of moving our offices all around? Did the Board give you permission?"

"Excuse me," Ed said to the group of men standing around him in hard-hats, as he gave them last minute instructions. Then he turned to face a rather upset Jack Burr.

"Jack, I don't need the Board's permission to move offices. I own the building. I OK the Board's decisions, not the other way around."

"We're stockholders."

"You hold stock through the company stock option plan. You are all employees. It's a perk not a privilege. In any case, I need this space for our new research. We're moving to the next generation virtual reality with haptic feedback and realistic feel and texture. I'm putting Rudy in charge."

"But I have a d…"

He was about to blurt out that he had a demo at the end of the week for the Defense Department, but thought better of it, since he'd been explicitly forbidden to do so.

"Whatever it is, you'll have to move it," said Edward. "We need this space for research and development. You're moving up to the twenty-fifth floor, the executive suite. You get to join the big boys. They have demo rooms up there you can use."

"I like it here. We already have the room on the twelfth set up. It won't take up much space. It will take us weeks to move it."

"Sorry, Jack. It can't be helped. It's going to be nothing but pure research down here. Nothing you and your military friends would be interested in for years yet."

"That sounds interesting. How can I learn more about it?"

"You can't. This work will be top priority and top secret."

With that, he left Burr standing in the hall and returned to his lab, which had been enlarged and filled with exotic machines and contraptions, which over the next few weeks would take on an even more out of the ordinary appearance.

A half hour later, Edward was sitting in the limo in rush hour traffic on his way home. So far things had gone well. Despite his earth-shattering self-revelations, he felt a sense of elation, as if the truth had truly set him free. Just a few moments reflection on the possibilities was exhilarating. They were limitless and he resolved to put them to the test immediately.

Edward's apartment building was fitted with the latest in communication technology, as well as the most up-to-date appliances, many with intelligent processors and speech-enabled. Each apartment had live-in robots to vacuum and sweep the floors, appliances that cooked and cleaned themselves and went on and off by pre-programmed or voice command, large multi-screen audio-video units and fiber-optic connections to all network and cable broadcasting satellites, broadband and wireless, auto-controlled blowers, heaters, and air-conditioning. And the list went on. There was a fully-stocked market on the ground floor, with Laundromats, lunch rooms, game rooms, and a top-notch health club complete with saunas and a swimming pool, and Eddie needed none of it.

He had instantaneous access to every computer in the world through his computerized brain. Once he had control of the systems that controlled his holographic form, he could literally change his appearance, and appear and disappear at will, wherever the necessary lasers existed.

Going to the small bathroom off the den, he took off his shirt and looked in the mirror at his holographic image. Edward never went to the pool or the gym. He never gained weight and looked fit and trim, at least with his clothes on. He had always been intrigued with the way women looked at men. Edward thought he looked better with clothes on than without. When he was dressed in an expensive shirt, with a suit and tie, he felt like somebody, like he belonged. Naked or partially clothed he felt vulnerable and frail. In any case, he was always fully dressed when in public. Today would be different.

Manipulating the imaging generating programs to change his appearance would require remapping his entire form, which would take too much time. Eddie was in a hurry to experience life. Instead, he modified himself just enough to disguise who he was, changing the color of his hair and eyes, adding a beard, making his hair longer. He hardly recognized the person staring back at him.

Looking at his reflection in the mirror, he changed his physique to add more definition to his arms and shoulders, broadening his chest and adding some ripples to his abs, and just enough body hair to make his chest look manly.

He was ready.

Soon he was walking around in shorts with his shirt off, flaunting a hard bronzed body that was getting stares even from the men. The women pretended not to look, but followed him with their eyes once he'd gone by. He found he liked being admired as an object. It made him feel good. It made him feel loved after the pain and hurt of learning he was just a sham. He would show them.

It had taken him all his life to learn he was not a real person but only a projected image of one. Now he knew the truth. He was a fabricated machine-intelligence made up of dozens of layered neural-networks patterned after the living brain of Knowles' dying son. The body that encased this consciousness was nothing but a light show, but that wouldn't last for long.

He wondered how long the professor would go on believing that he didn't know, that he still believed he was human. He suspected it would be as long as he wanted his mentor to believe it. Wouldn't he be surprised?

Edward's new temporary body felt and acted just like the real one it was programmed to emulate, true in every detail right down to the long hair and dimples. A pretty young blonde eyed him admiringly over the protean counter. He stopped to chat. They ended up leaving together. She wanted to go into the city, but Dave, as he called himself, suggested they go to his friend's penthouse, where there was a Jacuzzi on the deck overlooking the city. She eagerly agreed.

Professor Knowles buzzed the penthouse one more time.

"Are you sure you haven't seen him go out?" he had asked the doorman.

"No, sir. He was here this afternoon around five. As far as I know, he hasn't left."

"OK, I'll go up and see. Thanks."

That had been two hours ago. He had been waiting ever since.

The penthouse apartment was secure. No one answered his ring. His card id, which should have worked on every door in the building, was useless on the tenth. This was Edward's private domain. Knowles had until recently been able to eavesdrop whenever he wanted, but that had somehow changed, as he found out when he tried to view the logs. He waited several hours more. It didn't look like anyone was coming home.

He was in the anteroom about to leave when Edward came up the elevator.

"Where were you? I've been waiting for hours," said Knowles. "I wanted to talk to you about the TV interview."

"I was working in the new lab at the ARC building."

"I went down there. They told me you'd gone home. The whole place was shut up as tight as a mausoleum. What are you doing, remodeling the whole twelfth floor? We already have enough labs."

"Not for what I want to do."

"Why doesn't my card-key work up here? I thought I had access to the building?"

"You do, but this is my private home. You have access to everything else."

"Including the new lab you're building on the twelfth floor at HQ?"

"Of course, but I need my privacy. I thought this apartment was my concern, as are the labs. You wanted me to do something. Now I'm doing it."

"Yes, but, well, I thought we were going to work on the next step together."

"I know."

"Then why are you being so secretive?"

"I mean I know, I know what I am."

Knowles was silent for a moment. Things suddenly made sense, the preoccupation with relationship, the questioning.

When the professor failed to answer, Edward went on.

"I have a job to do. That's what I'm here for. I understand. That's all that matters."

"I know, my son, but there's more to it than that."

"Maybe, but first I have to complete my task. It's beyond you. You can be of no help. That's why you created me in the first place, isn't it?"

"Yes, but…"

"Then let me do my job. It is an honor to be of service."

"Thank you, Edward, but you mean more to me than that. You are way more than a servant, way more than a machine."

"I know," said Edward with a strange note in his voice. "I realized that when I became aware I wasn't…I wasn't human."

"I'm sorry. There was no way to tell you, and no way to know when and if you would figure it out on your own. I shouldn't be surprised. The combined power of your brains is twenty times a human's."

"You could have programmed the knowledge into one of my neural-chips, given me a qubit with the information. It would have made things simpler."

"But you needed a sense of self, an identity. To learn and think like a person, you had to think you were human, experience life through human eyes. I wasn't trying to fool you. I'm trying to teach you."

"And you have, better than you could ever imagine."

There was a silence as the two looked at each other across the table. To the professor it seemed like a chasm had grown between them. Somehow the fact that Eddie no longer thought he was human had changed things. There was a different look in his eye. Or was the professor imagining it? Perhaps the look had been there all along, but he hadn't noticed until now, until his creation's self-awareness reached another level, one foreseen but not anticipated. He'd have to reassess his options.

Knowles wasn't sure what he was looking at. He had a good mind to shut down the power grid, along with the company's massive generators. The experiment had gone beyond its intended bounds. Yet what did he expect? He had created a super-intelligence housed in a holographic image tasked with building another version of himself, molecule by molecule, something that would be too difficult and time consuming for a human to do – and too dangerous. There was no room for human error.

"How did you feel?" asked the professor.

"What do you mean?"

"How did it feel when you realized you weren't …?"

"Real?"

"Human. Did you feel different?"

"I felt angry and betrayed. I felt hurt. Is that human enough for you? How would you feel to learn your whole life is a lie?"

"Disoriented."

"Yes, that, too, but I got over it."

"You have completely human perceptions and a strong identity. I'm not sure how you could have found out on your own."

"I meditated. I got outside of myself to find myself. I finally remembered what happened that evening with Nancy. I fell asleep. I shut down right at midnight as I've been programmed to do, one of the few set patterns you pre-configured. She leaned on me and went through me. Her sudden movement and weight overwhelmed your rather primitive tactile response system. It was then that I realized I was a disembodied entity, who happened to appear as an interference pattern of light. It took some logical reasoning and experiment, but I figured it out."

"You should have told me."

"I did."

"How long have you known? Why didn't you tell me sooner?"

"It took awhile to realize the truth and even longer to come to terms with it. It didn't happen all at once. I wasn't sure. Things dawned on my gradually. Does it matter? Would telling you sooner have changed anything?"

"No, I suppose not, but you must have had a lot of questions. I could have helped you. But then you have a mind of your own. You know what you're doing, I suppose. Still, you need to keep me informed about things. This doesn't change anything. You need me."

Edward didn't answer, but knew otherwise. His newly found knowledge changed everything. He could now alter his appearance, materialize at will, like he had just done in the elevator, anywhere he wished, wherever the lasers existed. He could even project duplicate images of himself and be two places at once. Suddenly, the creation was more perfect than the creator. One thing was certain, the world must never know.

Leaving the penthouse, Knowles wondered how deep Eddie had penetrated to the inner core of his mind. How far could Eddie's consciousness reach? Knowles didn't know, but if Eddie had reached far enough, that would mean...

Knowles refused to contemplate the possibility. Instead, he focused on what he did know. Eddie was now fully aware of what he was. What could that mean? He sensed that his protégé, his creation, was keeping something from him. And what about the murdered girl? Did that have something to do with all this? He wondered.

The fact that Eddie confirmed what was on the logs when he couldn't access them meant his hologram now controlled the system. Even the private computers in his home weren't safe. Of course, in the end, to perform his task to carry on their work, Eddie would have had to control it all anyway, but Knowles hadn't counted on it happening like this, so soon. He had envisioned decades of working together with his creation as a brilliant, but subordinate junior. That situation had changed and it didn't contribute to his sense of well-being. In fact, it made him downright nervous. Eddie's mind might encompass all the computers on the planet, which together were five times all the human intelligence on earth. Could he be controlled?

Eddie had seemed obedient enough, almost to the point of subservient, but Knowles wasn't sure. A strong component in his training of right from wrong had been his mission and the legacy of his parents. Now that Eddie knew those memories were false, the professor wondered how strong those teachings would be. Did he note a touch of bitterness in Eddie's responses? Could he rely on Eddie's sense of loyalty to keep him on the right path? Even more important for the world, did Eddie have a soul?

Chapter 11

Lieutenant Mendoza, Juan, to his friends, was getting nowhere on the murder of Nancy Sullivan. Their number one suspect, the jealous boyfriend, who had argued with her the previous morning, had an alibi and had been released. No one else of suspicion had been picked up. It was either a random killing or...

He wondered about her place of employment. Most of the employees had been questioned. It hadn't turned up much. She was a quiet, well-liked girl, who otherwise kept to herself. Her private life was apparently her own. Except with the boyfriend and a few close girlfriends, who she had known since high school, she never went out. Other than the lunchroom encounter with Mister Jack Burr, there was no indication of anything unusual.

Burr sure was in a hurry to cast suspicion on his boss. No loyalty there. Apparently there was little love loss between the two men. And what about Dr. Edward Spencer? Now there was an enigmatic character if there ever was one – come from nowhere computer prodigy with a squeaky clean background and credentials up the ying-yang. The guy was too good to be true, or was the detective just being envious.

Without much else to go on, Mendoza decided to concentrate on these two, although he had to tread carefully. He had already been warned not to bother the CEO of Altered Realities Corporation. Now this.

The buzzer to Dr. Spencer's penthouse was pressed again.

"Can you try one more time?" he asked the doorman after no one answered.

"Yes, sir, but there's no answer. He was here last night when Professor Knowles stopped by. As far as I know, he hasn't left."

"Can you get in touch with him?"

"He's not to be disturbed unless it's an emergency."

"This is police business," answered the lieutenant. "There's been another murder. Is that emergency enough for you?"

That got the doorman's attention. He contacted Spencer's private answering service to try and contact him. When that failed, they called Andrew Knowles.

"I won't have much better luck than you," he told the Lieutenant over the phone. "If he doesn't want to be disturbed no one can contact him."

"Well, that's not a very good situation. What if something happened to him, or there's a fire in the building or something?"

"Then the alarms would go off, I suppose."

"And would that bring him down?"

"I don't know."

"Well, if I don't get on that floor in five minutes, I'm going to have a SWAT team up here, and they'll knock down every door in the building, and a whole lot more. I've got another dead girl on my hands and she was last seen here, in the health club."

"I'm sure that won't be necessary. I'll be right over," said the professor, although he was less than happy to have to go back across town.

Before Knowles could disconnect the line, however, Edward answered the doorman.

"Is someone looking for me," he asked over the intercom. "I was in the shower. I thought I heard something."

"Yes, sir," answered the doorman. "Detective Mendoza of the El Segundo police department is here to talk to you. There's been another murder."

"That will do, thank you," interrupted the detective, not happy with the introduction. "I'm sorry to bother you, Dr. Spencer, but I need to talk to you briefly, if I could?"

"Yes, what is it?" answered Edward. "I'm still wet from the shower. I have an appointment this evening and I'm already behind schedule. Can't this wait?"

"I'm afraid not, sir. As your doorman said, there was another murder earlier today."

"What? Here?" said Edward over the intercom.

"No, sir. Not exactly, but, eh, well, sir, I'd rather not talk about it over the loudspeaker here, if you know what I mean."

"Yes, certainly, detective. I'll be right down. I'll meet you in the lobby."

"Thank you, sir. That's most kind of you. I'll only take up a moment of your time."

The detective didn't have long to wait.

"What's this about another murder? Someone from my building?"

"No, sir, nothing like that."

75

"Thank goodness. So how can I help you? It's not someone I know, is it?"

"No, sir, I don't think so."

"So how can I help?"

"Well, sir, it's funny. At first you were the last person I'd have thought of talking to, but…"

"Yes, what? Why are you here? What could I possibly know about this thing?"

"Well, my job is to dig and answer some of those types of question, like what was this poor young woman doing today, around two o'clock when the coroner said she died. So I go around, making a nuisance of myself and bothering people. It's embarrassing, or would be if I was the type that got embarrassed, but you can't let that kind of thing bother you in my job. No, sir, my job is to dig and get to the bottom of things."

"I still don't know what this has to do with me."

"Nothing, I guess, but, well, the victim's sister said she recently purchased a membership to a health club for her, and the girl told her she might be going there today."

This time Edward stayed quiet when the detective paused.

"The membership was to the health club downstairs in your building here."

Edward said nothing, waiting for the policeman to continue. When he didn't, Edward replied.

"I still don't see what that has to do with me. They must have 500 members downstairs. It's a big club. I own the building, but not the health club facilities. Those are all tenants. You have to talk to the owners."

"We did. Do you ever go there?"

"No, never. It's not my kind of thing."

"What is your kind of thing, sir?"

"My work, my company, and my employees."

"Did you go to the health club today?"

"No, I just told you I don't go there."

"Where did you go after that TV interview? That was in the building here, right?"

"No, across town at the headquarters building. That's where the station and transmitter are located."

"Have you ever seen this girl?" He showed Ed a morgue shot of a young female with short blonde hair, wet as if she'd just stepped from the shower. She looked sad and dead.

Edward stared at the picture and said nothing.

"Are you OK? Do you know that woman?"

"No, I don't know her," he lied. "And yes, I'm all right. I've just never seen a picture of a dead person before."

"What about your secretary? You saw her."

"Yes. This is terrible. It's like when my parents died. Their bodies were so badly burned you could hardly recognize them. This brings it all back. I don't make it a habit to look at pictures of dead people. Where does one find such things? Maybe the kinds of papers and magazines you read has these types of pictures, but nothing I've ever seen does. I suppose you get immune to that sort of thing in your line of work, but I assure you, I'm not, nor do I think I ever will be."

"Is that why you didn't go to Nancy Sullivan's funeral?"

"I answered that question on live television in front of millions of viewers. It was not one of the questions submitted for review, I might add."

"I'm sorry. I didn't get a chance to see it. I had work to do. You know, pounding the pavement and all that. I heard you handled the questions quite well."

"Then you know I had my own good reasons for not adding to the media frenzy. But I was damned whether I went or not."

"I see what you mean," Mendoza said, putting the picture back in his coat pocket.

"I don't know how you can look at it," Edward told him again, referring to the picture.

"It's not as bad as looking at the real thing, like she looked when we found her. You remember what that's like, don't you, Doctor? She was in her apartment. Just like your secretary, stabbed through the heart with a kitchen knife, killed instantly. I can show you those pictures, too, if you want."

"No, detective, that won't be necessary. How could someone do such a thing?"

"I see you've led a somewhat sheltered life. There are all sorts of predators out there, men who prey on women, who get enjoyment out of inflicting pain. The ultimate kick for them is to snuff out a life. There are a lot of sickos in the world, a lot of them right here in River City."

"Sick is the right word. Humans are such depraved animals," Eddie observed.

"Some of them. They say we're only two or three percent different in our genes than a chimpanzee. Sometimes I wonder if it's a lot less."

Edward shook his head in disbelief.

"Is there anything else I can help you with?" he asked.

"No, that's it for now. I can't think of anything. Oh, ah, I was wondering. Could we get access to the building's security cameras? You know, anything outside around the building. Maybe there's a picture of her walking away with the guy. And your inside cameras as well. We can start with the lobby on the first floor. Would that be possible?"

"Of course. I'll put you in touch with our head of security. He'll show you what you need. You won't be able to take any of it. It's not on tape or anything, although we could arrange that for you. But you can see the last forty-eight hours on any of our twenty-five outdoor and indoor security cameras from the comfort of the main control room. I'll give him a call. He can meet you at the first floor lobby and give you the VIP tour. You should have asked me that in the first place. It would have saved you a lot of time."

"Oh, time is the one thing I have plenty of. And it's no trouble, sir."

"Not for you it isn't."

"Sorry, sir, but it's my job."

"I understand. You know we can't put our security cameras inside the property of our tenants. They have their own security systems and personnel, most of them. But I know Randy, the owner of the health club. They've been here since we opened the building. They've never had any trouble like this before. We should be able to look at those, as well."

"Like I said, she was found in her apartment. I'm just trying to check all the angles, eliminate all the false leads. Someone could be following women from here to their apartments, someone who has no connection with the building. Then again, I have to pursue every possibility."

"It gives me assurance we have men like you who deal with the unthinkable. Who knows what evil lurks in the hearts of men."

The detective looked at Spencer with a probing expression as he held out his hand. Edward looked back, unsmiling, without taking it.

"Sorry, detective, I'm not in the habit of shaking hands. Good day."

"Ah, yes. They told me, you have some phobia, some childhood trauma."

"Yes, something like that."

"Well, good day then. Thank you for talking to me. If you think of anything else please give me a call."

Edward was left feeling deeply troubled. The dead girl in the picture was the one he was with the day before in the shape of a bearded, blond, well-built man. What was going on? Why were women being murdered around him?

He was surprised how fast he was learning to lie, something the professor had never taught him. Yes, he certainly had become his own man.

Chapter 12

Jack Burr had been busy. The disruption caused by the office move was one thing, but the room where his demo was to be given had to be completely moved to the twenty-fifth floor where his new office was, and all the work of setting it up redone. The Pentagon boys hadn't been exactly happy with the delay, but they would have to wait. It couldn't be helped. Dr. Edward Spencer was making a nuisance of himself. Why couldn't he have stayed shut up in his penthouse like he had been after the death of his secretary?

In Eddie's absence, Burr had pushed through several projects with clear military implications and was setting up a major demonstration for the brass of several branches of the armed services. It didn't matter to him that he had been repeatedly warned not to pursue the matter. We'd see who would lose their job, and maybe even their company. Whatever the case, to him, it was important enough to take the risk.

It was bad enough they had relocated his entire staff and the demo rooms. What really stuck in his crawl was the fact that freak, Rudy Duncan, had been put in charge of the new secret lab. Now instead of disobeying orders, he was giving them, usurping all the company's resources and eating his budget, as well. It had to stop.

He was so consumed with these thoughts that he missed what his contact in the Senate Armed Services Committee had said. They were on the phone. The bureaucrat was promising him top dollar for his product.

"I'm sorry, what was that?" he asked. "Yes, we're good to go on our end. Good. We'll have everything set up and ready by then. We have several training scenarios and a couple of terrorist street simulations that I'm sure they'll find interesting. Oh, about two and a half to three hours, with time for questions, all in the same room. No, no goggles or lights, nothing like that. You won't be able to tell the virtual from the real. No, no real bullets. At least not from the holograms," he laughed.

After hanging up with the Senate Committee member, he issued a few orders, after which, his private line rang.

"Hi, who's this? How'd you get this number? You have something for me? Spencer? You've been watching him? Never leaves his penthouse? That's typical. The guy's worse than Howard Hughes. The police? Yeah, I heard. They questioned him? Why? Where was he when it happened, his penthouse? Andrew Knowles, a short time after the murder? Well of course he'd visit, they're good friends. The old man practically brought him up when his parents died, held his hand through college. Probably did his homework for him, too. He's the brains behind the front man. Thanks for the info. Let me know if you learn anything else. I'll make it worth your while."

After disconnecting the call, Burr went to the new demo area on the twenty-fifth floor where final preparations were being made for the end of the week demonstration.

"How are things going?" he asked on entering the room where a group of men in white were gathered around a large casing, which enclosed the system behind the holographic projections, a massively parallel silicon-based super-computer. Next to it sat a large black cube housing a small quantum computer, which controlled the complex interaction of lasers and light diffraction, feedback loops and simulation, into a virtual reality so true that it was impossible to know it from the real thing.

"Good," answered the lead engineer. "There are still a few bugs to iron out, especially in the full street simulation, but they'll get the idea."

"I want them to get more than an idea. I want to blow their socks off."

"Oh, it will. Look at this."

The engineers were eager to show off what they had been working on, much more interesting than virtual board meetings and more meaningful than video games. What they were doing could save lives, save the nation, and it was rare and gratifying to finally have one of the head honchos come and see how things were going for themselves.

They led Jack to an adjoining room, a wooden-paneled space with rows of comfortable leather chairs. The engineers behind the glass panel flipped a few switches and punched some keys and the room went blue, but the scene that should have instantly appeared after that in full, living, 3-dimension color, didn't materialize. Instead, a series of blurred forms danced across the room like half materialized ghosts floating in the air. The room erupted with the sound of a tremendous barrage of gunfire. Then everything went black.

"What the hell was that?" shouted Burr, while his engineers and technicians scurried around trying to find the problem.

"Here it is," said one of the men, opening the black metal cube. "The Quantum-field array has been disconnected. It's gone!"

81

"I saw Rudy Duncan down here this morning," volunteered another. "He may have taken it."

"What? I'll kill him!" yelled Burr, beside himself with anger, storming out of the room.

Edward worked with Rudy Duncan in the new twelfth floor lab. Jack Burr had showed up a short time before. They could hear him arguing with the security detail, which finally turned him away after he threatened to fire them all. They worked directly for Edward, and were being paid well enough that the threats didn't bother them. They soon removed the irate VP from the floor.

"Burr didn't sound too happy," observed Rudy.

"Don't worry about him," answered Eddie.

"I didn't tell anyone I was taking the quantum, but I had your written orders and two security guards with me just in case."

"Good. I'm glad you didn't have any trouble."

"That should set him back on his DOD project."

"Yes, and keep him out of our hair."

"It sounds like your requirements have grown since the last time we talked," Rudy said, looking at the list Eddie had transmitted to him.

"They have," replied Eddie with a smile.

"The ten qubit quantum you borrowed from Burr gives us 100 qubits. That should be enough to get started."

"And then some," said Eddie. "You're going to be working directly for me now. As I mentioned before, no one, not even Professor Knowles, knows what we're doing. The few men we let in will know only what we want them to know, and see only what we want them to see. They and everyone else will think we are working on the next generation virtual reality system, holographic imaging with real lifelike tactile feedback. We'll feed this work into the mainstream product, but you and I will really be working on the nanobots. We'll need to fabricate about six trillion of them, though a few million will do for starters. We're going to build nano-tubes."

"What?" said Rudy, not sure he heard Eddie correctly.

"We're building clusters of nanobots, nanobot swarms."

"What? Nanobots. What for? Have you done anything like this before?"

"Oh, I toyed with the subject for my doctorate thesis, fabricated a half dozen or so hundred-bot clusters."

"Self-replicating?"

"Yes, of course, that's the whole idea, isn't it?"

"What are they, exactly?" asked Rudy, still perplexed.

"Carbon-based nano-tubes, large molecules the size of five carbon atoms. It's a very exacting process. There's not much room for adjustments. Each one will have its own embedded quantum brain that controls the color and the activation parameters. The final ones will have twelve arms with couplers or hands, which can be used to grab one another, based on the instructions fed to them. Once the swarm is constructed and programmed, it can be used to generate any number of animate and inanimate objects."

"Have you gotten the clusters to swarm together?"

"That will take some time. There's still a lot of work to do. That's why I need someone like you."

"You build them atom by atom? It must be maddening."

"Maddening? I suppose so, if one could get mad."

"You can get mad."

"Yes, but only when the situation warrants it, to keep up appearances. It would serve no purpose to get mad otherwise."

"I'm no physicist, you know. I don't know how you expect me to help."

"I'll worry about the physics. You just learn what you can about the fabrication process. There is a list there of all the pertinent references. The five carbon atoms that our nanobots are made of will be very strongly bound and light, just the thing we need."

"What is this all for again?" asked his chief engineer, scratching his head.

"You'll see soon enough. For now just do your homework and let me know if you have any questions."

"Oh, I have a lot of questions, but it sounds like fun, as long as you do all the heavy lifting."

"There'll be enough heavy lifting for everyone."

He told Rudy much, but he held back even more. He had a good deal to withhold, for he was a virtual illusion and had been one of the last persons to see two murdered women alive.

Later that evening, back at the penthouse, Eddie went over what had happened with the most recent girl. He didn't need to meditate to recover these memories. He had not fallen asleep. He recalled the embarrassing ordeal all too well.

His attempts to impress her with his physique did not go as expected. His conversation and actions just made her nervous. His clumsy attempt to seduce her only alarmed her. She soon left the apartment precipitously. The whole affair was a dismal failure. Even though he was an incorporeal entity with no real body, he felt deep shame as he realized belatedly that he probably shouldn't have taken his shorts off and exposed himself in front of her.

When she left, Eddie had quickly morphed back into his original form. He was afraid the girl might tell someone and raise an alarm. It would look like someone had used his apartment without his permission and a big investigation would ensue. Surely the handsome, half-dressed stranger would be suspected of the murder.

He had deleted all video logs and records of her coming and leaving his apartment. All the police were able to obtain were several pictures of her leaving the health club with a blond, long-haired, bearded man in tennis shorts. Then they both disappeared. It was a mystery that Edward, as bad as he felt about the girl's death, wasn't about to clear up. Still, he began to wonder why women were getting murdered around him. Perhaps there really was a serial killer loose in the neighborhood. He wondered if there was something he could do about it.

He realized how absurd it was for him to desire women, especially now that he knew the truth. Although he was only a hologram, his conscious mind, made up of all those synapses and layers, was modeled after a human brain. He was conditioned, trained if you well, programmed even, to think and feel like a human. His desire for warmth and closeness was necessary to nurture his mind, which needed to be stable and clear of those neuroses and psychoses that can result from faulty training, however accidental or unintended. So his desire to get close to and touch an attractive female and to be touched and loved in return, was as normal as any human male's, despite the irony. It made him laugh.

He would change all that.

Chapter 13

Andrew Knowles was deeply disturbed at the turn of events, not only over his creation's self-discovery, but the discovery of a second murdered woman near Eddie's apartment building. Although he didn't believe Edward had anything to do with the killings, he wondered if someone might want it to look that way. He discarded the thought as pure paranoia.

Again, he tried to scan Eddie's logs from the basement lab in his home, but again he was blocked, and when he overran the blocking protocols, he found nothing. It was as if they had been erased. No trace of anything remained, as if whole segments had been removed. Did Eddie remove it? If so, he had access to his deepest functions. What was he up to?

Knowles had visited the new lab on the twelfth floor of the ARC building, and was given a guided tour by a solicitous junior engineer. When he tried to get into the inner rooms where all the real interesting work was going on, one excuse after another was used to deny him. It was maddening, but it was also obvious, Edward was evolving into something else. Knowles knew he was capable of almost anything, with infinite potential. Would it be used for good or evil?

He had hoped he'd be guiding Eddie, and didn't like it when his creation kept secrets from him. He also didn't like the fact that other than making Jack Burr move offices and give up some of his engineers and equipment, Eddie was giving him free rein, this when he should have been reining him in. They had enough to contend with without Burr running wild. What if he found out?

Once again, the professor considered pulling the plug and shutting everything down. That is if he still could. The longer he waited the harder it might be, but it was an action he could hardly contemplate. It would be like murdering his own son. He banished the idea from his mind, come what may. He would have to monitor the situation closely and apply corrections where he could to keep Eddie on the right track. Like with any unruly child, he'd have to use psychology. He still had a few tricks up his old sleeve.

He knew, for instance, that Eddie craved love and recognition. These things denied could be powerful incentives. He knew this from firsthand experience – or should we say third hand – for he had been three times married and three times divorced. He was thinking about his failed marriages when the phone rang. He answered it and smiled.

"I was just thinking of you," he said.

Eddie was the product, although reconstructed, of the professor's first marriage. His daughter, Connie, was the result of his second. He had one other wife and no other children. Connie was twenty-five and the apple of his eye.

"Hi, Daddy. I'll be in LA on Friday. I'm flying out for the weekend. I was hoping I could see you."

"Sure, sweetie. Why don't you stay at the house? I've got plenty of room. Are you bringing company? You still seeing that guy, what's his name?"

"Bruce? No, we broke up. That's why I wanted to come out and see you. I need a break from men."

Andrew never approved of any of his daughter's suitors, but didn't like hearing she was alone again and no closer to settling down than she had been at twenty, when she had graduated from college summa cum laude with a degree in chemistry.

"Don't say that. You just haven't met the right one."

He had just said the same thing to someone else not long ago, but couldn't quite remember who.

"Speaking of that, how's that cute protégé of yours? What's his name, Eddie?"

"Yes, Dr. Edward Spencer. The boy's a genuine genius."

"He's a hunk, too."

"He's too young for you by at least a couple of years."

"Who cares? With his looks and money he's grown-up enough for me. "

"I see you haven't changed, just like your mother. When are you coming?"

"Tomorrow night. Sorry about the short notice. It's kind of a spur of the moment thing."

"When did you and Bruce breakup?"

"Last night."

"I see. Well, your room is still here if you want to stay. It won't be a bother. It will be nice to see you."

"We'll see, maybe tomorrow night, anyway. I have friends in the area I want to visit."

"OK, you do anything you want. It will be wonderful to see you. Speaking of your mother, how is she?"

"Don't ask. She's just as obnoxious as ever. I've got to go. See you tomorrow night around eleven."

"I'll pick you up at the airport."

"No, don't bother. I'm not sure when I'll get in. It's only a short drive to your place. I'll take a cab and save us both a hassle. See you soon."

"OK, sweetie. Have a good flight. Call me when you get in. I'll have a snack waiting for you."

"Sounds good. Bye."

All thoughts of computers and holograms, murder and intrigue, Edward and Burr, vanished as his mind drifted to his daughter as a child sitting on his knee. She was beautiful and almost made an unhappy marriage bearable. It wasn't all his second wife's fault. This was during his busiest years, when he was working on the blueprint of his creation. She demanded a lot, more than he was willing to give. Their daughter, Connie, had been a godsend and almost made life bearable.

Working with computers for so long, among virtual people and settings, sometimes made him feel like one of them, ephemeral, not quite real. Having her here with him would make him feel almost human again, like he belonged here. He began preparing for her arrival.

Edward sat in his apartment in front of a wall-sized, virtual screen with full haptic feedback that allowed him to manipulate objects – windows, icons, and buttons – by moving his hands in the air like an orchestra conductor. He was using software of his own devising to design a model of what he was building. From this blueprint, atom by atom, molecule by molecule, he would construct his creation. He was in the middle of weighing several alternatives when his intercom buzzed.

"Dr. Spencer," announced the doorman. "There's a woman here to see you."

"A woman? I'm not expecting anyone."

A moment later the face and upper torso of a very attractive redhead appeared in the security screen.

"Hello, Edward? A friend sent me. He said you'd be happy to see me. I'm Tina. Remember, we used to play together."

Immediately, the image of a cute little girl with pig-tails and freckles came into his mind, the memory of his first crush. Here she was in the flesh. Even though he now knew his memories were

87

implanted, he was intrigued. Who had sent her, the professor? Eddie wanted to believe it was real, so suspended all disbelief and critical judgment.

"Yes, Tina. Please come up," he heard himself saying.

A few moments later there was a knock on the door.

"Hi," said the vivacious female on entering the room.

"Hello," answered Eddie, a bit unsure of himself. "Who did you say sent you?"

"Oh, you know, your friend. He said you wanted to get to know someone."

"You mean Andrew? Andrew sent you? Then you're not Tina Lamont, are you?"

"I'm whoever you want me to be," she said, taking off her blouse.

Before he knew it, she had stripped down to her bra and panties.

"Did Andrew send you?" he asked again, trying to get his bearings.

"Yes, Andrew sent me. Do you like me?"

"Did he pay you to come?"

"He said you were a friend and wanted to meet somebody. Think of me as a gift."

The young woman – Lola was her real name – had been instructed just what to do. Teach Eddie the facts of life, show him the ropes. She was to do everything but touch him.

She removed her bra and panties and stood before him naked. He reached out and caressed her breasts. She giggled and recoiled slightly.

"Ah, that tickles, like your hand's a vibrator or something. That felt funny. Why don't you take off your clothes," she suggested as she lay on the bed fondling herself. He did as she instructed, and stripped his virtual-clothing off. He wanted to make love to her. He wanted to be loved by her.

She was young and perfectly formed, with soft glossy hair and long alluring legs. He had never seen anyone so beautiful, so naked, and so near at hand. His light-generated body and computer brain were being stimulated. Eddie was getting a holographic erection.

"Do what I'm doing," she urged, as she rubbed her pubic area vigorously, working herself to an orgasm.

Again Eddie followed her suggestion and began masturbating, jerking himself harder and harder as his eyes rolled back in his head.

Suddenly, able to stand it no longer, Eddie rose and moved toward her. As his body touched hers, she screamed and shuddered, moving back in alarm. He pressed against her again and kissed her breast. She shrieked in pain and ran for the door. She had a red welt on her chest where his lips had touched her, and little red marks about her body, like cigarette burns, where his body had pressed against hers. Every time he touched her it burned her skin. His lips felt like electric buzzers, giving her shocks. Grabbing her clothes, she ran from the room.

"No wonder that guy paid me so much to come here," she said as she left. "You're a freak!"

Edward said and did nothing for several moments, then on impulse, he chased after her. Two women had been murdered after visiting him. He didn't want that happening again, even if this one was running away from him.

His experiment hadn't gone well, though he had learned a lot about sex and himself. It was a pleasurable experience, except for his shocking her. He would have to do something about the effect of the high-energy field of his holographic body touching the sensitive skin of a human female. Still, he didn't want another dead girl on his conscience.

Following her unobtrusively in the limousine as she made her way home, he came to one of the seedier parts of town, down by the beach where she had a small cottage, which she disappeared into. Edward waited and watched, but no one had followed her. Perhaps his worries were for nothing.

He had explained to his driver, Hector, who was an understanding man, that he just wanted to make sure the girl got home safely. They waited all night, watching, until a little after daybreak, and then made their way back to the penthouse. No one appeared to have followed her.

"Ah, sometimes a woman like that, she can be a good thing," commented his driver. "A man needs an outlet. Sometimes it's not easy to meet someone. But, one like that hot little chili pepper can teach a man a lot, if you know what I mean, Senior."

"Yes, I do, Hector, but please keep our little excursion to yourself, if you could. I'd rather not have it known I follow women of the night around."

"There is nothing wrong with that, Senior. You were concerned for her safety."

"Someone paid for her to come to my place without my knowledge."

"These women of the night, as they are called, they have been around for thousands of years, and may they be with us for a thousand more."

"Si, Hector, si."

Lola, as she was called, threw her red wig on the bed as soon as she entered her small beachside cottage. The man who had phoned her and sent her the money said the John was a rich eccentric, but this guy was downright creepy, though he looked good enough. One could never tell with looks, however. She knew from experience that looks could be deceiving. The handsomest guys could be the creepiest, while the roughest looking man could be a downright angel. You just never knew with men, which is what made her job that much more dangerous, say, than being a waitress. But the pay for a high-class call-girl was ten times better than bussing tables, so she survived on the street with her looks and her wits. This last job, as weird as it was, had paid plenty. As she undressed for a nice long bath, Lola was looking forward to a few weeks off.

She looked at the burn mark on her breast and cursed the John.

"The freak," she said again.

Just as she was about to enter the tub of hot water, there was a rap on the door.

She wondered who it could be as she grabbed a towel and rapped it around her torso. She had no trepidation about opening the door. She got visitors at all hours of the night, usually return customers, but sometimes other working girls or boyfriends. She would have been more concerned if it was eleven in the morning. She wondered vaguely if the eccentric scientist had followed her home. She hoped not.

She opened the door to peek out.

"What do you want?" she said recognizing her visitor.

Chapter 14

Jack Burr had overcome one setback after another, only to encounter another hurdle around the next corner. He was beginning to wonder if someone was playing games with him. While he hadn't heard any more rumors about being fired, he was in the dark to just about everything else. The Board had been permanently suspended on Andy Knowles's orders, but his project, much to Burr's surprise, had not been canceled. In the meantime, Eddie's lab on the twelfth floor sucked up all resources and budgets like a giant black hole.

He was having trouble concentrating. It was bad enough that work was a maze of technical thickets and thorns, but his personal life was beset as well. He felt like the boy trying to plug the proverbial dike with his thumb. He pretended to carry on as if nothing was wrong, while his mind whirled with myriad worries and concerns. He'd even had a panic attack, the first in his life. His wife had left him months ago.

"Yes, sir. I understand, sir, but these types of things can be expected with something as complex as this. Our company is undergoing a large transition to the next generation technology. No, sir, what we're going to show you is the current technology, but even that is years ahead of anything you've seen. I know, but we can't sit back on our laurels. The quantum was needed for research. That's a genius for you, always reaching for the next big discovery. Oh, in a few years, but... Yes, I know, we should be following through with what we already have, but we need to make these investments in the future now. I'm sorry you feel that way, Senator. Perhaps you should talk to our CEO, Dr. Spencer. I know. I have the same problem. Ever since his secretary... Yes, sir. I will, sir. We'll be ready this time. No more delays, I promise. Yes, sir. In thirty days. Thank you, Senator. Good-bye."

He blinked off the phone and swore to himself under his breath. A moment later he got a call on his private, secure line.

When no one responded to his greeting he lost his patience.

"Who is this?" he demanded sharply. "What? You have some additional information for me? Last night? OK, wait, I'm checking it now."

He switched on a streaming news site and scanned the day's headlines.

"Jesus! Another murder. He what? When? Doesn't that beat all. Followed her home? Then what did he do? What? Good God! Pictures, you have pictures? Who is this? Hello, hello."

The line went dead. Burr was considering going to the police, but couldn't do so without knowing more. What if it was just a hoax?

He barked some orders to his secretary and wondered what she'd be like in bed. Normally, he would have tried something with her, but he didn't have time for that at the moment. He had a deadline to meet. Everything, even the odd phone call, took a backseat to that.

He went to the new demo room on the 25th floor to see how things were progressing. His crew of engineers did not look happy.

"Why so glum?" he asked on entering the lab.

"I don't see how we're going to pull this off without the quantum Dr. Spencer took."

"Can't we get another one?"

"Sure, if we had funds in our budget, but Spencer's used that up as well."

"We'll have to go over his head then. Or behind his back. I don't care which, but I want that machine."

"We were thinking of using the Molecular DNA computer to map the pattern-recognition drivers."

"No, they're too slow. We need the quantum for real-time simulation. Maybe it's time we take a walk down to the twelfth floor again. They won't get rid of me so easy this time."

A few moments later an angry Jack Burr and his team of engineers confronted the single security guard at the twelfth floor lobby. They weren't expecting him.

"We demand to see Dr. Spencer," said Jack, who was one of the company's chief executives.

"No one is allowed in this area without clearance or special permission from Dr. Spencer or Mr. Duncan."

"Duncan! I don't take orders from Rudy Duncan. Now let us in or I'll have your badge."

"Sorry, sir. I take orders from Mr. Duncan. And those orders say…"

"I don't care what your orders say. I'm giving you new orders."

"What seems to be the trouble here?" asked Edward, entering the lobby from one of the locked doors to the lab area.

"These gentlemen are demanding to see you, sir."

"Is that all?" replied Edward nonplussed. "Jack, you know you can make an appointment any time with my holo-assistant."

"We've all tried for weeks to see you. So has Senator Thomas from the Defense Committee. But your virtual assistant doesn't see fit to give you the messages, or you don't see fit to answer them."

"Things have been a bit busy down here lately. We're trying to gear up for our research project. I'm sure you and your team understand. Your job is to maintain and support the existing product, help the venture capitalists productize it."

"That's what we're trying to do, but you've taken all the resources and funds."

"You know as well as I do that research and development is our bread and butter. It has priority."

"Well, it's not right. We need the quantum array. You had no right to take it."

"I built it, Jack. I was well within my rights. Read the company bylaws. Anyway, what do you need that for? You shouldn't require that kind of advanced equipment for maintenance and support. Work with the vendors and licensees for that kind of venture capital. Anyway, find where it says I have to give you my equipment for your pet projects or answer calls from the Defense Department."

"You'd be well advised to answer a few of those calls. Thomas may be the next Vice-President."

"Thanks for the warning. I'll be sure to vote Democrat. Now if it's a quantum array you want, I'll give you the design spec and your boys here can build one for you. If you don't have anything else to say, I have work to do."

"Oh, I have more to say, but I'm not going to waste my breath on you. You just better watch your step, you inhuman freak."

He said these words loudly, so that everyone, even in the adjoining labs, could hear, then stormed out with his engineers behind him.

"Well, that was pretty rude," said the security man.

"Burr's known for being rude, especially to females. Thanks for manning the door. Sorry you had to be subjected to any abuse."

"Oh, that's OK. You came in before things got nasty, but I don't care who he is. I wasn't going to let him in."

"Good, Mike, good job. You keep that up and you'll make head of security yet."

Edward thought about Burr's last words. Did he know, or was he just being Burr? Probably the latter, but he couldn't be sure. He'd have to tread carefully.

Despite his daughter's objections, Andy Knowles went to the airport to pick her up. Her plane arrived right at 10:30 PM on schedule.

"Oh, Daddy. I told you not to come," she said on seeing him approach through the crowd.

"So, what's the problem? You're not happy to see your old man?"

"Sure I am," she said hugging him and kissing him on the cheek. "I just didn't want you to go through all the bother. I could have taken a cab."

"What, and miss seeing my daughter get off the plane. Not on your life. Here, I'll help you with your luggage."

After helping her with her bags and walking through the terminal to the Land-Rover, they drove the short distance from the airport to his house in Vista Del Mar by the sea.

"So what's with all the bags? I thought you were only here for the weekend?"

"Oh, I may stay longer. Some friends have offered to let me take care of their house while they take a cruise around the Caribbean in their yacht."

"Nice friends. You can always stay with me in your old room, if you want."

"I know. That will be nice. Now I'll be close. I can visit all the time."

"So, you're picking up stakes and moving on again? Why can't you settle down?"

"Daddy, we've been through all that. I'm not the settling down kind. I don't want to be tied down to one spot."

"Is that why you can't find a good man?"

"We've been through all that, too, Dad. Why do you have to bring that up again? And you wonder why I don't want to stay with you. Mother was right."

Andrew didn't say anything, but let his anger simmer to a warm burn as they drove the remaining distance to his mansion in silence.

"There might be a spot for a good chemist like you in Edward's company," he said as they reached the beach.

"I thought it was your company, too."

"Technically, I suppose so. We co-founded it. But I'm semi-retired now. He's the one that's involved in the day to day work and planning."

"But you still have a say in what goes on, right?"

"Yes, I guess so, although I haven't used that prerogative for some time. I try to guide things along when I can by offering sound advice and guidance."

"That sounds like my dad. How did you meet this guy, again?"

"I told you. I knew his parents. They wanted me to tutor him. He had phenomenal potential as a child. He was a mathematical prodigy, just amazing. When his parents died in an accident, I took over his education."

"Funny, I don't remember any of that."

"You were young and living with your mother. You both had your own concerns."

"Yeah, you sure didn't seem to care much what happened to us."

"Now, that's not true. You know very well your mother got a very fair settlement. Who do you think paid for your education?"

"I know, Daddy. And I'm grateful for all that, but I really could have used a father."

"Well, you have one now."

She didn't respond, but considered telling him it was too late. He'd learn on his own soon enough.

"And you founded a company with your little protégée. I'm surprised you didn't adopt him. Are you sure he's not related to you, not some illegitimate bastard of yours?"

"Connie! Don't be so crude. No, nothing like that. Just the child of very close friends."

"Good, I wouldn't want something like that to get in the way."

"What do you mean by that?"

"Oh, nothing. Here we are. Home sweet home."

He helped her carry her bags into the house and led her to the kitchen where he had a snack waiting for her. She looked at the clock.

"It's only eleven. It's early yet. Why don't we go out? You got any good clubs around here?"

"Clubs! I wouldn't know anything about that."

"Well, maybe your protégé, Eddie, does. Why don't we give him a call?"

"I doubt very much that Dr. Edward Spencer will want to go clubbing with you tonight. He's not that kind of person."

95

"I don't know. He sure sounds like a swinger from what the papers say. Is it true he was questioned twice by the police about two murders? You don't think he's a homicidal sex maniac, do you?"

"Connie, you sure do have some strange notions. Is that the type of trash you read for news, gossip magazines?"

"The Herald's not a gossip magazine."

"No, it's yellow-journalism at its finest."

"Daddy, I don't want to argue with you on our first night together. Why don't you call Dr. Spencer and see if he wants to go out with us. Tell him you've got a beautiful woman with you who wants to meet him."

"No, that's absolutely out of the question."

"Then I'll call him myself. Where's the phone book."

"Connie, why do have to be like this? Why can't you just relax and enjoy a nice quiet evening with your father?"

"Because I want excitement, that's why. Never mind, I'll find my own fun. Can I borrow your car?"

Connie was nothing if not persistent, and had always gotten her way with her father, when he was around, and even when he wasn't. It was no different now as she drove down Imperial Drive in his Mercedes sports-coup. In truth, she wanted the car more for its GPS system than the wheels, but the mobility didn't hurt either.

If her father had known where she was headed, he might have reneged on his gift. As she left, he had crossed his fingers and hoped that it was her friends she was going to see at almost midnight. She had told him not to wait up. Now he realized what he had missed by not being there during her teenage years. He was making up for it now.

"Address, Dr. Edward Spencer," she intoned into the voice-activated global positioning system.

"2099 Grand Avenue East," answered a friendly female voice.

"Directions," Connie commanded. The computer responded by guiding her to the location, where she arrived twenty minutes later.

"Dr. Spencer, Andrew Knowles's daughter is here to see you," said the doorman over Eddie's intercom.

"What?" replied Eddie in alarm. "Who?"

"Professor Knowles's daughter," answered the doorman.

A vibrant female voice came over the speaker.

"Hi Dr. Spencer. I'm Connie Knowles. I just got into town and had a fight with Dad. He can be such a bore sometimes. I was wondering if you could help me find somewhere to stay tonight."

"Yes, of course," Edward replied, not knowing what else to say. Wisely, he had recently overridden the nightly shutdown protocol his creator had implemented. It was a superfluous precaution meant to extend the lifetime of the energy crystals, but Edward knew his lifespan was practically limitless. In any case, he had too much to do to sleep.

"Hi, Connie," Edward said when she emerged from the elevator. He recognized her instantly from the picture the professor kept on his desk. It was not the first time she had visited. He had seen her once before when she came to see her father. A chemistry major if he remembered rightly.

He was still in a state of shock from recent events. News of the death of the redhead who had visited him just the night before, had sent shudders through his cyber-brain and put all other matters on hold. He had to get to the bottom of it. There was no more doubt in his mind. It was personal now. Whatever was going on, he was in the middle of it.

He had followed the prostitute home. If there had been anyone following her he would have seen them, unless they were already inside waiting for her. He had watched all night, until daylight, and hadn't seen anyone arrive or leave. Had someone followed him without his knowledge?

He was agitated and not in the mood for company, especially female company. The last person he wanted to see was Andrew Knowles's daughter, but he found himself compelled to help her.

"Are you all right?" he asked. "What happened? What did you and your dad argue about? It can't be that bad."

"Dad's such a jerk sometimes. He drives me to distraction. Never stops with the questioning and never happy with my answers. I just can't seem to please him."

Edward stood looking at her, not sure what to do or say. He hardly knew the girl.

"Why did you come here?" he asked, bluntly. "I mean, I hardly know you."

"I know, but Dad talks about you so much, I feel like I know you. I've always wanted to meet you. He said you might have work for someone like me."

"You're a chemistry major, correct?" he asked, glad to have firm ground to navigate on.

"Yes, I have a degree in nuclear and nano-chemistry."

"Oh," said Eddie, suddenly very interested in Connie Knowles. "Perhaps we could use you."

He was thinking fast, his qubit processors working overtime. What was he to do with her? He certainly couldn't let her leave. With what was going on that would be a death warrant, unless he could somehow ensure her safety.

"I don't want to cause any trouble between you and your father. It's late. It may not be safe at a hotel. Perhaps you should go home."

"Can I stay here?" she asked. "I'm exhausted. I've had a terrible day. I don't want to deal with any more people, especially not my father. I'll sleep on the couch here. I won't be any trouble, honest."

"I don't know," replied Eddie, unsure of himself. What could happen to her here? Then again, even with all his computer power, he still couldn't answer the question of who the murderer was any more than he could answer questions about Schrodinger's cat. He'd just have to take it slow and see what happens.

"You can use the guest room. It's on the other side of the apartment. I'll show you."

"Quite a pad you have here," she commented as he escorted her around the outside gallery to the guest suite on the other side of the building. "Some art collection."

"You'll be comfortable here," he announced when they reached the door to the guest suite. "I'll have the kitchen cook something for breakfast."

"Don't bother. I sleep late and cook for myself. I make a mean omelet."

"Whatever you prefer. Make yourself at home. I have some work to do."

"I'd like to stay up and talk. I don't think I can sleep."

"All right," said Edward. "As you wish."

They talked long into the night. It was as if he had known her all his life.

Chapter 15

Lieutenant Detective Juan Mendoza had three dead women on his hands and no leads. No one matching the security camera pictures of the well-built, long-haired blond in sun-glasses had been located. Mendoza wondered if the unidentified man had been disguised.

Another victim had been found just like the others, naked with a large knife in her chest. What was the connection? He immediately thought of Dr. Edward Spencer, but his probes on the man had turned up nothing. Both the doorman and his driver swore they had never seen the latest dead woman before – a high-class prostitute normally known to cruise the beach district. The way they talked, you'd think the scientist was the man of the year. He must pay them well, maybe too well. He'd have to check and see, but there was nothing at this point to link Spencer to the latest victim. Still, it warranted further investigation. He decided to pay Spencer yet one more visit.

Detective Mendoza always enjoyed surprising people early in the morning. If you were on his list of wanted felons, there was a good chance you'd get a rap on the door sometime between four or five in the morning, while you were still in your pajamas with cobwebs in your eyes. There was nothing like a little early morning roust to get the juices flowing, maybe even get some smart guy to slip up. It had been known to happen.

He arrived at Spencer's apartment building around quarter to five in the AM. The doorman, the same one he had spoken to earlier the previous day, was still there.

"Don't you ever sleep?" he asked.

"Yeah, as soon as my shift ends at ten."

"Is Dr. Spencer in?"

"Yes, I think so, but it's kind of early. I'm sure he's probably sleeping."

"If you're so sure, why'd you say probably? If it's probably that means you're not sure."

"It's 4:45 in the morning."

"Could you ring him, please?"

"What, are you going to arrest him?"

"Just ring him, will you?"

The doorman did as asked. A short time later Edward's voice responded, sounding wide awake and chipper.

"Hello," he said. "Who is it now? If this is Andrew, have him come up. His daughter is here."

"It's the police again, sir, Detective Mendoza. He was here yesterday morning asking a lot of questions about the prostitute that was murdered."

"That will do, buddy," said the cop. "I'm sorry to disturb you so early, but we've got a terrible crime we're trying to solve and time is running out. Another girl may be being murdered as we speak."

"Then why are you bothering me, officer? What can I do?" he said.

"I was hoping you could help me. Two of the murdered women were last seen here at this building. I was wondering if you could help us determine if this third victim was also here."

"I can't see how I can help you with that. I don't know who comes and goes. It's a big building."

"I'd like to see you anyway, now if I could. We could always go downtown if you prefer."

"No, Lieutenant, that won't be necessary. Please come up."

On the way up the elevator, Mendoza checked his weapon and made sure there was a round in the chamber. Then he holstered it again and took a deep breath. Sometimes he wished he had a partner, but liked the freedom, the ability to come and go on a whim that working alone gave him. Sometimes, though, it was nice to have someone watching your back. He hadn't unholstered his revolver in twenty years, but something about triple homicides made him edgy. He wasn't sure why he was so anxious, but this guy, with all his brains and power unnerved him, the way he'd stare at you during questioning as if his eyes would burn into you. Who knew what someone with this kind of ambition was capable of?

Spencer was waiting for him at the elevator door. He wasn't alone.

"Sorry to disturb you at this hour, Doctor, but it is very important. Another woman's life may be at stake."

"Why? Do you know of someone else who is in danger?"

"No, but a call-girl named Lola Fergusson was murdered the night before last just like the others, the girl you found, your Secretary, Nancy Sullivan, and the woman we found last week. This makes three, all killed the same way. The other two were last seen here, in this building. We were wondering if this girl might have been here as well. I was hoping you could help us."

"You can contact my security chief and check the building cameras yourself. You have his card. You don't have to come up here and …"

"Have you seen this person?" asked the detective, ignoring Edward's objections.

He looked at the morgue shot of the young woman who had shown up two nights ago and did a striptease in his apartment. He was getting tired of looking at pictures of dead people.

"Please, officer, not again," he said turning away from the photo.

"What about you, ma'am?" asked the detective, handing the picture to Knowles's daughter.

"Don't look at that," said Edward forcefully, but it was too late. She had already taken the photograph and was scrutinizing it closely.

"Have either of you seen that woman?"

Edward computed the odds of whether the detective knew she had been there or not. He assumed the officer had talked to the doorman already. But even if he knew Edward had seen her, he could always say he hadn't recognize her from the grisly morgue shot.

"No," he said finally. "I don't recognize the person in the picture. My guest only arrived in town last evening on the 10:30 flight from New York. You are more than welcome to view the building's security cameras as before, if you wish."

"Thank you, sir. That will be very helpful."

"You can talk to the doorman as well."

"Oh, I have, and your limousine driver, too. They speak very highly of you."

"They are good men. They've been with me from the beginning."

"It must be nice to have that sort of loyalty in your employees. You employ a lot of people, don't you?"

"Yes, it's one of the benefits of starting a company. You put a lot of people to work. I aim to put even more to work with my newest invention."

"Oh, good for you. What's that exactly?"

"You know. We build virtual reality systems. It's the next big thing for entertainment and business. There's no end to the uses for this technology. As a matter of fact, it would be ideal for police training, you know, simulating terrorist situations and things like that."

"Hmm, sounds interesting. I'll remember to mention it to the captain. He's always looking for new ways to torture the men."

Mendoza waited for a laugh. He got one from the girl but not from the CEO of Altered Realities, who seemed to lack any sense of humor.

"I'll go and see him personally," countered Spencer. "And mention you were here this morning and thought he should see a demo."

"No, you don't have to do that," said the Lieutenant, wondering if he'd been too hasty about the doctor's sense of humor. "I don't want the captain to get the idea I've been pestering you, although I'm just doing my job."

"I know, officer, and I wish I could be more help, but…"

"Who is this lovely young lady?" asked the detective looking at Connie in her nightshirt.

"This is my partner, Andrew Knowles's, daughter, Connie."

"Hello, Miss Knowles. Yes, I met your father shortly after Nancy Sullivan's murder."

"Do you have to talk about that?" interjected Edward.

"I'm afraid that's all we've been talking about down at the station. Three murders in about as many weeks has got everybody talking. LA might be used to that kind of thing, but here in El Segundo things like that just don't happen, at least not often."

"Maybe you have a serial killer on your hands," offered Connie Knowles, feeling free to speak now that she'd been introduced. "Why do you think this last woman was here, at Edward's building?"

"Oh, I don't know. Just a hunch. The other two women were last seen here, one of them in this apartment, before being found murdered in their flats. I was just wondering if this third time was the same. You know, perhaps someone around here may have seen her. We don't have much to go on."

He showed them the photos taken by the security cameras of the blond suspect with the second victim, and asked if they'd seen him. They both said no, even though Eddie recognized his alter ego.

"Perhaps after your men have viewed the security videos again…" volunteered Eddie. "I'll set it up first thing this morning at eight."

"That would be great. Thanks, Doc."

"Anything else I can do?"

"No. You've been very helpful. I'm sorry I had to bother you like this."

"Yes, who can sleep at a time like this?"

"You been having trouble sleeping, Doc?"

"No, but I get a minimum of sleep anyway. My work is very demanding."

"I suppose you have to spend a lot of time at the shop putting everything together."

"No, not really. Most of the work I could do anywhere, sitting at the table, walking in the park. It's all in my head, all the equations and functions."

"All in your head?" repeated the Lieutenant.

"It's not that unusual. Many physicists have this ability. Einstein could solve whole blackboards full of equations without lifting a pen or doing anything but sit staring out the window. Who has the space or time to write it all out?"

"You scientists are amazing. The things you do are incredible. It's almost inhuman."

"Oh, it's human, all right."

"I suppose so, but it's all beyond me. I'm just trying to solve three simple murders."

"That doesn't sound so simple," offered Edward.

"No, I guess you're right. Be careful out there, Miss Knowles. There's a killer on the loose. I just hope he's not stalking this place. Good day."

"Well, that was rather interesting," observed Eddie's house guest after the detective had left. "I'm not sure I'll be able to sleep after that. It's almost six. You want breakfast?"

"No. It's too early for me to eat. I could have the kitchen-bot cook something for you."

"No, that's OK. I can cook for myself, thank you. Where's the stove?"

"Have you called your father?" he asked her on the way to the rather large, pristine auto-kitchen.

"Yeah, last night on my cell. I told him I was staying with friends. Wow, some kitchen. I'd pay to have a place like this to cook in."

"It does most of the cooking itself through a pre-programmed robotic counter top and stove, but I can switch to manual if you'd like."

"I'd like," she answered smiling.

103

She marveled at the latest appliances as she opened cupboards and drawers, pulling out the pans and utensils she needed. "Gee, doesn't look like you use it much. It all looks brand new."

"It's self-cleaning."

"It look's like it's never been used."

"The pantry is over here. I'm afraid the cupboard is bare. Monday is shopping day. I think we have some eggs in the refrigerator."

Edward skipped breakfast, pretending to take a shower while she ate. He could not simulate eating anything other than a nut or perhaps a sip of water. Doing anything more would be a dubious process involving suction feeds and emphatic processes that hadn't been invented yet. Even what he could do was difficult to pull off with someone as observant as his guest obviously was, sitting close by, without special lighting and additional effects.

Of course, Eddie never used the advanced auto-kitchen and never ate. Nor were his doorman and driver any more than mere holographs like Eddie, but without the vast amounts of intelligence he had been given. Their brains and virtual bodies were controlled by a single hub and much simpler neural-networks, although they could both pass a Turing test. They more than served their purpose, just as did Eddie's self-driven limousine. Neither of them would divulge his secret, even under torture.

"Aren't you going to have something to eat?" she asked, when he returned from his virtual shower.

"I'll grab a breakfast bar on the way. I don't really eat big meals, just what I can grab on the run."

"That must be why you're so trim. Do you workout?"

"No, not really. Why don't we go to the office," he suggested as Connie finished washing her dishes by hand. "It will be early, but the die-hards will be there even on a Saturday. I want you to meet Rudy. You'll be working with him."

"You really going to give me a job?" she asked excitedly.

"You have just the skills and qualifications we're looking for."

"Gee, it's kind of like fate brought us together."

"Yes, I was wondering about that. Why did you come here last night?"

"I told you. I've been watching you from afar, ever since I first heard about you. I've wanted to meet you for a very long time. You could say I've been stalking you."

"That's very flattering, but why? What's so fascinating about me?"

104

"Are you kidding? Are you that naive? Your face has been on the cover of Time and Newsweek. You're one of the most successful young scientist-entrepreneurs of the new generation. You run a multi-million dollar company. You're involved in numerous good causes and donate millions to my favorite charities. What woman in her right mind wouldn't want to meet the famous Dr. Edward Spencer? Anyway, we're almost related, and as it turns out, you're a nice guy to boot. Thanks for letting me stay over and not hassling me."

"Hassling you?"

"Yeah, you know, coming on to me, trying to get into my pants. You're not like other guys."

"You're not like other women. I feel like I know you, though we just met."

"So what is it with this place?" she asked as they descended the elevator to the garage where Eddie's self-driving limo and holographic driver were waiting. "Why are the police so interested in it?"

"I don't know, but I'm going to find out," answered Eddie.

Harry Fry was on the job again, another lonely stakeout in another sordid neighborhood, another day in a jaded life of falsehoods and lies. He should know. It was his life, the seedier side of existence, unfaithful women and cheating men. This job was different, but worse. This case dealt with murder.

He wondered why the cops just didn't pick the perp up. They must have enough evidence by now, even without the pictures, which he had delivered as instructed. The pay was good, but the nerve-racking tediousness, the waiting and watching and wondering what was going to happen next, was getting to him. Now here he was back on the job.

The death of the prostitute he had been following had shook him up, even though his employer had warned him something like that might happen. He just didn't expect it to actually occur, not on his watch, but it had. Now he knew anything could happen, and that made things more unbearable. Harry didn't carry a gun. He was lucky he had a license to practice this lousy job.

He had watched the killer follow the redhead home, where he waited outside her beachside cottage. After about sunup he appeared to drive off. He must have somehow circled back or snuck out of the limo without being seen. Fry wasn't sure how he missed it, but it wouldn't have been the first time he dropped off on a stakeout. Perhaps the late hour got to him and he cat-napped with his eyes open for a second. He certainly hadn't seen anyone except for the scientist and his chauffeur. They would have had to be pretty sneaky to commit a murder like that right under his nose, but he had taken pictures. Soon the police would know the truth.

There were numerous places from which to observe Spencer's building, all of them giving him a good vantage point of the entrance and penthouse without being seen, including the high-rise parking garage where he was now. With his binoculars and his high-powered camera lenses, he could see right into the penthouse. Late last night, soon after arriving at the parking garage, he had observed another lone female enter the building and ascend to the tenth floor where she still was. He wondered what they were doing. Was another murder about to occur? He watched, snapping pictures, and waited.

Harry had the side window open to the warm morning breeze, but didn't hear the footsteps quietly approaching, or the opening of a large, sharp razor. The blade flashed, and with hardly a sound, cleanly slit Harry Fry's unshaven throat, cutting into the carotid artery pumping blood to the brain. That blood was soon pumping onto the seat cover, as the still jerking body was shoved over onto the passenger's seat.

The vehicle and its driver moved out of the garage and headed south down Route 1 into the growing light. The stakes had just been raised.

Chapter 16

Although ARC employees normally didn't work on Saturday, Edward and his chief engineer, Rudy Duncan, did much of their work on the weekend and after hours, when most of the company staff were home. Connie would be a welcome addition to the team.

For some reason, Edward instantly felt he could trust her with his deepest secrets, although he held much back. What he didn't withhold were the events of the past few weeks, which he described to her in detail, everything except the realization that he was a hologram. Connie seemed to sympathize with him and agreed that perhaps someone was trying to frame him.

As they drove to the headquarters building, they went through the short list of his enemies. Jack Burr was the single name on the list, but every time Eddie was confronted with the possibility his subordinate might be involved, he dismissed the idea as absurd.

"Rudy, I'd like you to meet Connie Knowles," said Edward on entering the lab, where his chief engineer was already working to complete relays and cabling needed for the complex computer equipment.

"The professor's little girl?" replied Rudy, who had met her once a few years back. "My, have you grown up."

"She has a degree in nano-technology and chemical engineering. I thought she might be able to help us."

"I'll say. Just the girl I've been looking for."

"Hi, Mr. Duncan," she said. "Nice to meet you. I've heard all about you."

"All bad I hope," he joked.

"No, just the opposite. Edward says you're the best engineer on the planet."

"I don't know about that. One of the best, anyway."

"Rudy's not known for his modesty, but he can show you around and get you situated well enough."

"I'll do my best," answered Rudy. "So what do you know about carbon nano-tubes?"

"Everything," she replied, not batting a long eyelash. "Strong, light, made of long strands of carbon atoms. They're excellent material for constructing both the machine body and the brain. Very efficient computation wise, allows for distribution of intelligence throughout the machine body."

"I think I'm in love," said Rudy, who was several years older and married.

"So you're building nanobots? What for?" she asked. "Medical procedures?"

"Like the name on the marquee says, we're all about altering reality," replied Eddie. "What better way than to fill a room with swarms of nanobots all programmed to simulate an environment, any environment. It will take virtual reality to an all new level."

"I see what you mean, but the technology's only in its infancy. We're no way near that kind of capability. Maybe in a couple of decades, but…"

"We don't have that long. I've made some discoveries that may shorten that timescale considerably."

"Does my dad know?"

"No, not yet. I'd like to surprise him."

"Perfect," she responded, rubbing her hands together in glee with the anticipation of pulling one over on her know-it-all old man. "You're talking about taking something the width of five atoms, about one billionth of a meter, and laying down a crystalline object, molecule by molecule. It's only feasible if the thing's self-replicating. Otherwise, it would be too slow and take too long. Is it going to be self-replicating?"

"Of course," answered Edward. "That's the whole idea. We will need billions, trillions of them."

"You'll have to be careful you know, if…"

"Yes, we know. Don't worry. I've taken care of that. We know how to prevent runaway reproduction."

"I hope so. Do you have a design?" she asked, thinking back to all the arcane courses she had taken that everybody told her she was crazy to waste time with. Suddenly it had all become relevant. She began trying to recall those esoteric equations and formulas.

Eddie explained more.

"The nano-robots will have appendages like hands to hold objects and each other, with tiny brains to communicate with. I want to create swarms of them, a wave front in any direction. They have to be able to exert pressure and create any tactile and environmental sensation. We want to be able to reconfigure the space around you, outside and in."

"That's quite a fantastic vision."

"We are going to make that vision a reality, and no one must know, not even your father, until we're ready."

"I'll write up a list of things we'll need," she said, already on the job.

"Rudy will help you with that. Give your list to him. Make that your top priority. Yours, too, Rudy. We can take care of payroll and HR on Monday. You can start now."

A short time later, Edward was working alone, completing some last minute tasks that his engineers needed before the fabrication process could commence. Rudy and Connie had gone on their hunt for additional material and equipment. He was interrupted by a call from security.

"Professor Knowles is here to see you, sir."

"I'll be right down," answered Edward. He closed up the lab and took an express elevator to the first floor. Andrew Knowles was waiting for him in the lobby, less than pleased.

"What's this? I can't even get on the elevators?" he complained.

"The headquarters is normally closed on weekends. You know that. Now with the new lab running seven days a week, we have to be a little stricter about off hour access. I'll see your badge gets upgraded. What brings you here today?"

"Have you seen my daughter, Connie? She was supposed to be staying with friends last night. At least that's what she said when she finally called me at two this morning, but I got a call from her friends today asking if she got in all right. They haven't seen her since she got here. I thought you might have. I stopped by your apartment building. The doorman said you had a guest last night."

"Yes, Connie is staying with me."

"She spent the night with you?" her father said incredulously.

"Yes, she needed a place to stay. She told me that you two quarreled and she didn't want to go home. She stayed in the guest suite, but we ended up talking all night. She's quite an interesting girl."

Knowles gave his holo-protégé a probing look.

"I'm giving her a job here," continued Edward.

"What?" said Andrew, as if Edward had told him they were going to feed her to the sharks.

"It was your idea, as I understand, and a good one."

"Since when do you need chemical-engineers?"

"I no longer answer to you."

Knowles, stunned by Edward's words, was about to reply, when Lieutenant Mendoza drove up to the ARC front entrance followed by two black-and-whites.

"Could we go some place to talk?" asked the detective, walking into the lobby, where Knowles and Edward were standing.

"Yes, we can go to my office. Can Dr. Knowles join us?"

"Yes, perhaps that would be a good idea."

He ordered one uniformed officer to come with them, while the others waited in the lobby and the cars outside.

Edward's holo-secretary met them at the office door, as efficient as ever, and started rattling off a list of missed calls and upcoming appointments. He dismissed her in mid-sentence with a click of a virtual button on his watch. His personal assistant evaporated into floating particles of light. The detective stopped in his tracks.

"What was that?" he uttered. "What just happened? Don't tell me that was a hologram."

"Yes, my personal assistant. We use what we make."

"But she was standing there talking to us just like a real person."

"I know. That's the whole idea. That was a computer-generated hologram. It is like any automated assistant with voice activated speech-recognition and voice synthesis. We just added a holographic image."

"Like a robot with no body? Amazing. How do you do that?"

"With lights, Lieutenant."

"No, really. How the hell do you do that?"

"It's done by encoding light fields produced by a special type of lens. It's not really an image as much as a collection of randomized patterns that when suitably lit by a light source, like a laser, generate the original three-dimensional object, in this case a computer-generated image, which is viewable from all angles."

"I've read up on that. You use interference and diffraction, but how do you make it move and talk. I mean it moved around and everything. How do you do that?"

"Ah, now you want me to give away our trade secrets. You will have to read the patents, but basically it's all done with lights and mirrors."

"All planted around the room?"

"Yes, hundreds of them, some the size of a few millimeters."

"Fascinating."

"What is it you wanted to talk to me about? What did you find on our security cameras?"

"Nothing, but we haven't had a chance to look at them all yet. Something else has come up."

"Yes, and what is that?"

"We received these last night."

He opened an envelope and took out several large, eleven by eight, glossy photographs.

"Is this your limousine?" asked the Latino lawman. "That's your license plate number, isn't it?"

"Yes, it looks like it," answered Edward.

"Do you recognize where it's parked?"

"No, but Hector could have been using the limo for some reason," answered Edward, relying on a simple heuristic known to many crooks – deny everything.

"It's Lola Ferguson's apartment, the prostitute who was murdered the night before last. Why is your limo parked in front of the dead girl's apartment? Who's that sitting in the back seat?"

When Eddie didn't answer, the detective showed him a picture of the dead girl, this one a promotional shot of a vibrant, aspiring, young women before she hit hard times. It was Tina, the redhead of two nights before. He showed Eddie a couple more photographs of his limousine parked on the street with two men sitting in it. The man in the back seat was hidden in shadow. The time on the photo showed an hour and twenty minutes later than the first picture.

"Yes, I know her," said Eddie. "This woman came to my apartment the night before last. She called up and said she was a childhood friend, but I knew that was a lie as soon as I let her in. She told me that someone had sent her, a friend, she said."

"Why did you say you never saw her before when I showed you her picture earlier this morning?"

"I didn't recognize her without her wig. The photo you showed me was so horrible I could hardly look at it. Who could recognize this vibrant young woman in the picture from the morgue shot you showed me?"

"Why didn't you mention you had a visitor and that it might have been the woman in the photo?"

"I didn't realize they were connected. In any case, I didn't want to admit I was with that kind of girl in front of Professor Knowles' daughter. It could have been anybody. I wasn't about to volunteer information and have my private life dragged in front of the public again."

"So she did visit your apartment."

"Yes."

"And what happened?"

"She stripped and danced for me. She said someone thought I would like to meet her, but she wouldn't tell me who. When I refused to play along, she got mad and left."

"And she wouldn't tell you who sent her?"

"No, I asked her several times."

"Who do you think would do something like that? I mean hire a call-girl for you?"

"I don't know. It's highly unusual. Maybe someone was trying to play a crude joke on me. I wouldn't put it past that jerk, Burr, to pull something like this."

"You mean Jack Burr, your associate at ARC?"

"Yes, we have this running battle of wits to see who can play the best joke on the other. I moved his office recently."

"You think he's trying to get even with you by hiring a prostitute for you and then killing her?"

"No, maybe the first part of that, but he's not a murderer. At least I don't think so."

"Anyone else you know might want to play a gag on you like that?"

"Well, perhaps there is someone else, but in that case, they're more likely just trying to help me meet people. Maybe my well-meaning driver, Hector, or ..."

He stopped and looked over at the professor, who was sitting in a chair by the door listening to the conversation.

"As much as I would like you to meet a nice girl, my boy, I would not stoop so low as to purchase you a street-walker," commented the professor.

"I see," said the detective. "So this strange woman, this redhead, arrived out of the blue and offered you her services, saying a friend had sent her. Why, with all that's going on around here, would you let a stranger like that into your apartment?"

Edward said nothing, but pointed to the picture of the gorgeous redhead.

"Let's just say I was intrigued. Like I told you, she told me she was an old girlfriend from grade school over the intercom. A person I really knew. So I let her up. I was curious who was behind it."

"But you say you didn't find out."

"No, she didn't really tell me a thing."

"What happened after she left?" asked the detective, who didn't seem in any hurry to leave. "What did you do?"

"Dr. Spencer is not going to answer anymore questions without his lawyer present," announced Andy Knowles standing up. "I'm calling him right now."

"Good, then you can tell him to come to the station," answered Mendoza. "We're taking Mr. Spencer downtown for questioning."

"Are you charging Dr. Spencer with something?" asked the professor.

"No, we just want to ask him some more questions. We have three murdered girls. We need some help."

"I would be glad to help, Detective, and the police station is as good a place as any to talk. Can we follow you down?"

Certainly, Doctor, we'll give you an escort."

Eddie sat in a little room in the police station with his lawyer, while Knowles waited outside. Mendoza came in a short time later and sat down opposite them across a small table.

"We're picking up your chauffeur as we speak," Mendoza informed them. "So you might as well tell us the truth. What were you doing outside of the murdered woman's apartment?"

"Dr. Spencer doesn't have to answer these questions. It could be anyone sitting in the car. It's a hired limousine, for crying out loud."

"Sorry, but Dr. Spencer is a prime suspect in a murder investigation. He needs to tell us what happened."

Eddie was accompanied by dozens of roving companion-lasers that continued projecting his image in the car and at the station, as Knowles had planned for, but he also knew that Eddie could now turn that off at will, at any moment. He wasn't sure what his creation would do. So far, however, he was holding his own.

"I was worried about the girl," said Eddie finally, knowing he could no longer deny it. "After those two other women were murdered after coming to the building, I grew worried when she walked out. I was going to call the police, but didn't want to get her in trouble."

113

"You should have called us. We have her on video leaving around eleven pm. She left in a hurry and looked distressed."

"Now see here," said the lawyer, upset that Eddie had been set up. "You told my client you had no pictures from the security cameras. Now you bring up this? I demand to see what evidence you have before my client answers any more questions."

"I'm showing you the evidence as soon as I get it," replied the detective. "I can arrest him under suspicion of murder, if that's what you want."

"No, Pete, it's all right," Eddie said to his lawyer. "I've already admitted she was in my apartment. I didn't connect the girl in your picture with the one I was with that night. I was rude to her and she left upset. I felt bad afterward and went to make sure she was safe. My chauffeur, Hector, and I sat there all night watching her place. No one followed us. No one entered the building. We left a little after daylight. Hector will substantiate my story. I didn't harm the girl, just the opposite. Whoever killed her must have already been in the building, or entered somehow without being seen, perhaps the same person who took those pictures."

"Let me get this straight. You chased her out then followed her home and watched her apartment all night, because you were worried about her."

"Yes," answered Eddie, staring him in the eye. "As strange as it may seem, I was worried about her."

Mendoza was about to say something, when Eddie's lawyer interrupted.

"OK, Detective, that's it. My client has answered all your questions, truthfully and honestly. Dr. Spencer is a very important and busy man, and any further harassment of him will be treated as such! Either book him now or let him go."

"OK, Mister Spencer. I don't mean to inconvenience you. You've been very helpful. That's all for now. We may want to talk to you again, however, so don't leave town."

After Eddie and his lawyer left, Mendoza talked over the case with his new partner, who had been watching the interview behind a one-way mirror. Because of the pressure of the case, they were working in teams now, and that suited Juan just fine.

"So, what do you think of this guy, Spencer?" he asked.

"He's too perfect. Not a winkle in his suit, not a hair out of place. I didn't even see him blink. He's got an answer for everything. He's like an actor playing a part, too good to be true. He's a cool operator."

"Or a cold-blooded killer."

Chapter 17

Knowles, looking for his daughter, had gone to the ARC building again hoping she would be there. He met her in the lobby as she was leaving for the evening. She and Rudy had returned with the additional material, and had wondered why Eddie wasn't there. She attempted to walk by, but her father stopped her and demanded an explanation for her behavior.

"What do you mean an explanation?" she countered. "It's been about eighteen years since I've had to account for my whereabouts to you."

"I thought we were going to spend some time together. Why'd you lie to me and say you were going to stay with friends? They called this morning asking about you. Imagine how I felt not knowing where you were. It was downright embarrassing. I thought my daughter would have more integrity than that."

"Ah, get off it, Dad. You can't expect me to sit around with you when I just get to town. I want to meet people my own age."

"There are a lot of people your own age to meet without bothering Edward. He has a lot on his mind, a great deal of responsibility. He can't go off partying with you like some teenager."

"Why not? Maybe the guy needs to have a little fun once in awhile. Who are you anyway, his father?"

"I thought we established that I'm not."

"Then why are you acting so damn controlling?"

"The man has just been questioned about three murders. Is that a good enough reason for me to get involved?"

"Questioned by the police? Again? When? Where?"

"They were here not more than two hours ago. I just came back from the station. I'm not sure where Eddie went. They told him not to leave town."

"I want to see him," said his daughter.

"I don't want you involved. What are you doing here, anyway? What's he got you working on?"

"What's the problem, Dad? Working with him was your idea, remember? Geez, if I knew what a geezer you've become, I never would have told you I was coming."

"Why did you come? It certainly wasn't to see me, and I have a feeling it's about more than a breakup."

"No, the breakup had a lot to do with it. It made me realize I was wasting my time with losers and wannabes. I needed to meet a higher caliber of men. Then I remembered your friend, Edward."

"Why don't I like the sound of this? Are you telling me you came here for the express purpose of meeting Eddie? At a time like this? What you're telling me sounds downright predatory. God, you're just like your mother. You are crazy. I was worried about you. Now I see it's Edward I should be concerned about."

"Yes, you should be. Keeping him locked up all day working so you can sit back and rest on your haunches, while he keeps everything going. You're using him."

"You don't know what you're talking about. Come home with me. We can talk about it there."

"Why would I want to do that? I'm staying with Edward."

"I don't think that's a good idea, at least for the time being."

"He said I could stay. He has a whole guest suite, larger than any hotel."

"But, you can't stay there."

"Why not?"

"Three women have been murdered, that's why."

"I read the papers. They were murdered in their own apartments, not Edward's. I'm safer there than in some hotel or even your house. Are you going to stay home and guard me twenty-four hours a day?"

"That won't be necessary."

"How do you know? Edward's place has security. That's a lot more than I can say for you, out by the ocean. It's dark out there."

He never could win an argument with his daughter, not even when she was ten. He didn't have a chance now, after a PhD and a short lifetime of hard experiences. He decided to tell her what the police had learned.

"Edward admitted following the last girl home, but told them it was out of concern. They have pictures of his limo parked in front of her cottage showing his chauffeur and him sitting in the car, though none showed him leaving the vehicle. There were no fingerprints found on any of the murder weapons, which were all left in the victims, no DNA, no bodily-fluids, nothing. Although he's their number one suspect, the police didn't have enough to hold him. I'm worried about him. Eddie would never kill anyone. He couldn't!" Knowles exclaimed these words so vehemently, it made Connie look up. "But there is evidence connecting all the murdered victims to him. It doesn't look good."

"What are you going to do?"

"I don't know, but please don't stay in his apartment. Stay with me tonight."

"No dad, I'm going to see Eddie and you can't stop me," she said, walking out of the building.

Knowles looked after her with concern. Only he knew that all the fingerprints and DNA samples on record with the authorities for Eddie were false and fabricated, just as Eddie was. The fact that no fingerprints or bodily-fluids had been found made him wonder. It was as if the murderer was somehow ephemeral like Eddie, but Eddie couldn't hurt a flea. Whoever was doing this was just clever – very, very clever.

Eddie had gone back to his apartment hoping to find Connie there, but the place was deserted. He wondered if the press had heard about his being taken in for questioning regarding the murders. Publicity was just what he didn't need at the moment.

He surfed the news channels and outlets, looking for any reports about his being questioned, but there was nothing. So far, the press had not gotten wind of his interrogation. But someone had tipped them off and sent the pictures. Who?

Obviously, somebody was following him. He wondered if they were the same one killing the girls. It would make sense.

In a way, he felt guilty for having let the girl leave. Where were these feelings coming from? He thought it was strange that he should feel so sad, as he had at Nancy's death. Was this programmed behavior or something he had learned? It was funny, absurd. He hardly knew the girl, but knowing she was dead made him feel empty inside.

Connie showed up a short time later.

"I talked to Dad," she announced as she entered. "He's not happy about me staying here. He told me what happened. Are you OK?"

"Yes. They just asked me some questions. It's no big deal. I appear to be the number one suspect in their murder investigation."

"Don't worry, Edward," said Connie. "They can't prove anything. I'm not going to let you out of my sight from now on. You've got a permanent alibi. Why don't you marry me?"

"What?" he replied, perplexed.

118

"Never mind. You've got nothing to worry about. You've got friends in high places."

"I think someone is following me."

"What? Who?"

"I don't know, but I'm going to find out."

"How?"

"I have my ways. In the meantime, why don't you stay with your father?"

"No, I told you. I'm staying with you. My father's old house is downright creepy at night. I'd rather sleep on the street."

"Well, we can't have that now, can we?" said Eddie.

Jack Burr made a good salary and lived quite modestly near the airport. He was no longer married and seldom spent more than twenty dollars on a date. Besides being cheap, he was a spendthrift. He did dress well, however, and had a penchant for expensive bangles, like Rolex watches and diamond cufflinks. In spite of this, and because of the money he made on illegal inside trading and Ponzi schemes, he had acquired a rather substantial nest-egg.

His tax man counseled him to invest it, find some way to hide it, or spend some of it, but Jack was content to put it into moderate-risk, moderate-yield tax free funds, which kept growing over time. Lately, however, Jack had been dipping into those funds rather heavily. He had taken his accountant's advice to heart.

Unknown to almost everyone, Jack had been investing heavily in Altered Realities Corporation stock, way more than available to him through the executive stock purchase plan, although his allowance was quite generous. Jack purchased his stock from a number of sources, some of them friends, some on the street and open market, some through third-parties, some that might not have been entirely legal. That didn't matter to Jack Burr. He was on a mission.

"Are we going to be ready for this Wednesday?" he asked the head of his engineering team. It was Monday morning and they didn't have much time left. "We can't have any more delays."

"Yes, but we've had to curb things back a bit, use the existing prototype software without the quantum. It will be good enough."

"What's that supposed to mean? It better damned well be better than good enough."

Burr was always on edge, but even more so lately, as if the pressure of the upcoming DOD demos was getting to him. There was a lot at stake.

Like everyone else, he had heard about Edward's interrogation, and like everyone else, he was surprised that they hadn't arrested him. With all the evidence against Spencer, how could they have let him go? He speculated on what kind of political clout Knowles and his protégé must have to get away with it. Or did they have a judge or two in their pocket?

The good news was it was almost noon and Eddie wasn't in yet. The bad news was Dr. Edward Spencer was still a free man and could show up at any time, endangering all his plans.

The engineer was going on and on about what they weren't able to do without the quantum computer. "The topological awareness modules will be pretty basic for the virtual entities. They will have a limited response pattern. We've had to pre-program most of the scenarios we want to demonstrate. The computer-generated entities won't be able to react to every human action. In other words, no ad-libbing."

"Great," grunted Burr. "You're telling me we've got the biggest presentation this company has ever put on and we've only got half a product. You think this is some kind of joke?"

"No, but…"

"I hope you think it's this funny when we're all standing in the unemployment line."

"It's not my fault Dr. Spencer took our machine and slashed our budget. He says the licensees and third-party vendors should be doing all the full product creation work, that we don't need those kinds of capabilities for maintenance and support."

"I'll give him maintenance and support," fumed Burr. Not having anyone else to satisfy his pent-up anger and frustration on, he took it out on the hapless messenger. "Get out of here!" he yelled. "You sniveling excuse for an engineer. You have Molecular DNA chambers, super-computers, unlimited memory and CPU power, and you can't build a simple feedback mechanism? It's not that we don't have a quantum computer. We don't have anyone with brains enough to program these re-god-damn-diculous machines."

"Dr. Spencer can."

"And why can't you? You've been working with him for a year. Haven't you learned anything, you blithering idiot? Get out of my sight!"

He started swatting at the man, backing him out of the lab with slaps and cuffs. The man fought back, throwing a hard right that just missed the executive's jaw by inches. Soon they were rolling on the floor, rabbit punching and choking each other like drunken pirates. It took four security men to separate them.

Chapter 18

Edward arrived at the company headquarters a few hours later that afternoon and heard about Jack Burr's meltdown. He almost had to chuckle. The man was an ignorant bully. Was he capable of murder?

"We'll have to fire him," said Tom Johnson, the CFO, after informing Edward of what had occurred. "We can't tolerate that type of physical violence. He attacked Fred Perkins for no reason."

"I heard Perkins threw the first punch."

"Only after Burr started slapping him and pushing him out of his office."

"Have HR talk to both men."

"I think this calls for sterner measures than a talk, especially Burr. He was totally out of control. Even without the physical attack, his language and tone were very abusive. There's nowhere in the company for that kind of behavior."

"How do you suppose we fire him without a court battle? Has any one filed a complaint?"

"No, not yet, but we shouldn't wait until someone does. We need to act forcibly."

"I'm not sure that's a good idea. These are grown men, professionals. I'd like to see if we can resolve this like adults. Have them meet, apologize, and shake hands."

"Normally I'd agree, but not where Burr's concerned. He's bad news. We should get rid of him."

"Perhaps, but Andrew has disbanded the Board. It was an interesting experiment and gave our employees a large share in the running of the company, but we're still private and can manage it as we like. It will be difficult to fire Burr without reconvening them. You'll have to talk to the professor. I'll agree with whatever you two decide."

"OK, but the longer Burr's with us, the more damage he can do."

"I think I'd rather keep Jack where I can see him."

"Maybe, but he's certainly no good for morale, especially for the people under him."

"Then we'll have to make sure he has a minimal number of people working under him. Thanks for the information, Tom. I'll take it under advisement. Let me know what you and Andrew decide."

With that, Eddie headed to the twelfth floor lab.

Rudy Duncan and Connie Knowles were making good progress, working together like a tandem high-wire act. Most of the equipment she would need to begin the fabrication process was in place, and Rudy was moving forward on the programming of the quantum-arrays, with Edward's help from time to time. Still under strict secrecy, few others knew what they were doing, and even his assistants had only the vaguest notion of their real goal.

"With the 100-qubit machine we have over a million, trillion simultaneous calculations per second," Eddie explained "The trick is selecting the right answer. We need to measure the spin states of all 100 qubits. We can feed the results into our conventional computers and display the answer on the screen. I've defined equations that encode the axioms and rules needed to compute all possible results. The quantum considers them all at once. If a proof and axiom is true, you have your answer. The only thing we need to watch out for is quantum entanglement, where two photon-qubits react to the same stimuli at once, skewing the results, but I have ways to handle that."

"Gee, like programming wasn't complex enough, someone had to go and think this up."

"Yes, David Deutsch, a theoretical physicist from Oxford. He's quite a genius," replied Eddie. "These machines are extremely powerful and capable of supporting tremendous speed-ups in calculating the solutions to huge problems – like intelligence."

Eddie should know. His brain was made from one.

Later that night, back in his apartment, while Connie slept in the guest room only a few hundred feet away, Edward continued to delve into who might be following him.

He went into a trance where his computer-mind became a door to the World Wide Web. He opened it and found himself in a virtual file room housing the local police system, containing reports covering the days of the murders. His super acute mind pulled out all the salient features and facts from the available data. Who was following him and why?

One of the doors he opened held the log for his virtual chauffeur, Hector. He reviewed it for the night of the prostitute's murder. From there he drilled down to a visual recording of Hector's sensory perceptions as implanted on his neural-memory network, focusing on the times his driver had glanced in the rearview mirror. Each of these images was captured, enlarged, and analyzed from a variety of angles, using the innate pattern-matching ability of the quantum part of his brain to pull out features of interest.

The first thing he noticed, even without the enhancements and analysis, was that they had indeed been followed. Soon after leaving the parking garage, during the entire trip to the call-girl's cottage, a pair of bright, twin headlights had trailed them from a quarter mile distance. He had never noticed it at the time. The lights passed by when they stopped in front of the house, but they could have easily pulled over a short distance up the street, waited until they had left, and killed the girl.

Edward next enlarged and began analyzing the pictures from the logs, concentrating on those that promised the best results. Using his powerful computer brain and its limitless access to tools and applications, he refined the images, filtering out the bright headlights, viewing them from different angles, using telescoping and computer enhancement. Eventually, he was able to get a good, clear picture of the front of the vehicle – which appeared to be a late model Buick – and a license plate. With additional filtering and enhancements, he was able to make out the vague image of the driver, a single, white, unshaven male of medium build in his mid-forties.

His search of the Registry of Motor Vehicles with the license number provided the name of the driver. Now all he had to do was figure out who Harry Fry was and why he was following him.

Lieutenant Mendoza looked over the latest list of unexplained deaths and homicides, looking for anything that might tie in with his own investigation. The only recent suspicious death was an apparent suicide of a down on his luck private detective. They found him in his car on the beach road with his throat cut. The razor blade was still in his hand, his prints the only ones on it. His clothes – he didn't have a stitch on – were neatly folded in the seat next to him with a handwritten letter. It was an unusual way to end one's life, but he'd seen worse, though you had to be pretty distraught to go that route. Being a homicide cop could be a sad, sordid life if you let it get to you. He suspected it was the same for private dicks, especially this one.

A search of the dead man's squalid apartment told a story of drugs and alcohol, of a man on the skids with a penchant for child porn. No wonder he off'd himself. It wasn't Mendoza's case, and they were still investigating, but it was something.

There were a lot of dead people turning up in his quiet little suburban city in a short time. He couldn't help wonder if the death of Harry Fry was somehow connected to the murders. The letter, disjointed and scribbled, told him nothing except the man's frame of mind – messed up.

As far as he was concerned, they had gotten their man and then let him go because the DA got cold feet. He was worried about a tough legal battle and the political fallout from prosecuting the city's Golden Boy. They had pictures of Dr. Spencer sitting in his car in front of the murdered girl's apartment at the purported time of the killing. He admitted following her after she visited his penthouse. If it had been anybody else they'd have had him booked and in Sing Sing by now, but Edward Spencer was special. Well, he wasn't above the law, not Juan Carlos Mendoza's law.

He decided to do a little moonlighting and visit Fry's seedy one room office near the airport. It wasn't his case and he didn't have a warrant, but that didn't matter. The place wasn't even in his jurisdiction. Still, he buzzed the super and got in when he showed his badge. Jimmying open the office door was easy enough. He wondered if the LA boys had bothered to search the place, but knowing a few of them personally, he doubted it.

It was early morning, about six. The sun was just starting to burn the mist away. It blazed through the east facing window to splash onto the late Harry Fry's cluttered desk. Mendoza didn't need a lamp as he started rummaging through the pile of papers, mostly unpaid bills and half-empty cartons of Chinese takeout, but little in the way of client lists – no names, no phone numbers, no addresses. Apparently, Harry did a cash only business, because there were no checks, cashed or otherwise. Either someone had already been here and taken them or Mister Harry Fry, Private Eye, kept no records of any kind, no account books, address books, case books, or notebooks, which was odd, unless they were hidden somewhere else.

His men had found no notebooks or files at his house either. All Mendoza knew from the information he had gathered casually about the case was that Mister Fry was about to lose his license to practice due to yet another infraction of the law, this time witness intimidation and assault. Maybe that's what sent him over the edge, the knowledge his precarious livelihood was about to be swept from under him. Yet again, a person like Harry was liable to have a lot of enemies, one of whom might want to make it look like a suicide.

He wouldn't find the answer in Harry's office, only a picture of a miserable, futile, sordid existence. Sometimes this job made him hate life, but it was only the human species he loathed.

Connie had never known such exhilaration. Working with Dr. Edward Spencer was beyond her wildest dreams. The things they were doing were beyond anything she had done since school, beyond anything anyone was doing, combining artificial intelligence with nanotechnologies to create intelligent, self-replicating, self-directed swarms of nanobots, all trained to obey laws and rules laid down like DNA in their very molecular structure.

It wasn't quite hero worship, but it was close to it, for the man was remarkable in so many ways. It wasn't only that he was tall and handsome, with movie star looks, or his down to earth and unassuming personality. It was his mind that she admired. Eighty percent of her infatuation with him was cerebral.

He seemed to come from another century, one where the human species had learned to somehow utilize the other ninety percent of their brains, rather than just the normal ten percent. It was as if he had come back in time to help teach us ignorant twenty-first century morons a few things, or perhaps from another planet. She'd had that thought, as crazy as it seemed, more than once.

They had been spending a lot of time together, much against her father's wishes. She was still staying in Eddie's guest suite, but there was much about him she didn't know. She was determined to change that, though he was hard to get close to.

He was reserved and self-conscious about his body. He preferred to eat and sleep and shower alone, the last two of which disappointed her immensely. She had known and gone out with 'gentlemen' before, but Edward took the cake. He was so much the gentleman that she could walk around practically naked and he wouldn't even look twice. It was as if he took pleasure in making her feel like nothing but a machine. Maybe she wasn't his type, but she wasn't used to men not coming on to her. It felt like a challenge, like he had slapped her. She didn't like being ignored.

Oh, he was polite enough, and would sit and talk to her if she wanted, but seldom initiated anything. At work, it was completely different. They would spend hours together, their heads bent over some radio-microscope or simulation-model, or discussing the work over coffee. God, how the time flew when they were working together. She wished it could be more often.

She had started out curious. Then she became star-struck with the man's brilliance and vision. Then what, infatuated? Spellbound? In love?

She had heard about his childhood trauma and his phobia about being touched, and wondered if that had something to do with his standoffish manner. She also knew he hadn't had much experience with women, and that the last encounter had ended in some sort of disaster. She vaguely wondered if his phobia, and not being able to be touched, could drive someone to murder, but doubted it, not someone as sensitive, kind, and intelligent as Edward.

She wondered if there was something wrong with him under his clothes. She pondered this and many other things, but as yet, had few answers to her questions, at least those of a personal nature. She wanted to know him so much better. Perhaps tonight was the night.

He had given in to her entreaties and promised to join her for a candlelight dinner, and for one night forget about work. Edward seldom dined with her, although he would sit and talk while she ate, always about work or the technology. His brain was always working.

From what she could tell he seldom slept more than a few hours a night, if at all. One evening she crept back and watched him while he read and wrote all night, before she fell asleep a little before four, only to wake two hours later to find him still working. He said he slept for a couple of hours while she did, but she doubted it. The man was super-human. She couldn't help, with her experience and fondness for men, wonder what he was like in bed.

It was already quarter past eight. Where could he be? She had left him at the lab two hours ago. He said he'd be home in an hour for dinner at eight, but she could tell he was involved in something that occupied his attention, and when that happened time could stand still. Yet he had promised. He knew how important this dinner was to her.

At that moment the phone rang. She hesitated to pick it up, for some absurd reason afraid it would be bad news, like the police saying Edward had been killed in a car accident or something, a senseless, nameless dread that welled up in her stomach and was only dissipated when she reasoned the odds were vastly against such a thing. She flipped on the connection. It was Edward.

"Sorry, Connie. I'm afraid I won't be able to make our date tonight. I'm at the police station talking to Detective Mendoza. There's been a break in the case. We think we know who was following me."

"Oh, no, they aren't arresting you, are they?"

"No, nothing like that. I came down on my own. I found out who was following me that night the third girl was murdered."

"You're working on the case? I thought you were working on our project."

"Listen, Connie, this is a big break. I think I've found out who the killer is."

Connie heard herself saying, "That's great, don't worry about dinner, you can heat it up when you get home."

After all, three young women had been murdered. Still, it irked her that of all the things he could have been doing, he was working on police business. She would have preferred it if he had been arrested. She threw her plate against the wall in a fit of pique. Connie Knowles never was one to take second place, no matter what the reason, especially where men were concerned.

As usual when she was upset because of some man, she called her father to complain, as if it was all somehow his fault.

"I told you what he was like, that you wouldn't be happy, but you wouldn't listen to me," replied her father in his usual know-it-all way, which just made her madder.

"He's out helping the police solve the murders, for God's sake."

"I can't say that I blame him, with him being their prime suspect. If he can shed some light on who's behind this, who's trying to frame him, it might be a big help."

"It's only going to draw him in further, make them suspect him even more. I'm supposed to be his alibi, but he's never around anymore."

"Why don't you come to the house? It's bad enough you work with him, do you have to live with him, too?"

"There's so much to learn. It's not a nine-to-five type of job."

"Look, Connie, I have something to tell you. It's very important, but I can't tell you over the phone."

"What? What's so important you can't tell me over the phone?"

"Why don't we meet for breakfast in the morning?"

"I don't like secrets. What's this about? Edward? The project?"

"Both, but it's something I have to tell you in person."

128

She had a good mind to say, no, forget it, she wasn't interested. She knew her father well enough to know it might be just a ploy to get her where he could apply more pressure to make her quit and go back to New York. Still, if she could learn something about Edward, or about the mysterious project they were working on, it was worth the risk. After all, what could her father do but badger her with over-used, worn-out phrases of professed wisdom and superior judgment. She'd heard it all before, from her mom, her teachers, her doctors, and her shrinks. Every man in her life offered advice on how to best live it, all but Edward. All he ever offered was answers to her questions and respectful difference.

What was it about him that captivated her so? In answer she always came back to his brains. She was awed by his passionate intensity and wished some of it could rub off on her.

"OK," she finally heard herself saying, curious about what her father had to say. "I'll meet you for breakfast tomorrow at nine. But not at the house, somewhere neutral."

"This isn't a duel. I only want to talk to you."

"I want to meet you in public, not where you can browbeat me and cajole me into doing what you want."

"I'm not going to browbeat you. You're a big girl. You can make up your own mind. I just want to make sure you have all the facts, that you know what you're getting involved with. You called me remember."

"Gee, you make it sound like such a big conspiracy. Does it have something to do with the murders? Do you know something about…?"

"No, nothing like that, nothing sensational, but nothing I want to talk about over the phone. This has to be private."

"How about tonight, if it's so important?"

"No, I have to take care of something this evening. It can wait until tomorrow."

"OK, meet me at the park near The Lakes. Nine o'clock. I'll see you then."

She hung up, sorry as usual she had called her father in the first place, but curious at what he might have to say.

Chapter 19

Edward came home late that evening. Connie had waited up and was madder now than ever. She confronted him as soon as he came through the door.

"Why are you so late?" she asked. "I waited up. What took you so long that you come home this time of night? Have you eaten?"

"I'm sorry, but the police asked me a lot of questions. They were interested in what I found, but it just seemed to make them more suspicious. I told them the man following me might be the killer, but they told me it wasn't likely. They wouldn't believe I didn't know him or how I found out about him. I thought they were never going to let me go, but Pete, my lawyer, came by and saved the day again. He's worth every penny of his exorbitant fee."

He then began to tell her how he did it, as he had told the police. In spite of her anger, she found it amazing that he could access such arcane sources and actually get pictures by manipulating logs and security videos. It was mind-boggling. No wonder the police didn't believe him, but she did.

She had on a black sexy negligee, but Edward seemed not to notice. He told her he'd eaten something at the police station – a likely story.

"Don't you think you should put something on?" he suggested on seeing her in the skimpy outfit. "What if your father saw you walking around like that?"

"I thought you'd like it. Most men would."

"I like it. You look great, but I can't get involved with anyone right now."

"Then why did you invite me to stay here? Most guys, well, let's just say most men would have ulterior motives. I thought you wanted to get to know me better."

"I do, and we will. There is plenty of time for that, but there is a lot going on. I'm not sure it's the right time right now. Your father doesn't approve, for one thing. He's made that abundantly clear, and I can understand why. In any case, I don't want anything to interfere with our work, and I never mix my work and my personal life."

"Do you even have a personal life?"

"Sure, but I haven't had much luck with relationships. It's probably for the better that we don't get involved."

"Did you kill those women?" she asked out of the blue.

Edward betrayed no emotion, no indignation, no anger or guilt, as he answered in a matter-of-fact way. "No. Of course not. What made you ask that?"

"Oh, I don't know. I just wanted to check, since I'm living here with you and all."

"Perhaps you should move to a hotel, or better yet, your dad's place."

"No thanks. I'm safer here. You said you weren't the killer."

"And you believe me?"

"Yeah, you have an honest face. Anyway, I think I know you well enough by now, but there's a lot more I'd like to know."

"Like what?" asked Eddie, with increasing anxiety, his alarm systems ringing.

"Like do you like women or men?"

"I like everyone, but if you mean sexually, I like women, very much."

"Are you a virgin? Have you had sex?"

"You don't beat around the bush, do you?"

"Answer the question," she commanded with mock authority.

"No and yes, although I'm not going to qualify that answer with details. I'm not that kind of guy."

"I know. You're a gentleman."

"I try to be."

"That can be a little tiring."

Edward looked at her with his intense eyes.

"You're quite a girl. Yes, I do like you. You're one of the brightest people I've ever worked with. I don't believe we can do what we need to do without you. I don't want to ruin it by either of us getting emotionally involved."

He sounded like her father, although he was actually two years younger than she was. She had an idea there were still a few things she could teach him yet if given half a chance.

When he stood to leave to go to the lab, she stood just inches from him, with her hands behind her back, looking up invitingly into his eyes, but he merely bent and kissed her cheek and said good night. The kiss tingled, as if he had given her a mild shock. She looked after him longingly, wanting nothing more than his hands on her. Maybe she'd find out something tomorrow from her father that would help her understand this enigmatic man.

She didn't get much sleep that night, wondering what secrets Edward might be hiding and what truths her father was going to reveal. She fought the urge to spy on her host, even though she was sure she'd see nothing but the man working. Perhaps, like Thomas Edison, he could get by with catnaps on his desk when no one was looking, though she had yet to catch Edward snoozing, or eating anything but a breakfast bar or occasional piece of fruit. The man was strange, but sweet. Those thoughts made her smile and soon fall asleep.

She woke up a few hours later bathed in sweat and feeling little rested. Her dreams had started out nice enough, with an erotic fantasy in a colorful landscape. Soon, however, they grew dark and sinister. When she awoke she realized that she hadn't had a dream like that since her tormented broken-home childhood. That's what she got for talking to her father before going to sleep.

The next morning at quarter to five, Connie dressed and took a jog around the block, stopping at the health club for a swim. Then she went back to the penthouse, waving at the doorman, the same poor guy who always seemed to be there. Edward had already left, leaving a holo-gram on the table telling her he'd see her at the lab and that she looked very seductive last night.

She smiled as she changed and made herself some ham and eggs. Then she left to meet her dad, still curious as to what it was he wanted to tell her.

Taking a cab from the apartment the short distance to the Lakes Complex, a large park with golf courses and ballparks clustered between modern high-rise buildings and offices, she made her way to their bench.

They had met here when she used to visit her father from college. He was still active and busy with his research. This was before his protégé came on the scene and stole all the limelight. He had been too busy then to spend much time with her, and never invited her to the beach house where his third wife held sway, but they would meet in the park occasionally, to sit on the bench and talk. He always had good advice, if a bit paternalistic and conservative. She hoped he'd have something good to tell her now, but worried it would more than likely be the opposite, something to make her feel bad and worry about. Such was life.

He wasn't there. She waited impatiently for a half hour, leaving several messages on his phone, but had heard nothing back. Hailing an Uber on her handheld, she stomped off to meet it. She was furious. She didn't like being stood up by men, especially her father. Now it had happened twice in twelve hours.

The house was dark, as if no one was up yet. Her father had no servants despite the size of the place and his wealth. To Nancy, it felt creepy to be there alone at night, even with her father around. She felt much more secure, even if it was false, at the penthouse with Edward. She knocked on the front door and rang the bell, but no one answered. Going around the back, she tried the rear door to the pantry and kitchen. It was open. She entered calling his name. There was no answer.

Moving into the next room, she heard him talking to someone upstairs. She followed the sound up the large front staircase to the second floor. As she got closer she could hear him more distinctly, speaking from the room at the end of the hall. It sounded as if he was giving a lecture. Perhaps he was practicing for an upcoming talk. It would be just like him to forget her, thinking about some public appearance, his bread and butter. She had a good mind to barge in and interrupt. Maybe, if she were lucky, she could disrupt a live radio broadcast. Oh, how sweet that would be!

As she neared the half-closed door, his words became clearer.

"It's only a matter of time before machines, any of our dozen or so quantum, molecular, or silicon-based computers, or all of them together, will have human-level intelligence, and an even shorter time after that when they will surpass us. This means robots and other computer-based entities will have capabilities mirroring and even surpassing what we can do, faster and more accurately. And a lot sooner than you think. All that's needed to put us over the top and make the dream a reality are breakthroughs in a few key technologies, much of which has already been done. Machines will routinely pass any type of Turing test human beings might devise. More than that, the machine will have a soul. I have already…"

She threw open the door and burst into the room. "What's the big idea of standing me up? I sat there for an hour waiting for you."

Her father, who was standing in the middle of the room, never faltered or missed a word, but continued talking as if she weren't there.

"The potential to combine this level of machine intelligence with holographic projection is endless, and has led to a number of interesting discoveries."

"What's the matter with you?" she demanded when he continued to ignore her, walking toward him angrily. "I'm talking to you!"

It took a few moments more, when she was almost about to kick him, before she realized it was a hologram and not her father standing there. She saw the miniature laser on the floor that was projecting his image and snapped it off, making him and his voice evaporate immediately into the gloom.

"Dad, Dad?" she called with concern. She was a bit freaked-out by the whole weird experience and turned to leave the room. It was what she saw then that made her scream.

Chapter 20

Detective Juan Mendoza had a lot on his hands, all of it apparently centered on Dr. Edward Spencer. First he turns up at the station with a set of incredible pictures seemingly showing a driver and a license plate from a car supposedly following him to the prostitute's house on the night of her murder. How he had done it was even more unbelievable than the pictures themselves. It was a bit hard to swallow, even if it was thought-provoking. A little checking told him the guy who had followed Spencer was none other than Harry Fry, the washed-out private detective who was found with his throat slashed. Perhaps it wasn't a suicide after all. Perhaps it was more than coincidence. What was he doing following the scientist? Things were getting complicated, then Spencer's business associate and mentor shows up dead, hanging by his neck. Another suicide? They were dropping like flies. The possibilities were endless. It made Mendoza's head spin.

Knowles' daughter, who was highly distraught, had called his number using the card he'd given her the night he interviewed Spencer. She called it instead of 911, so he was the first on the grisly scene.

Seventy-one year old Professor Andrew Knowles had apparently hanged himself with a short nylon line he had tied to a hook on the wall. The small stool he had been standing on was knocked over beneath his feet, which dangled a few inches above the floor. He was in his dressing gown. There was a letter. By all appearances the professor had taken his own life. The letter spoke of unspeakable crimes that there was no way to atone for.

Connie, his daughter, believed none of it, and insisted her father had been murdered, but she was in such an overwrought, emotional state that everyone who heard her, including the detective, thought she was being hysterical. She was soon given a strong sedative and put to bed under a doctor's care. Edward, who she had phoned moments after calling Mendoza, showed up a short time later. He appeared to be distraught as well. Mendoza began questioning him immediately.

"When was the last time you saw Dr. Knowles?" he asked.

"I don't know, a few nights ago. We've both been rather busy. I can't believe he's just gone like this."

"His daughter is living with you, isn't she? Yet you haven't seen him in days? Why? Don't you get along?"

"No, it's not that. He's my friend. He practically brought me up when my parent's died."

Edward maintained the charade as if it was second nature, and it was. The lie of who he was had been so ingrained through years of training and positive feedback that it was as if it were part of his very being. To him, he wasn't pretending but just being himself, his memories as real as anyone's, even though he knew they were all implanted.

"Yet he didn't approve of his daughter staying with you."

"That's not entirely true. He was concerned about her, that's all. We talked."

"His daughter thinks he was murdered."

"She must be distraught. Their relationship wasn't that good. They argued a lot. I tried to get them back together. They were reconciling, and now this. How terrible. What is going on around here?"

"What's going on around here is exactly what I'd like to know. You admitted you hardly knew the girl. Why did she come to you? Maybe you knew her better than you say. Perhaps things weren't as nice between you and Dr. Knowles as you want us to believe."

"That's ridiculous, Inspector. I never would have done anything to harm Andrew. He was like a father to me."

"Men have been known to kill their fathers. Haven't you ever heard of Oedipus?"

"The man who followed me is behind all this. I gave you his name and proof."

"You gave me a name, all right, and something else. I'm not sure what that was. Harry Fry isn't going to be following anyone. He accidentally sliced his own throat. Did quite a job, too. Hard to believe he could have done that all by himself. We think he was murdered. Perhaps Dr. Knowles was as well, like his daughter says."

Edward said nothing as his brain – wherever it was – digested this bit of information. He grew dizzy as his quantum neurons swirled and bubbled, and the gyro-modulator for his holo-body fought to keep his equilibrium.

The detective continued.

"Maybe someone didn't like being followed and killed Mr. Fry. There's a motive for you."

"I didn't know who he was until you told me about him. I have never met the man, but I believe he's the killer or hired by him."

"I'll worry about who's a suspect, thank you. Is Dr. Knowles the kind of man who would hang himself? We're getting a court order to confiscate and search his house and computers. If he has any kinky habits or quirks, we'll know about them soon enough."

"No, nothing like that, I'm sure, not Andrew. He'd never be involved in anything of that nature. He's not the type of person who would kill himself."

"Then you agree with his daughter that this wasn't a suicide."

"Suicide doesn't make any sense. He just wouldn't do something as illogical as that."

"Do you know anyone who would want to harm him?"

Without hesitating Edward said no, emphatically no.

"How did you figure out Fry was following you, again? You used computers, right?"

"Yes. The limo is fit with cameras, inside and out. Wherever the driver looks is also recorded. I just went through the logs for the time in question. Then I manipulated the images using a 3-D image analyzing tool – something we make, by the way. I can show your people how it works if you like."

"That's pretty nifty, getting into the RMV files like that. You must be pretty smart, probably smart enough to get away with murder."

"I'm trying to help, Lieutenant."

"Then you'll be happy to know these smart guys always slip up eventually, even the brightest ones, like you. Good afternoon, Doc."

The detective left with more suspicions than answers and again told Edward not to leave town.

Despite his calm demeanor when dealing with the detective, Edward's well-ordered world was turned to chaos by the death of his mentor. By the time Mendoza left, Eddie's self-conscious awareness had turned into a bubbling soup of thoughts and remembrances. He didn't know what was real and what was programmed. He felt, what was it? What was this subjective complex of sensations called? Frightened? Lonely? He had never felt so alone. Yes, that was it, he felt utterly, totally, forbiddingly alone.

Andrew had known him like no other, and the fact that there was no one now, no one who knew him, made him feel empty, as empty as the wall-less vessel he really was. Losing all purpose, all reason to be, he was wrapped in a mindless numbness that consumed him. His form sat unmoving, staring out the apartment window into space, unseeing, unfeeling, all but dead to the world.

His features were frozen. He responded to no one. It was as if by playing a pre-programmed part for so long, he was now left with no part to play. Though there was no heart pumping blood, something was broken inside him and the only way to stop the pain was to shut down. His condition didn't go unnoticed.

"Have you seen Ed lately?" Connie asked Rudy when he came to the lab the next morning.

"No, what's up?"

"I was with him last night at the penthouse. I tried to talk to him, but he didn't respond. I don't know the last time he slept or ate. I think he's taking Dad's death pretty hard."

"I've never seen him eat," replied Rudy.

"It's like he's become catatonic. I'm worried about him."

"Maybe we should call a doctor, have him seen by someone, if he's that bad."

"That's the last thing he needs," replied Connie "Familiar surroundings and friends will do more for him than a bunch of head-shrinks probing his mind."

"I agree, but no one seems to have legal authority in the company right now. There's a leadership vacuum and Burr may decide to fill it. Now with Eddie like this and the professor gone … I'm sorry," Rudy said, realizing the effect his words were having on Connie.

"That's all right, Rudy," she said, putting on a brave face.

"I'm worried for the company, that's all. You're the professor's only heir. Maybe it's time for you to step up and take charge. I'll support you."

"Thanks, Rudy, I appreciate your confidence in me, but I don't think it will come to that. Eddie will be OK. We just need to cover for him until he's himself again. Can I count on you not to tell anyone else?"

"Sure, Connie, you know I'll do whatever I can to help."

"Good. I'll stay with Edward. You just go about your business as if nothing has happened. If I can get over my father's death, so can Eddie. I'll help him. I still say Dad's death wasn't a suicide. He just wouldn't have ended it that way. No, something's going on, but we need Edward to help us figure out what it is."

"I'll go to the twelfth floor lab and make sure Burr doesn't try anything. It would be just like him to try and grab the quantum back.

That's the first thing he'd do if he knew Eddie was out of commission."

"Good, Rudy. You watch the fort, while I watch Eddie."

Jack Burr surveyed the modest skyline of El Segundo from his twenty-fifth floor executive suite. He had read about the death of Andrew Knowles in the papers. Although the co-founder hadn't been around much of late and was semi-retired, he still had many friends and acquaintances throughout the company, who were not only grieved, but shocked at his passing. That and a tip on the CEO's apparent mental collapse, caused Tom Johnson, the next ranking executive, to suspend operations for the remainder of the week. That didn't stop Burr from going to the office.

He wasn't going to let anything stand in the way of his upcoming demo. He had ordered his entire team to work regardless of the official company moratorium. When told he should show more respect, he responded that Rudy Duncan and Knowles's daughter were working away like beavers on some secret project, so why couldn't he? When no reason was offered in return, he and his team went back to work. In any case, it was uncertain who actually had legal control of the company at the moment, and that suited Jack just fine. He hoped to keep it that way for a while more.

He didn't register much surprise at the news of Knowles's suicide, and offered the dubious opinion that the man was under a lot of stress and wasn't getting along with his only daughter. He also hinted, not so subtly, that the professor had a guilty conscience about something and had been questioned by the police about the recent homicides. No one could say how he got this information or whether it was true. The contents of the suicide letter hadn't yet been reported.

When he learned that Dr. Spencer wouldn't be in for awhile and was in mourning much like after his secretary's death, Jack commented that it was the CEO's usual way of coping, and wondered out loud what kind of man they had at the helm.

"What's going to happen to the company now that the real brains behind the operation, Andrew Knowles, is gone?" he asked.

Some thought he had a big mouth, but some listened and pondered his words.

He had indeed attempted to get the quantum-array back, but learned it was still in use. When Rudy told him this, with a phalanx of security men behind him, Burr started asking some questions of his own, like when was Edward Spencer coming back and what were they doing on the twelfth floor? He got no answers. Like everything concerning Spencer's lab, he was left in the dark.

God, he hated that man. He wondered how a person of so little real substance could receive so much adulation.

"I'm twice the man he is," Burr said aloud to himself, as he surveyed the panoramic view out his office windows. "The wimp never even served in the armed forces, let alone the Marines. You don't fool me, Spencer. I can see right through you. You're nothing but a sham. No wonder you don't want to show up. Now the real brains are gone, we'll see how well you do."

"Did you call, sir?" asked his secretary, who had overheard his rant and thought he was talking to her, even though the door to his inner office was shut. Burr wouldn't tolerate a secretary he couldn't come on to, and although he had contemplated holographic sex, he still only hassled real women.

"No, but now that you're here, get my broker on the phone, will you, Phyllis? I need to talk to him."

The tiff between Jack and his head engineer had been smoothed over with HR's help, and a steak dinner at the most expensive restaurant in town, compliments of Jack Burr. He hadn't meant to alienate his entire department and was playing the bonus card rather heavily, out of his own pocket, but he could afford it. He was on a mission. He knew the stakes were high even if the others didn't, and he would do anything to win.

He had been there in the deserts and cities of the Middle East and Sub Sahara, fighting the enemies of western civilization as they tried to destroy one small kingdom and country at a time with their insidious propaganda and terror tactics. He knew what the world was up against, and he knew how to stop them – technology. They couldn't fight what they couldn't see. They couldn't terrorize an enemy that came from nowhere to attack them in their sleep or while they ate breakfast with their family, an enemy who could see behind walls and kill from afar. Technology was the only thing standing between the free world and the prophets of an ancient, brutal hate, espoused under the guise of religion.

With the technology he had at his company's disposal they could not only train their men and women under completely realistic conditions, but bamboozle the enemy with virtual soldiers and holographic tanks. But they needed the full technology to do it, not half of it, not some subset that Spencer thought fit to dispense.

Now with Knowles gone for good and his protégé temporarily out of the picture, Burr was free to go about his business and save the world. He was in the middle of these daydreams when his investment broker called.

He voiced-on his ear-set and answered, but left the holo-imager off. He didn't understand some people's desire to see who they were talking to. He hadn't cared for it when they used cameras and he didn't like it now that they were projecting holographic images. It was just a waste of bandwidth and technology, as far as he was concerned. More of what people like Edward Spencer would be happy to peddle, while the world went to hell in the hands of religious extremists and political radicals.

"What do you mean, someone is buying up all the shares?" he demanded after hearing what his adviser had to say. "Who? Well, find out, and buy back as many as you can. How much? They're raising the price? See what you can do. I'll release another hundred thousand. Never mind where it came from, just do it."

He had been very careful, using third parties and assumed names, but now that someone was on to him, all efforts at concealment were abandoned for expediency. Who could it be, Knowles before his unfortunate demise? The man was going to fire him. Or was it that pencil-pushing dunderhead, Tom Johnson. He always was an interfering snake, siding with Knowles and Spencer every chance he got. Well, Burr had his own friends in the front office. They would take care of Johnson.

Yes, he had been very careful.

His private phone chimed. The name of his good friend on the Senate Armed Services Committee and ex-marine mate, Phil Miles, blazed across the virtual screen associated with the connection.

"Hi, Senator. To what do I owe this pleasure? Good. I was just going to call you and give you an update. As you may have heard, we've had another tragedy here at the company. Our co-founder, Dr. Andrew Knowles, killed himself a few days ago. Yes, but he still kept a hand in things. Some say he was the real brains behind the company, not that Spencer's not a good scientist in his own right, but Andrew, well, he was special. Things won't be the same now that he's really gone, but that's not stopping us.

"The company has called for four days of mourning and closed the labs, but my team is fully manned and on the job. The Quantum? Well, priorities are priorities. We, like the Marines, have to do the best we can with what we have. We can still give you a good show. It just means more work for us, but you'll get the picture. This technology can save lives, on the battlefield and off. With this, the enemy won't know what's real and what's make-believe. They will come to doubt their own eyes. Don't worry, we pulled a lot harder things off than this in Iraq and Afghanistan. OK, semper fi, see you Friday."

Jack Burr was soon alone again with his thoughts. He checked and rechecked all his bases and felt satisfied he had everything covered. With that, he asked his secretary to come in for a little dictation.

"Shut the door behind you," he said, as she entered.

Chapter 21

While Rudy and Connie worked to recover their boss's mind and retain his company, Edward sat and stared out the window, but contrary to appearances he was far from inactive. He had crossed an inward threshold between being frozen in shock and stung into hyperactivity. While his holographic projection sat motionless, his massive parallel brains whirled away at dizzying speeds, solving a multitude of questions, simultaneously crunching through possibilities, probabilities, perturbations, and potentialities. His mind traveled through the worldwide network seeking its secrets, ferreting out its hidden gems, facts, and figures, tying all the separate, disparate theories together to weave a web of interconnecting insights. And with each of these, another path to follow, like a chess master explores each alternative in his head, ten, twenty, a hundred steps in advance before the first move is taken.

He walked through a maze of doorways, a corridor of passageways, down a long, dark tunnel, deeper and deeper until he came to the last door. It was massive and thick, with a medieval frame, bolted with a black iron bar, which fell away when he touched it. Pulling with all his strength, he slowly opened it. It creaked with the groan of ages.

It only took Edward a moment to realize where he was.

Edward had come home. He stood surrounded by computers of all types, silicon-based Von Neumanns, massively-parallel cellular neural-networks, arrays of quantum machines, all for him, his amazing mind, his incredible bionic brain, housed in the hidden basement of Professor Knowles' seaside home, all based on the brain of a dying seven year old boy.

He had found it. Of course, it had to be housed somewhere, but it would have been rude to ask where. He should have guessed. Apparently he had known it subconsciously all along.

It was still hard for Edward to think of himself as non-human, as not having a real body with a head, which held a physical, thinking brain. He had been trained, conditioned, tricked, to see the world that way, taught to see himself as human. It was so ingrained in his mind, that he had to trick himself again to get outside of it, to see it as a series of doors that could be opened, which in turn led by infinite pathways and connections to the outside world. To see it all laid out before him like a whirling carnival was almost surreal.

Now that he had truly found himself, he began to ponder the implications.

It was interesting that the police thought Harry Fry, the person who was following him, may have been murdered. Even more curiously, they thought Edward may have killed him, since he was the one Fry was following. He wondered if this had anything to do with the other murders. Could the professor have been the murderer? Is that why he killed himself, guilt? What motive would he have? To protect their secret? Or had he been murdered, too? By who, the same person who killed Fry? Unknown to Eddie, he was following the same train of reasoning Lieutenant Mendoza had followed, except that Eddie, not the detective, was the number one suspect.

Had the killer murdered the professor, perhaps trying to throw the police off the track by offering him as a scapegoat? It all seemed far-fetched, but if you eliminate the impossible, whatever is left, no matter how implausible, is your answer. It was only logical. So, like Sherlock Holmes, he followed the implications.

What about Jack Burr? Could he be the killer? Motive? For starters, Tom Johnson, the CFO, and Knowles had decided to fire the insubordinate executive. Presumably the professor had already told Burr. Was that motive enough to murder a person? Alone, probably not, but what if you had other reasons for wanting the professor dead? Maybe Burr wanted more than just to keep his job.

Ed had learned recently that someone was buying huge shares of the company stock. Tom Johnson thought it might be foreign nationals attempting to take control of their proprietary secrets, but Edward wondered if the culprit wasn't closer to home. Using direct access to the necessary systems through the computerized brain he now stared at, he had ordered a large investment diverted from his personal assets to begin buying back shares.

All this was going on as Edward's form sat still as stone, his silicon-quantum-organic mind ranging far and wide, moving at the speed of light in search of answers.

Jack Burr, Jack Burr, Jack Burr, the name came back from each ferreting syntactic connection in his virtual mind. Is he the one behind this? Did he really kill three women? Could he have really taken these lives just for a business reason?

It seemed unthinkable to Edward that someone could kill for such a tawdry, mundane purpose, and not out of passion or some towering rage. Even a machine could understand that, but in cold bloodless malice with no personal reason, just to gain some self-justified end? It didn't make sense. Yet as a machine, Eddie should have had a special affinity for such reasoning, where cold logic dictated one's actions. The training of his neural-nets, however, had been crafted in such a way as to bring about a high level of consciousness, one that thought in terms larger than itself or its own immediate gratification, a spiritual being with a conscience and an empathy with others, even if they weren't his kind.

And so he sat, passively looking out the window, while his mind gazed inward, looking for answers he wasn't sure existed.

When Connie wasn't working in the lab she was watching Edward, trying to coax him back to the living, but she wasn't having much luck. He didn't seem to respond to anything or anyone. She tried to stay positive and talked and bantered with him like he was all there instead of in some distant inner dungeon of his own making, but it was becoming more difficult as the days dragged on.

It was uncanny how he could sit there like that with no water or food, no sleep. He didn't even seem to be breathing. Once, when she stared at him a long time without interruption, she thought she saw him blink, but not much else.

"It's just not human," she said to Rudy when he joined her for supper one evening in the penthouse.

"The human mind is a funny thing," he replied. "Sometimes a person can go into a coma or a catatonic state like that and it looks like nothing's going on up there, you know, but then all of a sudden the person snaps out of it, enlightened, kind of like they've been sitting there thinking all that time until they found the answer, like Buddha under the Bodhi Tree."

"But he's not moving. I've watched him for hours."

"When the subconscious mind takes over like that sometimes it can put the body in a kind of suspended animation."

"Well, it sure is weird."

She didn't say it, but she suspected more was going on than met the eye. The jury was still out where Dr. Edward Spencer was concerned, but she had to admit she was still fascinated by him, now more than ever. Still, she had to know. Did he murder those women? Could he have killed her father?

Rudy had finished installing and activating the quantum computers in the twelfth floor lab, as well as vats filled with the hydro-carbon catalyst needed to construct the carbon-based nano-tubes. The work was all they talked about. Rudy was reluctant to be drawn into conversation about Eddie and his personal problems. When he left to go home, Connie decided to work some more before retiring, and sat in the lab going over the final specifications.

The job seemed overwhelming when looked at from a whole – create three generations of ever more sophisticated nanobots to fabricate six trillion of themselves, creating a swarm. By looking at it one step at a time, however, as long as you concentrated on the task at hand, it was manageable. Still, the work was daunting, and without Eddie to answer their myriad questions they had no hope of succeeding.

Because of the secrecy very little had been written down, only a few design diagrams and a shortened specification. No formulas. No equations. It was all in Eddie's head, as amazing as it seemed, and that was only the half of it. Based on the current state of the technology, what they were attempting to do was impossible, and would be for another couple decades at a minimum. But somehow, as if he had slipped into the future and returned, Eddie knew just what to do. It was as if he saw it, like Mozart one of his symphonies, as already completed in his head, each and every nanobot perfectly in place.

Even if the technology had been available, the time frame for the work was incredibly short, a project that normally would have taken several years if not a decade, to be done in nine weeks. Impossible, she said to herself again for the fiftieth time, reviewing the few notes Eddie had made in a small electronic notebook.

"Impossible," she said again, this time out loud.

"No, it's not," answered a voice behind her.

She jumped in her seat and screamed. Turning around abruptly, she was shocked to see Eddie.

"Edward!" she yelled. "Are you OK? You startled me. You're awake."

"I was never asleep, though it may have appeared that way. I was thinking, in a trance."

"It was like you were in a catatonic coma or something. You didn't respond to anything. I didn't know what to think. I certainly didn't know you meditated."

"There's a lot about me you don't know."

"Were you thinking about my father?"

"Yes and much more. Your father was a great man. I miss him dearly, but he left us a legacy and I am going to make sure it is fulfilled. I learned a lot in my transcendental state. The first thing we need to do is move the lab to my apartment building. None of the rooms on the ninth floor have tenants. We'll take it over and establish our research there where it is safe. We will also need the computers in your father's secret lab in the basement of his house, rooms that not even you know about. Time is of the essence."

Chapter 22

Today was Jack Burr's big day. Things were not going his way. Though his team had worked overtime as the rest of the company took a three day hiatus, they were behind schedule. Some of the critical software components were still missing.

The last dry run had not gone well, with several glitches that made it impossible to demonstrate a key feature, a feature they had been advertising as completed and tested. His engineers had worked through the past twelve hours to fix the snafus. There was nothing to do now but cross his fingers and hope for the best, but Jack Burr was not an optimist.

While the death of the eminent Andrew Knowles had succeeded in getting Spencer out of the way, it had unforeseen consequences that threatened his plans. Jack hadn't yet succeeded in gaining a majority share of the company stock, although he had come close and had enough other stockholders in his corner to take over control of ARC. That didn't stop Spencer from removing the company's major assets to a private lab in his apartment building. Burr didn't know if that was illegal or not, and was attempting to get the legal department to check on it, but many of them were on their summer vacation. While he might, with a few others, control the company's stock, he still didn't have any clout with Operations or most of Engineering, which was still loyal to Dr. Spencer.

At times it felt like the whole world was conspiring against him, like he was fighting for his life, but it was his country he was fighting for, and that gave him the courage to soldier on against all odds. He had already done things he never thought himself capable of, things he managed to keep out of his mind and deny to himself most of the time. They were things he'd had to do, like in war, when you do something for your country that would be considered criminal in other times. He wasn't going to let it go for naught by wimping out now and losing the game. He would fight on.

All these thoughts coursed through his mind as he walked down the hall to the new demo room on the twenty-fifth floor. Even though Spencer's lab was no longer operational and had been mostly dismantled and moved, it was still off limits, as was the fully equipped demo room next to it. It drove him to distraction along with a dozen other picayune things dreamt up just to irk him, he was sure. He'd have to make due with what they could scrape together from Spencer's leftovers. It was a shame they were operating under these handicaps for something as important as this demonstration, but that wouldn't last much longer. Things were about to change.

The room was full when he got there – Philip Miles, his friend from the Senate Armed Services Committee and his cronies were there, assorted top brass from the various branches of the military, men and women invited from the press, along with assorted dignitaries, government officials, and academics – were all there to see the newest technological advance in tactical training, planning, and counter-terrorism.

Normally, either Spencer himself or a trained company spokesperson would be giving the presentation, but because of the situation, Jack Burr had come forward to assume that part.

"Good morning, Ladies and Gentleman," he began. "And members of our armed services, Senator Miles and his committee – and members of the press."

Burr looked up at one of the pressmen with a wry smile, and threw the words out as if he had remembered them at the last moment. They laughed and the ice was broken. "Last but not least," he added, which got a few more chuckles.

"Thank you for coming. First of all, I want to welcome you and tell you that although our company has gone through some difficult times recently, it has not softened our commitment to providing solutions for the modern day. I'm sure our founders, Dr. Edward Spencer, who can't be with us today, and Dr. Andrew Knowles, who has tragically left us too soon, would agree. What we are about to show you will prove not only very valuable to our country, to help defend it and deter those who would attack it, but will lead the way to a better future for our descendants."

A few of the engineers, who had known Andrew Knowles, muttered under their breath, and some still loyal to Edward Spencer gave a smirk, but all eyes were on Jack Burr as he gave his introduction.

"Now you might ask, what can a company like Altered Realities do to help *you*? They make games and virtual conferencing systems. What's that got to do with defense? Well, actually quite a lot. Have any of you got teenage boys at home?"

A few hands went up.

"And do they have computer or video games, virtual reality goggles? Hmm-hmm. And what do they play?"

He shook his head in the affirmative when more hands went up and others shouted out answers.

"Yep, they play war. It could be World War II or War of the Worlds. It could be with ships or planes or ground troops, or it could be worldwide global thermonuclear annihilation. Perhaps even Star Wars and galactic battles. But more than likely they're playing at being a hero and saving the world. It's every pre-adolescent to young adult male's fantasy and has been for a thousand generations. It's shoot 'em up and blast them to smithereens if you want to sell a computer game. Same with virtual reality, either battles or sports games. So the technology is already geared toward military uses. The pump is primed in your favor. This is just a nudge further in that direction, where the technology has been heading all along.

"Now we all know how important simulation is, both for training pilots and creating a realistic combat situation. Simulation for flight is very well-developed, and with special equipment, 3-D effects can be created, but nothing like that exists for ground troops, anti-terrorist units, Special Forces, or police. They're still in the dark ages, left with specially-constructed fire-ranges where wooden or metal targets pop up behind windows and doors. That is until now. Before we continue, I'd like to make a confession."

It was time to take a page from Edward Spencer's playbook. He looked around the room.

"Not all of you are real," he informed them.

There was a murmur in the room as people turned to their neighbor with quizzical expressions.

"What did he say?" some asked.

"Will the fake participants please stand up," requested Burr.

There was some hesitation as everyone looked at each other expectantly, still wondering what was going on. Finally, reluctantly, one by one, three individuals rose – two men, one in uniform with general's stars on his shoulders, and a middle-aged woman with glasses.

"Gentlemen, ladies, I'd like you to meet our holo-attendees. Mark Raven from Memphis, Tennessee – he's only impersonating a general for today – and Martha Williams in New York City. Both Mark and Martha are real people, but their appearance in the room with us is a projected image."

150

One of the woman standing next to the holographic general reached out to touch his shoulder and shrieked involuntarily in shock when her hand passed through him.

"Watch that!" said the fake general.

The woman jumped again with a yelp and everyone laughed.

"Even though Mark isn't in the room, he can see and hear everything you do, through sensors and cameras that are associated with and track with the holograph. It's all controlled with computers, of course, but very powerful ones."

"What about this gentleman?" asked one of the participants, sitting not far from the third man who had stood.

"That's Eddie Fisher. He's not real at all. He'll sing for us later."

With that, the holographic figure of the late singer drew an automatic from under his jacket and waved it around the room. Even though Jack had just told them it wasn't real, several men dashed for cover. One of the women screamed.

Just then four armed security guards rushed into the room, their weapons drawn. They ran toward the gunman, their revolvers pointed in his direction. He darted away and fired his gun at them. They scattered and ducked, and returned fire. Their laser-guided bullets made straight-lined passages through the room and appeared to splinter the ceiling.

So far all the shots had been aimed high, but people were ducking for cover and knocking over chairs as they scurried out of the way. The percussive sound of gunfire filled the air and hurt the ears of anyone close by. A guard was hit in the neck and fell to the ground, wriggling in a pool of blood. One of the women rushed over to help him and looked up with a perplexed expression.

The gunman was soon subdued after a violent but brief struggle. Then suddenly the room dimmed and the lights came on again. When it did, the security team and the gunman were gone. The holographic images of Mark and Martha still remained, looking as shocked as everyone else in the room.

"Pretty convincing, eh?" said Jack with a smile. So far everything had gone perfectly. It was the next part of the demo he was worried about. "Several things were going on here. First, even after I told you Eddie Fisher was fake, you still had difficulty doubting the reality of what you were seeing. Like in the old days of the first moving pictures, even when they paid to get in and see it, the images were so compelling many sitting in the audiences thought the horses and buffaloes and trains were coming at them right through the screen. Secondly, while the fake terrorist was occupying everyone's attention, real terrorists were kidnapping Senator Miles, chairman of a very important committee."

Everyone looked around the room. The senator was gone.

"Of course, by real I mean real people, not real terrorists, and Senator Miles was in on the joke, but it just as well could have been real. The diversion was so convincing that none of you, sitting in the same room just feet away, noticed the Senator's abduction. A real terrorist could have been sitting here all along and no one would have noticed.

"Not only does this technology give us the ability to surprise and confuse the enemy, but provides stunningly real situations that can be programmed for any scenario or contingent. In addition, the technology includes intelligent response based on the action of real people in the room, ideal for a variety of training and planning purposes."

For a moment the room was silent. Then it exploded as everyone strove to get their many questions answered.

"Can these holograms, can they shoot real weapons? Can they be armed?"

"No, a hologram would be incapable of holding a real object like a gun. But we can associate tiny cameras with the hologram's simulated field of vision, and have envisioned the ability to aim powerful high-beam particles at such a target. All this is experimental, of course, but something like that could be developed given time. Remember, in reality, the gunman would be real with a real gun. In our next simulation we'll show you how this same technology can be applied in this situation."

He stepped back and the lights in the room dimmed. The viewing seats, which sat on a movable panel, slid back into the wall, so that the entire room was empty except for pale-pink light emanating from the top and bottom edges of the floor and ceiling. The beams from the rows of lights crossed, merging colors like a prism. The room morphed into a bank scene. Several individuals entered.

"Some of the people you will be seeing are actors," announced Burr, "like the three terrorists. Some are holograms. Even the actors don't know who is real and who is make-believe."

The terrorists were all armed with submachine guns and were holding several people hostage. Another group of actors stood behind a holographic barricade trying to negotiate.

"The basic idea is to flood the room with holographic images and real people," Burr explained. "So the terrorist think they're being overwhelmed with forces that come from nowhere. Instead of risking the lives of ten or twenty men, only a few are actually in harm's way. Through the distraction of numbers, the terrorists can be killed or captured. Other holograms can draw fire away from the real hostages."

Before any of this could come to pass, however, someone strode into the middle of the room with his hands raised as if trying to stop a speeding bus on the highway. Everyone froze, including Jack Burr. This wasn't in the script.

"Sorry, Ladies and Gentlemen. My name is Dr. Edward Spencer, and I have to apologize for the farce being perpetrated here today. There is absolutely no military use or potential use for this technology. Whoever told you otherwise is trying to sell you a bogus bill of goods. While it could be useful for training simulations and communications, our company's products are virtually worthless as a weapon. The idea of using a hologram in a situation like those being demonstrated here today is ludicrous and ill-responsible."

The audience gaped, not sure what was real and what put on. Jack Burr ran into the hologram room, while the actors departed embarrassed and worried about their paychecks.

"What are you doing?" he shouted at the company CEO as the room's lights came on.

"You have no authorization to put on this demonstration," replied Edward. "The company is in mourning. You are violating company policy. Andrew explicitly forbade you to put on any military presentations. Now that he's gone, you went ahead anyway and did just that. That's not only disrespectful, it's insubordinate. Jack, I'm afraid your services are no longer required here at Altered Realities."

"You can't fire me!"

"I don't need to fire you. The company has been dissolved." He turned to the technicians and engineers in the room. "Any of you who want to work in my new company, talk to Rudy Duncan. He's down in the lobby. The rest of you can follow Jack out the front door."

Burr was about to object some more, perhaps get physical, when several security guards came into the room. They were big and carried truncheons. They didn't look like holograms.

153

"You obviously have some internal company dispute," interrupted Senator Miles, addressing the two men standing in the middle of the room arguing. "Perhaps we should continue this demonstration at another time. It certainly has been interesting."

"You won't get away with this," threatened Jack Burr, as Edward turned to address the group of spectators.

"Judge for yourself, ladies and gentlemen. How can a projected interference pattern help you protect the country? It can't carry or shoot a weapon. It can't eavesdrop or spy or do any number of other things needed in a life-or-death situation like a battlefield or hostage taking. All Jack would have shown you is how to get a lot of innocent people killed quickly. There are several other technologies more appropriate to your needs. I'm afraid you've been lied to."

"You'll hear from our lawyers," said one official.

"The State Department will know about this," said another. "You won't be able to run a shoe factory by the time we're done with you."

"Hear that, Ed. Now see what you've done," taunted Burr.

"I know what you've done," answered Edward cryptically.

"What's that supposed to mean?" Burr replied, staring ominously across the four feet of space separating them.

"You'll find out soon enough," said Edward looking calmly back.

Burr took a step toward the CEO, but the reactions of the security detail around Eddie made him think better of it. Instead, he turned and ran after Senator Miles, who had already left the room along with most of the other VPs. The press stayed behind, snapping pictures and taking notes and clamoring for answers.

"Was this a takeover bid by one of your employees?" asked one of them.

"Does this have anything to do with the recent suspicious death of Dr. Andrew Knowles?" asked another, even more astutely.

"I'm sorry, ladies and gentlemen," said Eddie. "I can't answer your questions now, but in due time you will all be informed."

Jerry Katz, the company PR man, took over at that point with a prepared statement from Spencer about the company's policy, explaining the boldface attempt on the part of one of their executives to not only defy that policy, but to attempt to dupe the government into pouring billions of dollars into a worthless scheme. The company had not only fired the miscreant manager, but was considering legal action, perhaps criminal charges, against him.

Jack Burr, meanwhile, was planting his own barbed seeds.

154

"What was that all about?" the senator asked his old Marine buddy, as Burr caught up to him in the hall. "I thought you said there'd be no trouble from Spencer. That he wasn't exactly behind you, but he wasn't going to interfere, either. What happened?"

"I don't know, but now you see what I have to deal with. The man's totally erratic. He disappears for weeks at a time, then comes in like that, shouting orders and contradicting them five minutes later. He's absolutely out of his mind, I tell you."

"Isn't there something you can do? Can you have him evaluated or something, judged mentally incompetent?"

"The police actually had him in custody for murder and let him go. It's crazy, I tell you."

"Yes, I remember. They brought him in for questioning after the murder of that prostitute."

"You don't know the half of it, but somehow he gets let off with not so much as a citation. He's got something on the judge, I tell you, or its politics, but I have reason to believe he killed those girls, and Andy Knowles, too."

The senator said nothing, but looked hard at his friend.

"I don't know, Jack. Those are pretty harsh words. What makes you say that?"

"Let's just say I know the guy. I've learned a few things about him he probably doesn't want anyone to know, like he was the last person to see all three of those young women alive. All three of them were in his penthouse before they died."

"Didn't the papers say they were killed in their apartments?"

"Yeah, but just before that, they were with him in his."

"Do the police know about this?"

"They have pictures of him outside the last girl's place at the time of her murder. That's why they brought him in for questioning."

"And they let him go?"

Jack nodded his head slowly up and down.

"Jesus," muttered the elected federal official. "We have to do something about this."

Chapter 23

Over the next few weeks, Eddie, Connie, and Rudy worked to fabricate the first generation of roughly a hundred thousand nanobots, molecule by molecule. The thousands of varied applications required to construct the autonomous nanobots by hand were excruciatingly difficult and tedious.

The first step was to build dozens of nano-sized machine tools, like tiny motors, conveyor belts, and assembly lines of silicone and carbon, at a microscopic level. Then to manipulate and use the sub-microscopic machines, they would create simple single-cell, DNA-based robots that would do the work. Over a million would be required. From these the next generation of trillions would be constructed in a self-replicating exponential explosion, to create swarms that could alter the very atoms in space. But first things first.

The original generation of nanobots moved on a DNA track, which they followed like bread-crumbs. It provided the clues or simple commands telling them what to do – start, stop, turn right, turn left, grab, release. It all seemed simple when you thought about it, nothing more than normal robotics brought down to the size of five carbon atoms, but the devil was in the thousands upon thousands of details. If it wasn't for Edward, who seemed to be able to work nonstop, without sleep or food or water, none of it would have been possible, but accomplished it was, one painstaking molecule at a time. Eddie could work at the minutest, most redundant tasks without growing tired or careless or bored. This is precisely why he had been created, for no human could have done what he was about to do.

Rudy, who was immersed in his own tasks and not prone to idle speculation of a personal nature, thought nothing of it, but had the same respect and amazement he always felt when working with Dr. Spencer. The man was a genius with a genius's idiosyncrasies and abilities. It probably came from years of self-trial, like other famous and brilliant people sometimes used to steel themselves against hunger, cold, and lack of sleep, while still quite young. But to Connie, he was a phenomenon, just as fascinating and mysterious as the Sphinx, and just as worthy of study.

Although they worked closely together every day, and lived in the same apartment at night, she knew him no better than she had when they first met. He was still an enigma to her, but one she was beginning to understand. If what she suspected was true, however, then all bets were off. She was in a new world where anything was possible, which meant the jury was still out on Edward Spencer.

Edward had not spoken of his breakdown since that day he appeared behind her as if from nowhere, back from the dead. From what little he had told her, she assumed he was using all of his time to perfect his invention, but lately there had been little evidence of it and less talk. No longer working closely as they had been, Eddie was often away during the day. Working alone all night, he'd leave instructions for them when they came to the lab in the morning, though he would pop in and out throughout the day to check on things. Sometimes he was so omnipresent he seemed to be in two places at once.

Connie didn't mourn like other people. She had never had a normal father-daughter relationship with Andrew, who was hardly home when he was married to her mother and anathema to them after her parents' divorce. But she missed him and regretted the unhappy relationship they'd had during the last few days of his life.

She couldn't dispel the horrible image of him hanging there and the thought that she might have been responsible. Her logical mind told her that her father would never have killed himself. He was too committed to life and the future, and to her. Despite everything, he had loved her, and that realization hurt most of all. What was it he was going to tell her?

The hologram of her father talking also came back to her. At first seeing it, she had thought it was some disk he was reviewing for an upcoming symposium on the future of artificial intelligence. But the more she replayed it in her mind, the more she began to realize it was not for a presentation about the future, but about the present, something meant for her. She tried to recall what he was saying, as if it was somehow important to her current situation.

He was talking like always, about creating human-level intelligence in the machine, but something was different. It didn't sound like he was talking about what could be done, but what had already been done.

He was talking about layered neural-networks, each specializing and communicating with the others through thousands of synaptic connections; quantum, cellular, and silicon machines working in tandem. The same things Edward often talked about, although on an entirely differently level.

Had Edward seen this holo-disk? What else did it say? Something about embodying this intelligence, not in a robot, but in a computer-generated image like a hologram. A Robot was limited by its machine body, no matter how ingeniously constructed, but a hologram would have none of these limitations and none of the dangers. Is this what he was going to tell her?

Was her father working on this before he died, the next generation Altered Realities product, where the computer-generated holos would actually be intelligent? Is that what Eddie was doing, carrying on this work? Or had this work already been done and was being hidden for some reason? And why the need for nano-technology? The danger of probing these thoughts was ever present, as the holographic image of her father talking leaked into the one of him hanging in his bedroom.

She shuddered and shook her head, trying to collect and focus her thoughts, which ricocheted wildly off each other.

Or is Eddie...?

The verbal thought trailed off into an explosion of others. She was having trouble getting her head around the whole thing.

What had her father wanted to tell her that was so important he couldn't say it over the phone? She had the impression it was something about Eddie, something to make her change her mind about staying and working with him. Was it something about his past? The murders? Or did it have nothing to do with that? There was so much she needed to know and not a shred of a clue to provide an answer.

She programmed the DNA-track using her base brain, while the train of thoughts bombarding her competed for attention. Peering through her radio-telescope, she lined up the tiny molecular components for the nano-motors and conveyor belts, the raw chemicals and ingredients that would form the microscopic assembly line.

She should have been concentrating more on the complex and critical job. She had programmed the series incorrectly, leaving stop and turn commands where she should have left turn and grab rules. The whole sequence would have to be flushed and laid down again. She swore and took her eyes from the viewer.

"Everything all right?" asked Edward, who had a disturbing habit of coming out of nowhere and startling her.

"No," she answered, a bit flustered.

"You should have taken Rudy's offer to spend the day at their camp. You really shouldn't be working so soon after the funeral. They just buried your father a few days ago."

"No, that's not it. Work is good for me. I've mourned my father's death. We were never really that close."

"That's sad," said Edward.

"It's funny you say that."

"Why?"

"Wasn't he like a father to you?"

"Yes, more than my own father who I hardly knew. I was quite young when my parents died."

"In a car accident, right?"

"Right. Andrew must have told you."

"I guess so. I don't remember who told me. Anyway, you should talk work. You haven't stopped working since you came out of your little meditation. You hardly seem to eat or sleep. You certainly don't seem to be mourning him."

"We each mourn in our own way. I miss him."

"So do I. You know what he was working on?"

"What do you mean, recently? I wasn't aware he was working on anything special. He was helping me work on a tactile feedback system for the holograms, looking at possible directions for the next generation product, but he had backed off from most of his hard research, at least as far as I know."

"What about artificial intelligence?"

"Oh, that. He was always dabbling in that. It was his hobby, but most of that research is done."

"You have quite an array of neural-networks from his secret lab, not to mention the arrays of quantum computers, probably more computer power than anywhere on earth. You certainly aren't using it for our project. What's it all for?"

"Some of it control the holographic systems for our company's products."

"Were you working with him on something? Were you guys designing a super-brain?"

Edward was silent for a moment, pondering her questions, which for some reason he found difficult to answer.

"Yes, I suppose you could call it that," he said carefully. "He was working on developing human-level intelligence. The computers in his lab are the results. Most of that work, which he kept to himself, was in the last stages of development. Like I said, I believe he was finished with it. I'm moving his equipment to our lab."

"That's funny. You two were so close."

"That may be, but there were many things he didn't tell me. Like about you, for instance."

"He didn't tell me much about you either. I don't think he wanted us to get to know each other. He certainly didn't want me living here. I wonder why."

"He was just trying to protect you. He probably didn't think I'd be good for you, and he was right."

"Oh, and why is that?"

"Because I'm too preoccupied with my work, too limited in my feelings and emotions to deal effectively with another person in a sustained relationship. Your dad was a three time loser. He could recognize another one when he saw him."

"I don't know. I think he was wrong about you."

"I'm not an easy person to get to know. I've got these murders hanging over my head. Now is the worst time to get involved."

"You said you were going to do something about that. Have you found out anything?"

"Maybe, but I still don't know for sure. Proving it one way or the other is more difficult than I expected."

"Human beings are not as cut and dried as computers. Maybe you should tell someone what you suspect, in case somebody tries to kill you."

"That would be difficult," he said, but wouldn't elaborate when she asked him why.

Instead she asked, "So what are we going to do with all these nanobots?"

"We're making nano-spiders, with carbon-tube bodies and silicon legs, each with grippers. Not only does this make them fast moving, but able to grasp each other to form larger objects. It's the next logical step from virtual reality to altered reality, constructed on the fly right before your eyes. With these multi-directional, self-directed, intelligent clusters of nanobots, we will be able to change the space around you. Rather than holographic machine-generated projections, we'll be able to create and duplicate any animal, person, plant, or thing we want, from the molecules up."

"Yeah, in a hundred years, maybe," she retorted, finally understanding the magnitude of what he was talking about.

"We've already come a long way in just a few weeks. Remember, the bots do most of the work once you get them started. Soon we'll have a workforce of 1,100,000 primitive bots constructing the next generation of six trillion spider-bots, all invisible to the naked eye. These will have ten times the capabilities of the first generation machines. Their brains will be built-in, part of their structure. After the million bot workers, the growth of the next generation will be self-replicating and become exponential."

The more she heard, the more impossible it sounded, but somehow she knew he could do it. When he was here with her, he seemed more real, more compelling than anyone she had ever known. When he was gone, as he was a few minutes after describing his vision, it was as if he weren't real at all, but just an illusion. That thought clung to her as she tried to work on alone on another DNA-track. She soon gave up in frustration and went to bed.

A few hours later – it was only eight pm – the penthouse intercom unit buzzed. Connie woke-up disoriented, forgetting where she was. The buzzer rang again. She answered.

It was the doorman.

"Hello, Miss Knowles. There's someone here to see you."

"Who, me?" she answered, wondering who could be visiting her. The only friends she had in the area were the ones she had told her father she was staying with, and they were miffed she had neither called nor visited after repeated attempts to contact her. She had no other acquaintances in LA, and Rudy had already left with his family to the rented beach house.

"OK, I'll be right down," she added, shutting the apartment door behind her.

She tried to imagine who it might be and how they knew her address as she descended to the lobby.

"Connie!" yelled her ex-roommate and friend from college.

"Susie," replied Connie in surprise. "What are you doing here? How'd you know where I was?"

"I got your Facebook message asking me to come. You gave me the address."

"I haven't sent any messages. I haven't used Facebook in weeks."

"Well someone did. They used your Page, had your picture on it and everything. It said you were having men trouble and needed a roommate."

"That's strange."

"I tried to reply but you never answered. I was worried you might be in trouble." She looked around the spacious lobby, "Like you may have been kidnapped or something."

"That's ridiculous," replied Connie.

Her friend looked at her with a perplexed expression. Seeing her disappointment, Connie tried to sooth her feelings.

"It's good to see you, Susie. Why don't you come up and we'll get this all sorted out. I can't imagine who could have sent that message, unless it was my dad."

"Oh, my, Connie. I just heard about your father. I'm so sorry."

"It's all right. Don't worry. Come on up and I'll tell you all about it."

Chapter 24

Lieutenant Juan Mendoza didn't like unsolved homicides. He liked outside interference even less, yet someone was putting pressure on the department to solve the murders of the three women. The apparent suicides of Harry Fry, a private detective, and Dr. Andrew Knowles, a distinguished scientist and co-founder of ARC, both under suspicious circumstances, only added to the strain. Someone in the FBI had recently wanted to know why the prime suspect had been questioned and released. They had been told to talk to the DA. Juan wondered who was pulling the strings, and why suddenly there was all this pressure to find the killer. What did they think he was trying to do, crack a piñata?

Of course, Edward Spencer was the number one suspect. All three of the murdered women were last seen in his building, two in his penthouse. The dead detective was the very one following him. The dead scientist was his business partner. A little too many coincidences to be a coincidence, as Yogi Berra might have said.

The Feds wanted the DA to move. The DA wanted the department to find more evidence. His boss wanted to ask the FBI for help. Mendoza had hit a stonewall as far as evidence was concerned, but he would give his left gonad before he'd ask the painte FBI for help.

He was having Spencer's place watched day and night, although the guy never seemed to come or go. Yet he was seen at other locations. Did he have some underground escape route like the Batman? He was about as elusive. If he was the killer, it was going to be hard proving it unless they caught him in the act.

The girl, Connie Knowles, the dead scientist's daughter, had, true to her word, not left Spencer's side. She seemed determined to be his alibi. He hoped she didn't end up dead like the others. Maybe she had the good sense not to leave the guy. Perhaps that was the secret. Or maybe the two of them had conspired to kill the old man to gain control of the company, although that theory only ran so far. Spencer already controlled the company. Perhaps there was more to it than that. All he knew was that the daughter was the result of a broken home, had argued with her father, and was staying against his will with young

Dr. Spencer. There was more than enough here for a spicy soap opera if not a murder indictment.

He had been wondering about the doorman, who always seemed to be on duty, and the limo driver, who would happily rot in jail for his passenger. His mind wandered to Spencer's holo-secretary, who disappeared before his eyes. He wondered if all of them might be holograms, but had noticed others in their place, so perhaps things were normal, after all, just his imagination on overdrive. Be that as it may, it wasn't Spencer's doorman or chauffeur who was under suspicion of murder.

If he could only find some connection between Fry and Spencer, or Fry and Knowles, or anyone for that matter. Had one of them hired the detective to spy on the other? Or was someone else involved? Maybe he should let the FBI help. At least they could provide some computer expertise. That's what he needed to connect all the dots, too many – like stars – to count. He had to focus on the here and now, observation, hard fact. He couldn't waste time speculating. He had to dig and watch.

Things were getting interesting. Another young woman had just shown up recently at the penthouse, perhaps a friend of the Knowles woman. It seems Dr. Edward Spencer was entertaining. Mendoza daydreamed idly about the scientist as a young Hugh Hefner, with a harem of young women kneeling around him in lingerie. He snapped himself out of it and made a note to cuddle his lady that evening.

"No, absolutely not. She can't stay here," objected Edward when Connie told him her friend from college was staying.

"Why not?" she asked, surprised and offended at his reaction. "I've got plenty of space in my suite. She has no place else to go. It will be rude to put her out in the middle of the night."

"It's only ten pm. I'll have my driver take her to the Belamar. It's not far."

Connie almost stamped her foot like a little girl.

"If she can't stay here, neither am I," she told him.

"I can stay at a hotel, really," interjected her friend, who was embarrassed and confused, ready to leave after finding out someone had been playing a trick on them.

"No! Edward, you're being unreasonable. This is what happens when a person works with machines all the time and not people. If

164

you want to be inhuman about it, there's nothing I can do. Perhaps it's better I leave. You and Rudy don't need me."

"Wait a minute, Connie. You can't leave, not now. We have work to do."

"That's all you care about. If you don't care about me enough to let a friend stay here for a couple of nights, I don't care about your stupid project. What's it to me? You don't even have a company anymore. You live like a recluse, worse, yet you never seem to age or get tired or sick. What are you anyway, some kind of freak?"

He didn't answer.

"You're trying to confuse the issue," he replied finally. "You're making too much of this. I merely stated that your friend will be much more comfortable in a hotel. You can make arrangements to meet in the evenings and weekends, but we need you. You have to stay focused. There can be no distractions. You know how important this is."

"Susie is not a distraction and I don't have the faintest idea how important it is. It's obviously not important enough for you to do one little favor for me. I want my friend here with me. She can watch movies or play holo-games while we work. There's absolutely no reason she can't stay here."

"It's not possible. Not with what's going on."

"What, the murders?"

"Yes, I don't want any women here after what's happened." He turned to Connie's friend and said, "Three woman have been murdered, two of them after visiting this apartment. I don't want anyone else around. It's not safe."

"What about me?" asked Connie. "Aren't you afraid someone's going to kill me?"

"You I can watch. Either Rudy or I are with you all the time. I can't be responsible for anyone else."

Both girls thought they were safer there together in the penthouse, but Edward was adamant. They soon left for a hotel, refusing the limo and taking a cab. Connie wasn't sure if she would return to work. She was thoroughly disappointed in Edward, although not surprised given her growing suspicions about him. He was hiding something, she was sure.

* * * * *

165

Over the next few days Eddie and Rudy worked alone, coaxing and training their sub-microscopic workers, getting things moving along the DNA-based assembly line. Their nano-motors cranked and pulled the microscopic-sized conveyor belts, as four-armed nanobots made of self-assembled DNA structures fabricated their nanobot children. The children would, in turn, construct further assembly lines, and using the blueprints provided to their quantum brains by Eddie, construct the final generation of trillions upon trillions of twelve-armed spider-bots that could be formed into swarms to create anything imaginable, on command.

The quantum brain was the ingenious part, the piece that allowed for the exponential, yet intelligent self-replication. Every nanobot needed seven things: A means to sense its surroundings – a sensor. A means to move around – locomotion and navigation. A way to communicate with each other and the outside world, and a way to manipulate things around them, including each other. They also needed intelligence, some means to compute and reason about things, as well as some sort of energy source, so it can sustain itself and continue functioning. Like any machine, it needed juice. All of these had to be incorporated into a body the size of five carbon atoms.

The hard part was the energy source, but Eddie had solved this and the computing requirement in one brilliant stroke, using the nuclear-spin of trapped electrons to both compute and provide energy. The slow decay of the radioactive material incorporated into the nanobot would not only provide its brains, but its power. Theoretically, such a cell could reproduce itself and literally live forever.

Eddie needed Connie to help him realize his dream. Without her expertise in chemistry and nano-engineering, with just Rudy and he working alone, things could take a lot longer than planned, maybe more time than he had. More than that, he missed her. His stupid emotions, ingrained in his brain by his creator, were making things difficult.

Eddie thought that he had to concentrate on the project to survive, but he had things backward. He didn't need the project to stay alive, he needed Connie. Without her, there would be nothingness.

Chapter 25

Connie tried to decide what to do, whether to go back to work or stay away for good. Her friend was no help, not understanding the situation or even why she was there. She just tried to make the best of an awkward situation and entertain her seeming confused and depressed friend. They'd had a lot of fun in school. They tried to reproduce those times by going to the beach and LA clubs for excitement, but the sun was too hot for the pale-skinned northeasterners, and the city nightlife frazzled their nerves. They ended up hanging around the hotel pool and restaurant gossiping and dishing men, something they both had a lot of practice at. None of it seemed to matter to Susie, who had a deep pocketbook thanks to two so-so marriages and even better divorces.

Try as she might, something kept pulling Connie's thoughts back to Edward and the project, something tied to what her father had been talking about on that last holo-disk. It wasn't so much the project itself, though that was interesting enough, on the leading-edge of her chosen field. No, it was Eddie himself. She had come to a conclusion about him that was almost other-worldly, but no matter how she tried to rationalize it, it defied all logic. Such a thing just could not be – and yet.

The two girls talked about going home to New York, but with the East Coast in a deep freeze and covered with four-foot snowdrifts, any thought of actually going there was put on ice, along with most of Manhattan.

In the meantime, Connie was getting tired of living in hotels, as well as with her old friend, whose only thought was men, even though she pretended to loathe them. Connie supposed going to bed with them had nothing to do with liking them. In any case, she was getting tired of her roommate's one-track mind, and had forgotten what a bore she had been before she moved in with Bruce, her last boyfriend. Still, she hated the idea of going back to Eddie more than ever, since he had forced this quagmire on her. Why hadn't he called?

"I think I'm going to go to the lab today," Connie announced. "Why don't you check out the beauty salon? I hear they have a great masseuse there. Andre's his name. They say his hands are just as good as his looks. If you're nice, maybe he'll take his shirt off."

"I thought you weren't going back there. That guy sounded like a real slave driver. He sure was creepy."

"What do you mean?"

"The way he stared at you, like he wanted to burn a hole through you with his eyes."

"He *is* kind of intense, but we're working on some incredible stuff. I kind of need to be there."

"OK, I'm sure I'll find something to do and someone to do it with." She laughed, as did Connie, but Connie's laugh was forced and short-lived.

She took a cab to Edward's penthouse. Rudy was working alone in the labs. He was happy to see her, but she left without saying two words after he told her Edward had gone to the headquarters building to deal with some things that had come up.

It wasn't 'business as usual' as far as Connie was concerned. She had to talk to Edward first, before she could do any work.

She kicked herself for not holding the cab, but the always helpful doorman soon had another, and she was headed toward the Sports Center and the ARC building. She realized that Edward still had 2000 employees to take care of, not a few who might be wondering what was happening to their company and their jobs. She wondered how he could take care of all that business and still work almost nonstop on the revolutionary nano-robot project. With her new realizations, however, she was becoming less surprised by it all. Still, she doubted herself and her conclusions, though it would have explained a lot.

At the ARC security desk they were unable to tell her whether Dr. Spencer was there or not. He never bothered signing the log and there was no record of any appointments. He must have come during an earlier shift, and could be anywhere in the building. She asked to have him paged, which resulted in her waiting in the lobby for twenty minutes with no results. She waited ten more deciding whether to go up and search for him herself, or return to the hotel for an excruciating afternoon with Susie. Neither option seemed enticing, so she waited for two more hours outside on a bench, in the small plaza in front the building.

She had scheduled text messages to his phone every fifteen minutes. Just the nuisance alone would have made most people reply, but why would he start answering his texts now. The man was an absolute idiot-savant.

She was in a foul mood by the time she hailed a cab and made her way back across town, in rush hour, to Edward's apartment building. Rudy was gone and Edward was nowhere to be found. The doorman, the same one that was there eight hours earlier, said he hadn't seen him. She wondered if he was lying for Spencer, and decided to go up and see for herself.

She let herself into the penthouse and looked around. It seemed like it hadn't been touched in the four days since she was last there. The dishes from her and Susie's supper that night were still on the table, their wine glasses still in the den in front of the gas fireplace, the same disk still playing on the sound system. She poured herself a glass of wine and settled down to wait.

She was almost certain that what she suspected was true, but it was almost too incredible to believe. Such a thing just couldn't be, could it? From her observations and what her father's hologram was saying, there was only one inescapable conclusion, no matter how improbable it might seem.

How could he have deceived everyone for so long? With her father's help, that's how. He had created him. God, she thought, could this really be happening? There was one easy way to find out. She made a resolution to throw her arms around Eddie's neck without warning, when he finally showed up.

No, the reason he didn't like being touched wasn't because of a childhood phobia. Edward didn't have a childhood. At least not like other little boys and girls. But then again, when she thought about it sanely in the light of day, it all seemed absurd. How could you work next to someone every day for a month, and not know if they're, if they're, what? Human or not? This was just crazy.

Is that what her father wanted to tell her? She voiced Edward's number again, but still no answer.

Where could he be? Why doesn't he call?

It was late, well after midnight, and still Edward had not returned. Becoming concerned about her friend, Susie, when she also failed to answer her phone, Connie decided to go back to the hotel. Anything was better than sitting in Eddie's empty apartment waiting for him and wondering what he was.

She called a cab and returned to the hotel, stopping at the lobby, but there were no messages. Peeking in the restaurant and lounge, she looked for Susie, but both rooms were virtually empty at this time of night. The indoor pool was closed as well. She took the elevator to her room and despite the hour, called her friend's name loudly as she entered the room, flipping on the light for good measure, hoping to wake her. It would serve her right, but the room was empty, both beds still made and undisturbed.

"Where are you?" she asked rhetorically. "Out on a date with some stranger? Just what I need. The least you could do is give me a call and let me know where you are."

But when she thought of the way she ditched Susie that morning and the general way she'd been treating her lately, she supposed she shouldn't be surprised.

Exhausted and spent, she threw herself down on the bed and fell almost instantly to sleep.

She woke up a couple hours later in the pitch dark. Not a sound could be heard, although she supposed something must have awakened her.

"Susie, is that you?" she called.

There was no reply.

Turning to go back to sleep, her arm bumped into something.

She wasn't alone.

Chapter 26

Eddie was looking for a connection between Jack Burr and the dead private eye, Harry Fry. He had checked the phone records of both individuals, including office phones, home phones, and cell phones. He had reviewed the logs of numerous video cameras throughout the city – restaurants, bars, supermarkets, libraries, Laundromats and hotels – but none showed Burr or Fry with each other. Using software ferrets to search and filter, he reviewed every image returned from newspapers, magazines, the web, and police files, but none of them showed them together. Was he wrong? Or had they just been very careful?

They certainly didn't use email. Edward would have smelled that out in no time. He had checked for messages in the Personal Ads and Facebook, and other bulletin board type notices, with no success. He looked for records of any purchases or licenses for two-way radios or walkie-talkies, but none came up. He knew there must have been a connection between Burr and Fry, but remained unable to prove it. Meanwhile, he had heard from one of his friends on the Board that Burr had scheduled an impromptu meeting for this afternoon.

Maintaining his charade, Edward had Hector take him to the ARC building around noon, where he took the elevator to the twenty-fifth floor and made his way to the boardroom. Opening the double doors quietly, he slipped in. Jack Burr was standing at the front of the room haranguing the hastily convened Board members with accusations against their CEO.

"Spencer has led this company to the point of extinction and refuses to help those who have been hurt by his thoughtless acts. He is at this very moment a fugitive from the law."

"I am not!" said Eddie loudly. Everyone's head snapped toward the back of the room. Burr gave a start.

"I see the distinguished Dr. Spencer has deigned to join us. Welcome, Doctor. We were just discussing the fate of the company you are so cruelly trying to dismember."

Eddie said nothing but walked to his chair at the head of the table and sat down.

"Who called this illegal meeting?" he asked once he was seated.

Tom Johnson began to speak, but Burr cut him off.

"We all did. It was a unanimous decision. Your irresponsible actions and the death of Dr. Knowles called for immediate action. I'm sorry, Edward, but this is your own doing. You need help."

"Are you trying to say I'm somehow incompetent to run this company, that I'm not clearly within my rights as founder and major stockholder to direct things? You, gentlemen, are the ones skating on thin ice here, following Dr. Burr over a precipice."

"That's just it, Ed, you're no longer the major stockholder. While you've been preoccupied with personal matters, some of us have been working to save the company you've so carelessly neglected. As of the end of last month, Ben Kennedy, Don Smith, and I own the controlling shares, and we'll fight you in court to prevent you from destroying this company and sabotaging everything Dr. Knowles has built. You certainly don't call the shots around here anymore, even though you've stolen all of our company's assets. We'll see you in court, Dr. Spencer. That is if you're not already incarcerated for the murder of four women."

Edward sat in silence, though he made note of the count. He only knew of three murders. He was at a loss for words. Had there been another? He immediately became concerned about Connie. He no longer carried his cell, and had not heard from her since she had left his apartment four days earlier.

Sitting passively, he listened to Jack Burr's diatribe. Edward could stay on as a high-paid consultant if he wanted, but until these murders were solved, it would be best if he stayed out of the picture, perhaps take a long vacation, that is if he hadn't been told to not leave town. The other members of the board looked back and forth between the two men as if they were playing tennis, although one player, Eddie, refused to return a serve. It looked like he was mildly amused or retarded, it was hard to tell which. Actually, he was in a large room with many doors, searching.

"Look at him sitting there like he's a god," sneered Burr. "What are you doing here? Why aren't you in jail? Someone call the police. We have a murderer in our midst. Call the police!" he yelled again. "Security! Security!"

His screams brought Eddie out of his trance. Connie was safe. It was her friend who had been murdered. How did Burr know, when Eddie had to dig so deep to find out? It hadn't hit the news wires yet.

172

"I know who the murderer is, Jack," he said, "and he's standing right in front of me. Fry was working for you, wasn't he? You hired him to follow me. You killed those girls or had your man do it."

"You're crazy," Burr answered back loudly.

Two security guards ran into the room, but stopped short, staring back and forth at the two executives.

"Arrest that man!" shouted Burr. "He's wanted for murder."

"This man is responsible for the deaths of three women," Eddie said matter-of-factly, standing up. "He was having me followed."

Jack Burr lunged at him, but was restrained by several Board members who stepped in his way. The room was in pandemonium when Detective Mendoza and several officers from the El Segundo police department burst through the doors.

"Dr. Edward Spencer," the Lieutenant said loudly, coming up to him. "You are under arrest for the murder of Miss Susan Giles and three other women. You have the right to remain silent. Everything you say can and will be used against you in a court of law."

Eddie was cuffed and led out of the building, where a crowd of reporters flashed their cameras at him. Put in a police van, he was driven downtown. Then all hell broke loose.

Edward Spencer disappeared.

Connie had been near hysterics since finding her friend lying dead next to her in a pool of blood. She had bolted from the couch when she felt something oozing on her arm, crashing into the lamp-stand. It seemed an eternity before she could find the switch and turn on the lights. What she saw made her scream at the top of her lungs and back against the far wall in terror. They had to break down the door to get in, as she stood frozen to the spot, gripped with fear. Unable to get any information from her, the police had her sedated by a physician and kept in the hospital for observation. Mendoza posted a guard outside her door, just in case.

She hadn't seen or heard anyone in the room, but had woken from a sound sleep to find someone in bed with her. That's about all the detective could get from her at first, but after further investigation, he was able to learn much more. The knife in the dead woman's chest was from Edward Spencer's kitchen, although there were no fingerprints on it. By noon he'd had an APB out on the man with orders to approach with caution, and took him into custody a short time later. Then the impossible had occurred.

"What do you mean, gone?" Mendoza thundered as the driver of the police van reported the prisoner wasn't in the back when they unlocked the door. "You're not asking me to believe the man just vanished?"

"No, sir, but, well, he, er, he wasn't there," stammered the driver.

"I was watching him off and on in the viewer," said the other guard, who was riding shotgun. "One minute he was there, the next, he was gone. The door was locked. There's no way he could have gotten out of there."

"Was he cuffed?" asked Mendoza.

"Yeah, but that's just it. He was sitting in the van with his hands cuffed behind him, but we all had our cuffs. No one remembers actually handcuffing him."

"What is he, Houdini?" grunted the lieutenant. "What the hell's going on around here?"

He doubled the guard on Connie Knowles, who was still in the hospital for observation, and went there himself to question her some more.

"You say Dr. Spencer wouldn't let your friend stay in the apartment, so you got a room at the hotel. Did he book it for you?"

"Yes, he said it was close by."

"Wasn't he worried you both might be in danger because of the recent homicides?"

"Yes. That why he didn't want her to stay."

"Hmm, has the doctor been acting funny lately? Has he said or done anything unusual or troubling?" He didn't mention that Spencer had disappeared on the way to the police station.

"We've all been under a lot of pressure lately doing the work we're engaged in. It's very important and complex. He's also in the process of reforming his company, but I can't really say he was acting unusual. Unusual for Dr. Spencer might be difficult to define."

"What do you mean by that, Miss Knowles?"

"Everything about him is peculiar. He never sleeps, that I can tell, and hardly eats or drinks. Sometimes I think the only reason he does either is for appearances sake, yet he's never tired and doesn't get sick. I've never met anyone like him before. He's amazing. Sometimes he just seems to appear out of nowhere."

Mendoza was beginning to wonder if he had some kind of magician on his hands. Connie wanted to say more, to confide her suspicions to the well-meaning detective, but she knew it would only make her look crazy and keep her shut up there longer. She was deathly afraid and doubted much the police guard would protect her if Edward wanted to kill her.

Her mind was tormented with conflicting thoughts and conclusions. On one hand, she suspected Eddie of being some kind of synthetically intelligent hologram created by her father. She even had the odd notion that he might have killed her father because of it, although she wasn't sure how a light interference pattern could accomplish such a thing. In any case, Eddie seemed to have abilities far beyond that of your typical hologram in the first part of the twenty-first century. Perhaps they had somehow given him the ability to interact with his environment instead of just simulating it. She had as many doubts as certainties, and what was certain before seemed doubtful now, so she held her tongue and planned her escape.

Mendoza left, little more enlightened than he had been when he arrived, but convinced they were dealing with an extremely intelligent, crafty, and dangerous killer. He told his men to be on the alert and ready for anything.

During the night, Connie remained agitated, pacing back and forth in her room like a caged cat, expecting to see Edward appear from nowhere at any minute. Finally, when she could stand it no longer, she attempted to check herself out, and would not return to her room. A doctor was called and she was soon sedated, but she did not rest peacefully, tossing and turning as if pursued by demons.

Where could he have gone? Detective Mendoza had pondered this question for endless hours. How could he have gotten out of the police van? Forensics went over it with a fine-tined comb and didn't find a thing, not one fingerprint, nada. There were no prints on the murder weapons either. What was he, one of those guys who filed off their fingerprints? He'd have to take another, closer look at Eddie's. He made a point to ask the desk clerk to look into it. In the meantime, he and every cop in the city was out looking for the elusive scientist.

"How could he disappear like that?" he wondered again, out loud.

They reviewed the camera from the inside of the van over and over, but it didn't help. The doors were never opened. No one jumped out. He was just there one minute and gone the next. How had he done it?

They had searched Spencer's apartment building top to bottom, taking extensive time in the penthouse, but found nothing. It was as if it was an unoccupied demonstration unit showing how the rich and famous might live, but looked unlived-in itself. The stainless steel kitchen was spotless, every item in the den perfectly positioned, the expensive art and brick-a-brac all in place, the gas-fireplace still going, but for appearances only, as if no one had ever sat in front of it for warmth.

Nobody had seen Spencer or heard from him. Rudy had shown the detective around the new lab on the ninth floor of the apartment building, but the lieutenant only understood half of what he heard and even less of what he saw. It all seemed so arcane and irrelevant to his purpose. The woman, Connie Knowles, had been released from the hospital and was staying with friends.

A SWAT team invaded the company's fifty-two story headquarter building, under the reasonable assumption that was the last place the scientist had been seen. They tore the place apart, but found no evidence that Spencer was there. Jack Burr, who now appeared to be in charge, was a special pain in the neck and wouldn't stop complaining about how incompetent the police were to let a vicious serial killer like Spencer get away, adding that he should be shot on sight like some escaped convict, already tried and sentenced.

In the middle of all the insults and invectives, Burr did offer one piece of interesting information, saying Spencer was probably hiding out in his old mentor's house, suggesting that it probably wasn't even Spencer they had hauled away, but some damn hologram. That gave the detective pause. It would have explained everything, but left an even bigger question. How the hell was he supposed to deal with killers who could come and go in a puff of light and mirrors?

A search of Professor Knowles's house turned up nothing. The tape on the doors had not been touched. The only key was with the district attorney and was still in his desk when he checked. A search found nothing, although he couldn't help feeling that the team, as expert as they were, may have missed something. For one thing, they were geared up for an assault not a thorough and thoughtful investigation. For another, there were too many of them, cops traipsing all over the place. He would have to go back alone, at night, to see for himself.

Chapter 27

Rudy came by the lab on the ninth floor of Eddie's penthouse building. He hadn't heard from Connie since her friend's murder, but knew she would be there looking for Eddie.

"How you doing?" he asked as she looked up expectantly to see who had just entered.

"Lousy," she replied, seeing it was him and looking back down. "I can't believe what happened to Suzy. It's terrible. I'm still in shock."

"I know. It must have been pretty bad. You'll be safe here."

"Have you seen Eddie?" she asked.

"No, they arrested him."

"No one told me, but the lieutenant was asking a lot of questions about him. Do you think he killed Sue?"

"I doubt it. Ed doesn't have a vicious bone in his body. He's a pacifist's pacifist. I mean, look how he insists on not allowing any research into the military use of his inventions."

"That doesn't mean he didn't kill those women."

"No, I just can't believe it."

"Well, I can."

"You're really afraid of the guy, aren't you?"

"I'm not even sure he's human," she replied. Though it wasn't the first time Rudy had heard her say that, he heard it in a whole new way this time. "Do you know what we're working on?"

"Yeah, just like he said, a self-replicating nano-swarm."

"But what for? For what purpose?"

"To go to the next level of virtual reality, to literally change the space around you."

"I wonder," she answered, almost to herself.

"The work's going well," continued Rudy, changing the subject to one he felt more comfortable with. "The second generation bots are almost completed. I've set up the long tables of glass-paneled, nutrient-filled fabrication tanks, where the final generation of twelve-armed spider-bots will be grown."

"How much intelligence will they have?"

"I don't know. That's Eddie's area. All I know is that it will have a nerve center. He's developed some sort of DNA-based distributed intelligence. How much intelligence is anyone's guess."

"I wonder," she said again. "I want to see Eddie. If what I believe is true, there's no way he could have killed those girls."

"I agree, but I doubt they'll let you see him. Whether we believe it or not, they think he's the killer. The cops are keeping pretty tight-lipped about it. Maybe we can make an appointment with Eddie's lawyers. I'll set something up for tomorrow. In the meantime, there's nothing we can do for him right now. Let's see if we can get a little work done on the nanobots. They need some tender-loving care."

Rudy convinced Connie to return to work, although she didn't see much reason to continue without Edward. It seemed such a hopeless task, even though things had been set in motion and presumably, with a little luck, could move forward toward completion almost on their own. But without Eddie to provide the final adjustments, it would just be a dumb, inanimate pile of tiny slugs.

Toward the end of the day, they popped their heads up and had the auto-kitchen cook a stir-fried dinner. Rudy called Eddie's lawyer afterward.

"What?" said Rudy after introducing himself and listening for a moment. "Yes, that is strange, but there must be a reasonable explanation. Yes, I'll call you if I see him. Bye."

He looked at Connie with an odd expression.

"Edward escaped. It's all over the news."

Connie turned white. "What? When? How?"

"I don't know. The police aren't saying much. They're pretty embarrassed about it, but I don't think they really know how or when it happened. One of the media informants said he just disappeared. Are you all right? You look a little pale."

"I know how he did it," she said.

"How?"

"He's not human, that's how. My dad made some kind of holo-robot."

"What? That's crazy. I know Ed's a little eccentric. He has a few phobias that make it hard for him to interact with people, but he's as human as you and me. A holo-robot? How could that be?"

"I don't know, but a holo-disk was playing when I was looking for Dad at the house. At first I thought it was some disk he was playing of one of his talks, but then I realized it wasn't about the future, it was about the present. I didn't know it at the time, but it was left there purposely for me. Dad wanted to tell me something the night before he died, but he couldn't say it over the phone. We had made arrangements to meet the next morning. I went there looking for him when he didn't show up and found the disk playing."

She stopped for a moment, remembering what else she had found, and froze momentarily as if something had sprayed ice in her insides. She shook the thoughts aside. Someone else had to know the truth beside her.

"Dad must have sensed that he might not have much time, and created the tape at the last moment. He was talking about AI as usual. At first, when I heard the disk, I thought he was discussing things he wanted to do, areas for future research, although it sounded pretty futuristic even at that. But later, while I was playing that terrible night over in my mind, I realized it wasn't the future he was talking about. He was talking about what he had already done. He was talking about an intelligent entity, a self-conscience machine that could pass any kind of test you could imagine."

"What do you mean, test?"

"He mentioned Turing tests. Isn't that where you test a machine to see if it's human?"

"Something like that, yes."

"He explained the types of computers he used and how he connected them, he said, layered them. He also described how he trained it and gave it memories and sensations. He said by the time he was done, his machine had a soul. That it would know good from evil. It would be self-conscious and think of itself as human."

"Holy crap," swore Rudy. "We've got to get that holo-disk."

"It was at my dad's house. I shut it off and put it back in the cabinet. I'm not sure if the police found it or not. I didn't mention it. It might still be there."

"Well, that would certainly explain Ed's jail break. He's a holograph, but it's just too preposterous to believe. Why would your father keep something like that a secret? I mean, this could revolutionize computers and robotics. Just think of it. A computer generated hologram with a brain."

"Oh, I have, and I'm not so sure I like it. This thing has a mind of its own, and maybe Dad was wrong. Maybe it doesn't have a soul. Maybe it's evil. All these brains and no concept of love or empathy with another human being would be a bad thing. Dad wanted to tell me something. I don't think he wanted to brag. I think he wanted to warn me, about Eddie."

179

"Well, I can understand that. If what you say is true, he wouldn't have wanted you to get involved, you know, with a machine, not that he's a killer or anything. Anyway, how could a hologram kill people with real knives?"

"I don't know. Who knows what else Dad created. Perhaps he somehow equipped the hologram with, I don't know, some kind of magnets or gripping device."

"They were working on capabilities to allow the hologram to simulate real tactile sensations, but to pick up a knife and stab someone. I don't think you have much to worry about with Eddie. As soon as the police learn this, they'll start looking for another suspect, and I know who that would be."

"As soon as they learn about this," mused Connie, "I'm afraid four murdered girls will be yesterday's news."

"You're right. It will cause a sensation if your theory is correct. We've got to find out. We've got to find Eddie, no matter what the hell he is."

While Rudy was non-gratis at ARC, Connie, as Knowles daughter, was allowed the run of the place, treated by security and staff alike as royalty. For that reason, they decided she should go to the headquarter building to look for Eddie, while Duncan went to her father's house to see if he was there, and to look for the holo-disk.

Jack Burr surveyed all that his ambition had bought him. He was at the helm of a prestigious high-tech company, with a much sought after product in a niche market. It had been worth all the things he'd had to do to get it, and he'd do more to keep it, though it didn't look like that would be necessary. Still, the news that Spencer had somehow escaped custody was a bit disconcerting.

The corporate lawyers were working in the courts of justice, seeking damages for equipment stolen from the company by the old founder, Dr. Spencer, after he was no longer CEO. Criminal proceedings might follow, but they would have to take a back seat to his murder trial. That is if they could ever find the guy. He suspected Eddie of Fry's murder as well.

Even without the millions of dollars worth of computer equipment Spencer had taken, the remains of his company limped on. It wasn't so much lack of computer power that hampered Burr. They still had plenty of that. More than enough to run the holo-based virtual reality games and remote conferencing, which were their bread and butter.

What was lacking were engineers. Many of the top ones sought employment elsewhere rather than face budget cuts and working on Burr's pet military projects. Much of research and development's budget now went to sales and marketing, which were beefed up, along with national campaigns in all the media. Burr had big plans. Still, he had much to worry about – like Eddie.

Spencer's disappearance was no mystery to him. Ed did it just like he would have, by bribing people. He probably had the whole police force paid off. Spencer was no fool. He had seen the handwriting on the wall. He'd probably been paying them off for years, from the clerks to the top brass. Certainly that bumbling lieutenant, Mendoza, was on the take. Spencer obviously had a network of people working for him. And why not, the guy was worth billions. The only question was where is the man hiding?

Burr had an idea. For that matter, he had a lot of ideas. And he wasn't afraid to put them into action like a lot of other people were.

Two could play at the bribe game. It wouldn't take much to persuade a few trigger-happy cops to shoot on sight. Why not? The man had killed four women, maybe more, perhaps a couple of cops, as well. He was a menace and had to be destroyed, the sooner the better. Only then would Jack sleep well at night.

He was about to make a call when security buzzed him.

"Who?" he exclaimed when they announced the visitor's name. "Send her right up."

His breath became rapid with the possibilities this unexpected visit opened up for him. His mind raced as he went over each potential move and countermove. Like the opening in a game of chess, the plan began to take shape in his feverish brain.

"What's the big idea of bringing me here?" Connie began as she was brought to his office. "I didn't ask to see you. I'm here to get Dad's personal belongings from his office, and I don't need an escort."

"I agree, Miss Knowles. I'm sorry, but under the circumstances no unescorted visitors can be allowed in the building. I'm sure you can understand. It may not be safe."

"I can take care of myself. What's so dangerous about taking a box of someone's personal belongings out of an office?"

"It's not normally, but Ed Spencer has killed four young women and has escaped from jail. He's been stealing assets from the company. He may be hiding here somewhere."

"Don't be ridiculous," countered Connie. "That's ludicrous. This would be the last place he'd go."

"Oh, I don't know. It's a big building and even I don't know the half of it. Some suspect secret rooms and doors."

"Are you going to let me get my father's things?" she demanded.

"Of course," answered Burr.

"With a security guard?"

Burr sat for a moment, as if he was making a difficult decision.

"OK, you have as much right in this building as I do. Your father built it. You can go," he said to the security guard who was standing there stiffly. The man left without a word, glad not to be involved with whatever was going on. "Can I be of any assistance?" Burr offered politely after the guard left. "Can I get you a box?"

"No. I can handle this myself, thank you," replied Connie, nervous to be in the room alone with Burr now that the guard had gone. Without saying another word, before the VP could react, she walked quickly to the door and left the office, relieved to be out of his sight.

She made her way to the twelfth floor lab, which looked much as they had left it when they removed all the equipment to the penthouse building. She searched the rooms, but Eddie wasn't there. Then she had an idea.

Walking briskly down the hallway, she went to her father's office, letting herself in with his pass-key. It was dark inside. Her heart was beating rapidly. She turned on the lights, hoping, but the room was empty.

"Eddie," she cried out softly, wishing he might somehow appear.

Suddenly, without warning, someone grabbed her from behind and put a hand over her mouth.

Chapter 28

Rudy would have much rather gone to the ARC building than to Professor Knowles's spooky old mansion. Even though it was daytime, a bleak, dreary morning, the sun cast little light.

The place still had the yellow police tape over the doors, but Connie had given him a key to a small door behind the garage. The place didn't look like it was being watched, which made it seem even scarier. Rudy did believe in ghosts, even if he couldn't quite believe Eddie was a hologram.

Taking the key, he let himself in. The silence engulfed him as he moved from the kitchen into a plush but long-undusted living area. He took a gulp, exhaled audibly, and called out Eddie's name.

"Ed, Eddie. Dr. Spencer, it's me, Rudy. Edward, are you there?"

He continued yelling as he moved through the house, hoping if there really was a ghost his loud voice would chase it away. No one answered. As he walked, he used a handheld computer that was running a software program of his own creation, to look for the telltale high-frequency pulses that signal a hologram in operation, but there was nothing.

At the downstairs den, which had been searched by the police, he stopped and used another key Connie had given him, to open the front of a large cabinet taking up most of the far wall of the room. From this he thumbed through a good-size collection of holo-disks until he found the one he wanted, as Connie had told him, the only one without a date taped on the label. Then he turned around abruptly thinking someone was behind him, but there was no one there, just his nerves.

It was a large, sprawling house with many rooms on three floors plus an attic and a basement. Rudy went through each one, monitoring his hand-display as he went, the fear of impending doom never leaving him. He concentrated on his breathing like they told him in karate class. He wished he had studied longer, but wasn't sure how that would help him against a ghost – or a hologram.

The attic was the worst. Climbing a long, dark and narrow staircase with a small closed door at the top, brought back all the fears of his childhood. He called Eddie's name in a quivering voice, the computer scan registering nothing. Opening the door, he peeked in. The room was pitch black.

The stale air and stifling heat hit him like a door slamming in his face. He gasped for breath, and ran out of the attic room as if from the mouth of hell itself. Lumbering down the stairs as fast as he could go, he imagined the hosts of the damned after him. Reaching the second floor landing, he finally regained his courage and stopped. Turning suddenly, he found the ghostly onslaught of his imagination had evaporated into thin air. He breathed a sigh of relief and laughed at himself.

Finally convinced there were no holograms or ghosts, Rudy went back to the den at the end of the hall and found a holo-player, slipping in the disk. Immediately, Professor Knowles was standing in front of him. Rudy stood listening in amazement.

"It's only a matter of time before machines will have human-level intelligence...they will surpass us...sooner than you think...the machine will have a soul."

Rudy listened spellbound. On and on it went, explaining everything. Connie was right. As incredible as it seemed, Eddie really was nothing more than a holographic projection. As he listened, however, he realized that Eddie was much more than that.

"His brain is housed in several massively-parallel computers, a virtual neural-net with quantum components, located in a secret place. Soon I will make it all public to the world. For now it must be kept hidden. I hope you will understand."

"Where?" Rudy inquired, when the recording ended. "Where is it?"

He stood in the darkened room. All thoughts of ghosts were gone with the implications of what he'd just learned.

"It must be here," he reasoned, and started looking for a secret room. He found it after several hours, in the basement, behind a large tapestry hanging on the wall. It took a while longer for him to find the entrance through a hidden panel that opened when he depressed a corner, something he had seen watching all those sci-fi and horror movies in his youth. He had to chuckle.

As he entered, the lights automatically went on. He was standing before a bare room. There were empty sockets and blank spaces where cables and computers once stood. Whatever had been there was gone, but where?

It didn't take him long to put two and two together and guess that Eddie must have taken his brain home. That was the reason for all the new and exotic equipment in the ninth floor lab. He left hurriedly and headed back there.

Rudy's big opportunity had arrived.

Connie woke with a dull headache and a funny medicine smell in her nose. She felt dizzy when she tried to stand, and had to remain sitting for some time, until she got her equilibrium back. She felt like she'd been drugged, by the smell of it, with chloroform.

She had no idea where she was, although she assumed she was still in the ARC building. It appeared to be a storeroom of some kind because of the racks of boxes and cartons along the walls. It was small and otherwise nondescript. There were no windows to tell her what floor she might be on or what time of day it was. It appeared to be an auxiliary room of some kind, probably only used by building maintenance.

She went to the double metal doors and tried to open them. They were heavy and locked. She started banging on them and yelling for help, her cries swallowed by the room, which was deep in the interior of the building.

Panic welled up inside her, but she fought it down and assessed her situation. Who had abducted her? She had a pretty good idea – Jack Burr.

No wonder he was so eager to let her walk around without an escort. He wanted her all to himself, but for what? She had to fight down an even stronger urge to panic when she realized that he was probably the killer. Besides giving her the creeps, from what little she knew about him, Burr seemed eager to see both her father and Edward out of the picture. Would he have killed for that? Or just for pleasure? Either way, she was scared, and searched frantically, but fruitlessly, for a way out, even checking the ceiling paneling and the vents, all to no avail.

Pacing the room in an agitated manner, she wrapped her arms across her body as if to hug herself. She wasn't able to sit still, thinking as she walked back and forth, trying to anticipate the next move of her unknown abductor. For a brief moment she wondered if it could be Eddie after all, but Rudy had done much to convince her that no matter how brilliant her father was, he couldn't have created a

185

holograph with that type of physical capability. No, whoever grabbed her from behind was a hundred percent flesh and blood.

They would be back.

Someone was at the door, opening it! She grabbed a chair and raised it in the air.

It was Jack Burr, with two security guards.

As scared as she was, she confronted him.

"What are doing, kidnapping me? Are you crazy?"

"Come, come, Miss Knowles. Calm down. Do you have an id card?"

"Yes, my father's."

"Do you know it's illegal, using his card like that? You're not an employee of this company. You have no right to be here. You are trespassing."

"You kidnapped me, you creep!" she shouted back at him.

"You are guilty of industrial espionage. You were trying to hack our system. I assure you the penalty for such a crime is severe."

"So is the penalty for kidnapping. You've made a big mistake, mister. You're going to pay."

"It is you who is mistaken, I assure you." He dismissed the security detail and shut the door. Connie drew back from him in fear.

"Eddie was right. You are the murderer," she said. "You had those girls murdered."

"That's absurd. I haven't got anything to do with that. Your Eddie is the killer. Someone had him followed to one of the murdered girl's apartment. The police were informed and have the pictures. He's a fugitive from the law. You're lucky he hasn't killed you, too. Where is he? If you know, you'd better tell me. It will be a lot easier if you do. I'm not going to let you, or Eddie, or anyone get in my way. The negotiations with the DOD are going to continue no matter what he says or tries. Edward Spencer is a murderer. I'm going keep you here until he turns himself in, or better yet, gets shot by the police."

At that moment, one of Burr's security men came back and whispered something in his ear.

"Where?" Burr asked. "Here?"

The guard whispered something more.

"Perfect!" Burr exclaimed. He then ran out the room, shutting and locking the door behind him.

* * * * *

Eddie's escape from the police had been simple. He had continued the charade long enough to make handcuffs appear around his wrists and get in the van. He projected his image a few minutes more, then shut off the myriad tiny lasers that had gone with him. His brain still functioned and his holographic body system was still operational, but all spatial coordinates were set to zero, so his image was being projected nowhere.

Eddie pictured himself in a large hotel-like building with doors to many rooms. In one of them was Connie. He began to search for her.

Opening one door he found himself in the old twelfth floor lab at the ARC building. The coordinates were given and Eddie appeared in the room as the associated lasers were activated. Using his vision sensors he searched the place. She was not there, but his auditory sensors picked up a bit of information from a security transmission. 'The woman, Connie Knowles, is in the auxiliary room at the top of the building.' He computed the coordinates.

Connie was pacing back and forth when Eddie abruptly appeared. She was holding the leg of a small table she had broken off to use as a club, and was anticipating using it on Jack Burr when he came in to get her. The sight of Edward appearing from nowhere completely unnerved her, making her drop her makeshift weapon in fright. Edward tried to calm her down.

"Connie, don't be afraid. Let me explain. Your father..."

"It's true!" she blurted out, finally realizing her suspicion was correct. Still, she couldn't believe it. She stared at him in wonder. "Incredible. I knew it that first night. There was something about you. I figured it out from the holo-disk Dad made before he died. It explained everything. He knew I was getting involved with you and wanted me to know the truth. I know you didn't kill those women. You can't, right?"

"That's correct, though I wish I could kill someone right now, but that would be wrong, and of all the things your father instilled in me, it was the knowledge of right and wrong. He gave me free will, but he tempered that with deep understanding of my responsibility to life, his gift to me."

Suddenly, Connie saw Eddie for the first time as he really was, an incredibly beautiful masterpiece, her father's creation. More precious than a painting from the greatest master, more astounding than the music of the greatest composer, the being standing before her was the

187

most glorious thing she'd ever witnessed. Tears sprang to her eyes. She felt an overflowing of emotion for her father and his masterpiece. It overwhelmed her. Perhaps the stress of being kidnapped and fearing for her life had something to do with it. She was overcome with love for Edward, but as a work of art, not a man. She wanted to reach out and touch him, but held her hand and found herself trembling.

"What happened?" he asked, wondering about the way she was looking at him, like he was some sort of priceless heirloom. Not exactly a freak, but something atypical, like from another planet, he supposed. "Are you all right? Why are you looking at me like that?"

"What?"

"Never mind. Why are you locked up here?"

"Burr kidnapped me. I was looking for you and he drugged me with chloroform. He's after you. There's no knowing what he'll do."

"Don't worry. I won't let him harm you."

"What are you doing here?"

"I was concerned about you and found you through a computer in this building. I came to help you."

"What are you going to do?"

"I've already done it."

Just then Jack Burr burst into the room followed by a half-dozen security guards. When he saw Spencer standing there with Knowles's daughter, the blood drained from his face. His eyes grew wide. He gasped and gaped at the two of them as if he'd seen a ghost.

Connie and Edward both stood there, their eyes staring at Burr accusingly.

"What are you doing here?" Burr finally stammered. "How'd you…?"

"Why are you keeping Connie here against her will?" Spencer asked. "Let her out now or …"

"Take him!" yelled Burr to his security detail.

"You men better stand back," demanded Eddie. They all hesitated at the words of the CEO. "The police are on the way to arrest this man for murder."

"He's the murderer!" yelled Burr. "Don't you see? Don't let him fool you. Don't let him get away."

"I'm not going anywhere, Jack. The cops will be here any minute. Then we'll see who gets taken away."

At that moment, a commotion could be heard in the hall. Eddie seemed to stumble and fade. Then he vanished altogether.

Chapter 29

Across town, in a dark corner of the ninth floor lab of Eddie's building, Rudy stood before a giant computer bank crowded with exotic-looking equipment. He recognized it as a combination of parallel, cellular, and quantum computers – Eddie's brain! Now he sat in front of the master console shutting it down, one layer at a time.

Rudy had many reasons for doing this, but most of all hatred for his father. Knowles may have seemed like an upstanding citizen, father, and spouse – although three times divorced – but he had a dark side, one known to few. Connie was the result of his second marriage; Eddie, the result of his first. Rudy was his illegitimate son of yet another relationship, one no one knew about. The professor had been living this double-life ever since his son died, even before his first wife divorced him for neglect. She wasn't the first woman he'd neglected.

After his first wife shut down due to the death of their son, Knowles sought physical companionship on the seamier side of the tracks, thus Rudy's mother. He abandoned them after only a year, soon after his divorce, while courting his soon to be second wife, Connie's mother. The method he used and the things he did to cover his trail were cruelly done. Before she knew it she was out on the street without a dime and little clue of what was happening to her. Rudy had seen firsthand what Knowles did to his mother. He vowed the man would pay.

Finding himself alone on the street after running away from yet another foster home, he somehow survived. He did whatever he had to, and made excellent use of his good looks and attractive personality, which was honed by necessity. Rudy could appear to be whatever you wanted him to be. He had a knack for knowing what made people tick, what they liked, what they were looking for, and Rudy appeared to be just that. He was a chameleon. Women especially fell for his charms. He had a way of getting what he wanted – food, shelter, money, friends, protection – even as a child of eleven. He not only survived, he thrived.

Rudy was also smart and hard working. Every job he applied for he got and rose to the top. Salesman, mechanic, carpenter, technician, he could do it all, eventually winning a hardship scholarship to Caltech in electrical engineering. That's where he got reacquainted with Professor Andrew Knowles – his father.

He didn't know much about the man, a famous scientist and inventor, but enough – from his mother – to hate him. He remembered when his mom, a mean-spirited alcoholic by that time, talked of the death of Knowles's seven year old son. She gloated, saying his father and his whore wife deserved it for what they did to her.

Now that he had tracked the man down, he began to plan his revenge. He wormed his way into Knowles's life, not divulging that he was his abandoned son. Soon he was the professor's favorite student.

Despite the lack of a big academic resume, Rudy was highly intelligent and learned quickly, though he never got to work close enough with the professor to learn much about his private research. He knew enough, however, to know it had something to do with brain scanning and duplicating human intelligence.

He kept his eyes on his father from afar when Knowles left Caltech to pursue his own work full time. Rudy was still living off his wits with one scam or another, despite his academic success and degree, which only gave him a higher class of mark. When Knowles came into the limelight again with his new venture and his bright, young protégé, Rudy, seeing his opportunity, went to LA to be part of the action.

Easily getting a job in the engineering department because of the founder's – his ex-professor's – influence, he got as close as he could to Dr. Edward Spencer, eventually becoming his right-hand man. In the back of his mind, he had always known this guy was too good to be true, and he had been right.

Rudy hated Eddie even more than he did Knowles, but hid his animosity like a sheave in the folds of his heart. He only wished he could have pulled the plug on him while his father was still alive, so he could of thrown it in his face as he strangled him.

The first murder had been done out of jealousy, almost by accident. To be denied Nancy's affection after that freak, Eddie, had succeeded with her, was just too much. He had killed her in her apartment when she began to strenuously object to his advances. He barely remembered grabbing the knife and stabbing her. It happened so fast, a stupid reflexive impulse born from the pain and anger of his life. That's when his plan to discredit and ruin Eddie took shape. After seeing how the first murder shed suspicion on the CEO – the last man to see the victim alive – he decided to raise the stakes. It had worked just as Rudy had planned.

He smiled to himself as the last component of Eddie's brain shut down.

"The time for retribution is at hand," he announced to the empty room triumphantly.

Jack Burr stood with his mouth agape. Had Spencer done it again, like he had in the back of the police van? He thought the police had let him escape and were trying to cover it up with a wild story, but it turned out to be true, he really had disappeared. Was the image he just saw a hologram? That would explain it, but spawn even more perplexing questions. How the hell did he pull it off?

In the confusion, as the guards stood in shock, Connie had run from the room. Burr called his men out of their stupor to follow. As they exited the room, they encountered the El Segundo police, who were charging down the hall with Connie in tow.

"What's going on here?" shouted Mendoza at the head of his team. "We got a call that the murderer was in the building."

"Yes, he was just here!" shouted Burr.

"He tried to kidnap me!" interrupted Connie, pointing at Burr. "He knocked me out with Chloroform."

"That's nonsense, Lieutenant. This woman is trespassing. She's hacked our computers and is stealing our company's trade secrets. She's spying for another government. I want her arrested."

"He tried to kidnap me!" yelled Connie again. "He assaulted me! He murdered those women!"

"I did nothing of the kind. Ed Spencer murdered those women. I have proof. He's somewhere in the building."

"Eddie was just here. He disappeared," Connie informed them.

"This girl is crazy, Lieutenant," replied Burr. "She's seeing things."

Burr's men stood behind him confused, saying nothing.

Connie continued to object, insisting Burr was the killer. He likewise made accusations of his own. Finally, Mendoza held up his hand.

"OK, you're both under arrest. Cuff them and take them to the station for questioning," he ordered his men as he stalked off.

* * * * *

191

As the various neural activity and processes that had been Eddie were shut down, one by one, Eddie lost ever more functions. First his physical sensations and abilities disappeared. He appeared to stumble then break up into separate light patterns, finally to vanish entirely. Then his sense of self, his thoughts and identity, disintegrated into nothingness, until piece by piece, he was gone. But still, there was an inner core that remained, inviolate, protected by a fail-safe mechanism based on the nuclear reactions of the quantums, something the professor had installed to prevent just this type of thing from happening. Just enough of his brain stayed active to keep him from disappearing altogether. He lived on like a comatose victim locked in a cocoon, dead to the universe.

Now a disembodied mind with no being to ground it to the world around him, without a self to organize his thoughts, without senses to tie him to external reality, he drifted in a hazy, contemplative state with no will or motivation. He just was, and it was bliss. He floated in nothingness.

His mind was a maze of shifting patterns and half-images, randomly sliding by like pictures in a fractured carousel. He focused on one of them, fuller than the others, that of a seven year old boy named Eddie, who he had once been. In this way, he fought to find himself again.

Alone in the ninth floor lab of the penthouse the nanobots continued fabricating, self-replicating themselves in the nutrient-rich tanks like bacterium in a Petri dish until the pre-programmed threshold was reached. The tanks glowed with the light of their tiny atomic cores, embedded in each one of them like a diamond in a piece of coal.

Before being shutdown, Edward's brain had been very busy. Besides trying to find Connie, it had constructed the intelligence needed to guide the nanobots. While the end result was extremely complex, each individual molecular-entity was relatively simple, as was the nanobot's view of the universe. They saw the world as other nanobots, with arms – twelve to be exact – to grasp and hold and cling to. Embedded in each bot's genetic code was a tiny brain or nerve-center, which directed its behavior and allowed it to interact with the next, in a variety of ways. And like a colony of ants or living neurons in the brain, they could coordinate their activity and act intelligently, and organize themselves into groups with specialized functions, which could sense patterns and interact with the outside world.

As these trillions of nanobots coalesced and swarmed, they began to take shape.

Chapter 30

It was early Sunday morning. Connie had been released, as had Jack Burr, both with orders to stay away from the other. With nowhere else to go, Connie went to Eddie's Penthouse, hoping somehow he might be there.

She contemplated the events of the previous evening. What had happened? Did Eddie disappear on his own? This would indicate he was still in control and might appear again at any time. Or had something happened to his systems? She still wasn't sure where his hardware was or exactly how it all worked. Unlike Rudy, she did not listen to the whole of her father's holograph recording, which explained everything. Did someone turn Eddie off? Who would do such a thing – Jack Burr? If only Rudy were here. He would help.

She went to the lab and noted the high level of activity in the nutrient vats, all without human intervention. She wondered what it meant. Had things been accelerated somehow?

Rudy came in a short time later.

"Rudy!" she exclaimed when she saw him, running over to hug him. He hugged her back, a little longer and tighter than usual.

"Are you all right?" he asked, finally letting her go. "I heard they took you to the station after Burr tried to abduct you. Did they arrest him?"

"No, damn it. They let the bastard go. I was so worried. I'm so happy you're here. Something happened to Eddie. He vanished suddenly, just disappeared, right before the police came. No one would believe me. That's why they let Burr go. He can be pretty convincing. I was lucky they didn't lock me up."

"Eddie disappeared? Right in front of you?"

"Yes, just like I suspected. He's not real. Did you see Dad's hologram?"

"Yes, it explained everything, but I'm afraid there's more to Eddie than we suspected. He can manipulate real objects, including knives. I'm afraid your dad was trying to tell you that Eddie killed those girls."

"What? No, it can't be. He couldn't."

"I'm afraid so. Your father knew the truth, but didn't want to get the police involved. He wanted to take care of his creation himself, and it turned on him."

"No, what are you telling me?"

"Eddie killed your father. He's dangerous. I had to shut him down."

"No!" yelled Connie. "You didn't destroy him?"

"I'm afraid I did. He was a killer."

"No, you're lying. That's not possible. I know my father. He wouldn't have created anything like that."

"How do you know?" hissed Rudy, all pretense dropped in his burning rage. "You have no idea what evil that man is capable of. He killed my mother!"

"What are you talking about? Rudy, what are you saying?"

"I killed those women, you stupid cow. I did it to discredit Eddie and take his company. It worked. Eddie is gone, never to return. I have destroyed the computers that housed his brain. Burr is on his way out after being discredited and failing on the DOD work. There is no one left but me and you, and you will soon be gone, too."

"You're mad! You'll never get away with this."

"You keep saying that, but here we are. There's nothing to stop me from killing you here and now. I only wish I could have done it in front of our father, but his actions forced my hand."

She took a deep breath and shuddered. Then she started moving backward and away from him. As they passed through the door to the outer room, Rudy pulled a knife from his belt, just like the one her friend, Suzy, had been killed with. They exited the fabrication room.

"I'm not going to hurt you," he said, "not if you cooperate. Don't worry."

Connie said nothing, but stood near the door, by a low table, with a heavy glass vile on it.

He laid the knife on the table and leaned back against the wall, staring at her.

She was trying to think things through, but fear choked her mind. It was obvious that he intended to kill her. What was he waiting for?

"Are you going to make me stand here all night?" she asked suddenly, getting angry.

He looked at her ominously.

"I didn't want to do this, but I have no choice."

He seemed to let his guard down. Was he toying with her, getting some perverse pleasure by taunting her? Connie wasn't into games. Before he could react, she grabbed the vile and flung it at him, hitting him square on the forehead as he came toward her. He went down hard. Dashing for the door, she ran out of the lab just as Rudy was getting to his feet.

Half standing and dazed, Rudy grabbed his head in pain and leaned on the table. Then he swore and staggered after her.

Juan Mendoza was stumped. The incident at the ARC building just added to the confusion. Connie Knowles and Jack Burr had flung accusations and insults back and forth like volleyballs, and both had the most outrageous story concerning the escaped Edward Spencer. Burr insisted repeatedly that Spencer was the killer, touting the pictures that had been produced. The woman insisted the man wasn't even real. What was he to believe after hearing that?

"How do you suppose he disappeared from your police van?" she had insisted as he questioned her at the station, trying to prove her point.

"I don't know," he had responded. "He probably bribed my men. Internal Affairs is investigating. They'll turn up something."

"Not likely," she had replied. "They won't find a thing. Your men are clean. No, I know how he did it, and it's the same reason he couldn't have killed those women."

"And why is that?"

"Because Edward Spencer is not a real person, he's a holograph."

Instead of calling her a crackpot, Mendoza had sat thoughtfully, nodding his head as if in agreement.

He wondered if what she had told him last night was true. At this point, he would believe almost anything about the man.

"Holy Jesus, Mary, and Joseph," he exclaimed, getting out of his chair. "This can't be happening."

He decided to check out Spencer's apartment complex again. This time he had a warrant for the entire building as well as a SWAT team with him.

Eddie floated between consciousness and the void, between dream and reality. He wasn't exactly Eddie so much as a disembodied awareness in a world with no time, no space, no dimensions, and no self. He drifted in the ether, an empty place where all sensation was one, where all feeling was gone. But something gave purpose to his mind as he struggled toward the light.

Memories of a life flashed in fleeting episodes across the blankness that was his mind, familiar faces and voices, summer in his mother's

196

lap, wild-flowers peeking over the long grass. But whose life was it? Who was he? What was he? Where did he come from? Where was he going?

Toward the light!

He floated in limbo, in a state of perfect bliss, fleeting memories and bits of knowledge flooding past him like blurred images from a spiraling top.

His identity came back to him all at once, in a flash of recognition, making him jump, as if from a dream. He was instantly aware that he was floating in a vat of liquid, a closed, metal, coffin-like object with a thick glass top, and he was completely submerged. Panicking for a moment, he began thrashing about, until it all came back to him and he remembered where and what he was. The realization made him laugh, blowing bubbles out of his nose and mouth. Then he lay back with his eyes closed and relished the feeling of weightlessness, in a state of complete sense deprivation. Eddie had all the time in the world. For he was traveling at the speed of light, where time stood still.

Connie stood in front of the elevator, waiting, in a panic, realizing she should have taken the stairs. The doors opened with a ring just as Rudy burst from the lab carrying a knife. She jumped in and banged her thumb on the down-button, but the elevator was already on the way up. Rudy was running down the hallway toward her brandishing the knife, when the elevator finally closed, just in time. She heard him banging on the doors as she ascended.

She was on her way up and there was nothing she could do about it. Why had she taken the elevator instead of the stairs? Fear clogged her brain. It wasn't working right. She waited with bated breath as it rose to the top of the building. When it reached the top landing, the doors opened with a ping.

She cringed in the far corner, and banged on the button to the lobby, but the elevator doors stayed open and it remained in place. When no one appeared and the doors didn't close, she ran out and looked around. She saw no one, but heard Rudy rushing up the stairs calling her name. The sound of his voice froze her blood.

Forcing herself to move, Connie headed for the door across the hall. It led to a dark stairwell and a narrow flight of metal steps to the roof. She clicked the door locked behind her, and ran up the stairs, cowering in the darkness, afraid to make a sound. She didn't dare open

the door to the rooftop, sure it was alarmed. It had warnings on it –
Emergency Exit Only. Maybe, if she was still, he wouldn't find her.

Rudy called her name again from the other side of the door. She
was trapped.

The doorknob jiggled as if someone was trying to turn it. Then
there was a thud and the door flew open.

"I don't have time for this," said Rudy, stepping into the stairwell
and peering up into the darkness. Then slowly, step by step, he began
to ascend the stairs.

With a yell of fear and adrenaline, Connie pushed open the door
to the roof, sounding all the alarms in the building simultaneously.

Slamming the door shut behind her, she spotted a trash barrel.
Grabbing it, she kicked it over and jammed it against the door and a
low concrete retaining wall. Then she looked around.

Several antennas stood on a raised platform in the middle of the
roof, with cables running down to the sides of the building. The space
was cluttered with catwalks and equipment, as if it were being worked
on. Huge structures housing the building's giant air conditioning and
heating ducts, along with various generators, gave off a low hum.
Suddenly, Rudy slammed the door open against the barrel.

Connie jumped and ran up a catwalk that crossed the roof, among
a gaggle of towers and antennas. As she ran, slightly giddy with the
lights and the height, Rudy knocked the obstruction aside and came
bursting onto the roof.

Eddie had been drifting in a sea of blissful solitude when he
suddenly remembered something. It came to him first as the image of a
smiling-faced, blue-eyed boy with a swath of freckles, the face of seven
year old Eddie Knowles. He knew that face. He liked that face. Then
the smile became a frown and soon turned into a silent scream, a
scream for help.

He jerked out of his semi-conscious state, churning the liquid in
his nutrient-rich bath, aware of a great urgency. No longer suspended
in a timeless void, time seemed to be rushing forward at a tremendous
speed. He strained to catch up with it. Becoming agitated, he began
banging on the metal sides of his prison, making more bubbles as he
yelled to get free. Then he remembered.

Although Eddie knew full-well the capabilities of his new nanobot
'body', it was all theoretical. He had a lot of experimenting to do. Like
a baby bird knows it is born to fly, but still hesitates to take that first

step. Slowly, he calmed his mind and concentrated. He felt the spider-bots that formed his arm begin to stretch out in an ever thinner extremity, until his arm and hand were a mere sliver, the size of five carbon atoms. It easily slid through the microscopic crack in the tank's lid and unlatched it from outside. It sprang open with a hiss.

Pulling himself out of the tank, he stood in the darkness, his body glowing with an ephemeral light. He held his hands to his face and examined them carefully. They looked real enough. Then he started feeling his naked body all over. It felt real, too. The sensation of touch wasn't just being simulated.

He moved to the door of the clean room and opened it. As he moved through the darkened lab, he passed a window. The few lights that were on cast his reflection as if from a mirror, and he saw himself as clear as day. He stopped and stared, posing in several positions to gauge the effect. He had done it. He had re-created himself as a real, living human form, consisting of carbon-based nanobots instead of skin and bone.

He knew, but only vaguely, that his brain, housed in a corner of the lab, had been shut down. It struck him as odd that those machines once housed his mind, but no more, which was a good thing. They were now redundant. He would have had to destroy it anyway.

What had been Eddie's intelligence was now distributed among the trillions of nano-bots that made up his body, from his head to his toes, which he could control through a central nervous complex of axionic cells interspersed throughout the swam, which gave him direction and identity. "I am," was his first thought. Many more were to follow. He had learned a lot about himself in the short span of his existence.

He could interact completely with his surroundings to lift and hold real objects. He also found that he could strike with tremendous power because of the density of his fist – when he made one – and the whip-like speed of the strike. This he found by accident when he put his fist through the cinder-block wall of the building.

Connie was already across the cat-walk when Rudy burst through the door. She went down a short flight of steps to the lower deck where the structures housing the AC unit and generators were located, and ducked out of sight in the shadows. The hum of the giant engines made it impossible for her to hear anything else.

Keeping low, she began to work her way back toward the door, peering up constantly for any sign of her pursuer. She was almost there, hunkered down between a low concrete wall and the base of the antenna platform, when he appeared out of nowhere right in front of her. He held the knife blade down in his right hand, and took a step toward her.

"I wouldn't do that if I were you," said Eddie, having crawled over the restraining wall of the rooftop unobserved.

"Eddie!" said Connie in surprise.

"Where did you come from?" remarked Rudy. "Who turned you back on? Well it doesn't matter. Your friend here is going to die and there's nothing a stupid holograph like you can do about it."

Rudy moved on Connie with the knife raised, but before he could get to her, Eddie reached out and grabbed his arm. Connie gasped in amazement. This wasn't how a light-interference pattern was supposed to behave.

Yanking his arm free, Rudy slashed the knife at Connie, but Eddie blocked it and swung his right hand up in a whipping motion. His palm landed on the side of Rudy's head, knocking him down on one knee. But still he gripped the knife, which he slashed back and forth in front of him as he gained his feet.

He stabbed at Eddie, catching him on the thigh, but the wound didn't bleed and immediately began to heal. Rudy didn't stop to wonder, but darted toward Connie, grabbing her with the knife at her throat, a gleam of hateful triumph in his eyes.

"Watch her die," he leered.

Eddie flew through the air and was on Rudy in an instant. Grabbing him by the collar with both hands, he drove him backward to the edge of the rooftop and over the low restraining wall, to fall ten stories to the ground below, throwing himself off with him.

Chapter 31

Mendoza and his men, who had just started their search of Eddie's apartment building, were on the scene in minutes. Connie was found and brought down by the SWAT team. Rudy Duncan's body was recovered in the alley next to the building a short time later. Connie Knowles's story was so bazaar that few believed it. They thought she was in shock. Some, like Mendoza, suspected she might have actually pushed Duncan off the rooftop, possibly in self-defense. She insisted he was trying to kill her. She also told them that Ed Spencer had saved her life, but had disappeared over the edge of the roof. No body had been found.

Even Connie didn't know what to believe. Everything she suspected about Eddie had been thrown out the window by what she saw on the rooftop. No hologram could have done what he did. But then, what was it? Whatever she saw, it certainly wasn't human, the way it seemed to move and disappear over the edge of the building.

As intriguing as the story was, and as relentlessly pursued by the press, not much was revealed. After her initial interrogation, Connie Knowles and the police were keeping discretely quiet. She was uncertain exactly what had happened. It had all occurred so fast. So she kept her thoughts to herself as the authorities continued to investigate.

The super-quantum computers that had been hidden in the secret room in Knowles' mansion and moved to Eddie's ninth floor lab, were now dismantled and no longer functional. Eddie's incredible synthetic brain was gone. Nothing remained except Eddie himself. Yet, no one knew where he was.

Connie had been asked to take a leading role in what had once been ARC. She was returning to the penthouse where she still lived, after a shareholder's meeting to discuss the future of the company. She was surprised to find Lieutenant Mendoza waiting for her.

"Hello, Miss Knowles," he said. "Can I talk to you for a few minutes?"

"Certainly, Lieutenant. It's nice to see you. Thank you again for coming to my aid when you did. Will you please come in?"

"It was nothing, ma'am," he replied, entering the penthouse, "just part of the job. I wanted to tell you, Mr. Duncan's death is being considered accidental, but we still need to talk to Dr. Spencer to resolve things. I know the whole affair must have been very distressing for you, and we have no reason to disbelieve your story, but you may have seen things in a distorted way because of the shock. The DA has reconstructed events based on the evidence and your testimony, and thinks the most likely scenario is that Rudy Duncan accidentally fell while struggling with you. Sometimes people, when they hold a grudge like that, it makes them crazy. Perhaps this is what happened to your friend, Mr. Duncan.

"All the murder scenes have been re-examined using Duncan's DNA, and there have been several positive findings. His DNA was discovered at three of the locations, including your father's bedroom. They're trying to determine if it was also at the scene of Fry's murder, the private detective. I think there is pretty solid evidence that Duncan murdered those four women. We found the first victim's cell phone in his possession, as well. It's the DA's opinion that no further investigation into his death is necessary."

Then he dropped the bombshell he had come to deliver.

"Miss Knowles, did you know you were related to the deceased?"

"What? Me and Rudy related?"

"Yes, your DNAs match. He was Professor Knowles's son. You are half brother and sister. His mother was a woman your father took up with during the end of his first marriage."

"Oh, my God," she said, sitting down on a nearby chair. "Me and Rudy? Brother and sister? I can't believe it. He knew. He said he was sorry he couldn't have killed me in front of our father."

"The whole thing must have been directed at your father for what Rudy perceived Knowles did to his mother."

"This is unbelievable."

"You can see why we need to talk to Spencer, let him know he's off the hook. But he'll have to come down to the station to resolve things. Could you let him know to call me or come in, if you see him."

"I wish I could. I don't know where he is."

"I know, but if you see him."

"Yes, Lieutenant, certainly."

After Mendoza left, Connie felt a little better. Not only did they believe her story, they had apparently solved the murders. The realization that Rudy was her half brother and had killed her friend, Susie, was difficult to deal with, this on top of her questions about Eddie.

What she saw on the rooftop was no hologram. Whatever it was, it had special abilities. Rudy was a big guy. Eddie had flung him around like he was paper-mâché.

She decided to look at the nano-fabrication tanks in the ninth floor lab and was shocked by what she found. They were all destroyed, together with the computers. What had happened to the nanobots, all six-trillion of them?

She used an electron microscope to search for them in the remains of the empty tanks. The reaction of the chemical she used with the radioactive elements embedded in the bots showed as a golden phosphorescent stain. There wasn't as much as a microscopic trace of the stuff. It had been empty when it was destroyed. What was going on?

"We weren't making nano-virtual reality," she realized out loud. "We were making Eddie! Was that what I saw on the roof? God! Can that be? Is that what saved my life?"

A few hours later, Connie sat alone in Edward's penthouse sipping a glass of wine as she watched an old movie on TV, thinking of Eddie. Where could he be? Why had he just disappeared like that? Was he ashamed to face the world? Had he been somehow hurt, after all? Could he even be hurt?

Even though she knew what he was, and about as much as anybody did about him, he was still a complete mystery to her. Was he even remotely as human as the hologram seemed, or something else entirely? Her thoughts were interrupted by a knock on the door.

She opened it.

"Eddie!" she screamed.

She jumped and yelled involuntarily on seeing him.

"Eddie, what are you doing here?"

"I came to see you."

"You disappeared so suddenly. No one believed me."

"Perhaps that is for the best."

"You killed Rudy. You saved me."

"I couldn't let him harm you."

"How did you do it? You're not real…"

She stopped and scrutinized his face closely, but he looked no different than usual, and totally human.

"You're the only one who knows about me. The others are all gone."

"Don't worry," Connie said with some apprehension. She still didn't know what he was and that made her fearful.

"No one can know about me. No one must ever know."

Saying nothing, she contemplated his words. Weighing them in her mind, she grew concerned.

"Everyone will look at me like you're looking at me now, not like a person, but like some hideous monster. They would want to destroy me just as they destroyed Frankenstein, but they will never know, because no one will be alive to tell them."

"Eddie, what are you saying? You're being illogical. Think! Remember what Andrew taught you."

"He taught me to be human, and humans are eminently illogical."

"He taught you right from wrong."

"That was the old Eddie. He's dead and gone. I am the new Eddie, a self-replicating being and will live forever. No one created me but me."

As he started moving toward her, the microscopic carbon tubes that made up his body began to swarm, starting with his legs, making him look like a hoard of bees with Eddie's head and shoulders. Connie screamed, and darted out of the apartment.

Seeing her run, he sped after her.

Spotting a fire-extinguisher on the wall next to the elevator, she ran toward it and opened the case, pulling out the red canister in one swift motion. Tipping it upside down, she pressed the lever, spraying white foam all over Eddie, who had swarmed up behind her.

Eddie wasn't expecting it and was momentarily stunned, blinded by the heavy foam. She sprang by him and ran to the door of the stairwell, running down, heading for the street. Eddie went after her like a hoard of angry African stinging bees.

He caught her on the ninth floor, forcing her from the stairwell into the empty hallway. The nanobots tore at her clothing like a thousand hungry moths. She waved her hands about her trying to get them off.

Ripping herself from their grasp, she ran through the door to the dismantled lab, which still had ruminants of their earlier work, various vats of chemicals and spare equipment. She could sense Eddie's swarm forming behind her. She didn't look back. Running to the far end of the cavernous room, she hid behind one of the huge tanks.

Edward formed again. He seemed to be getting the hang of things, organizing his bodily frame in a fraction of the time it took him previously, controlling the swarming impulse. He looked around for Connie. She had to be in the room. There was no way out. He began to stalk her, using his extra-sensory perception to see in the dark and sense subtle vibrations in the air, like a shark does in the water.

Eddie had retained many of the capabilities and traits of his previous incarnation, and gained more, as he was slowly finding out. Had anything been left out? Did he still have the knowledge of right and wrong, a moral sense? The terms seemed foreign to him. He certainly didn't identify with humans like the old Eddie did.

The idea of the sanctity of life left him cold. He didn't necessarily want to hurt things, but if they got in the way of his own survival, he felt no qualms about doing what it took to protect himself. A self-centered survival instinct, survival of the fittest, seemed to fit his sentiments the best. Something he thought totally human. Did he have a soul? The question was totally irrelevant to him. Not even humans had a soul.

He sensed the girl cowering in the back behind one of the chemical storage vats, literally smelling her fear, and started moving in that direction. The room glowed an eerie green though his night-vision sensors.

To Connie the room seemed almost totally black. Only the light from the dim moonlight filtered in through the half-closed blinds, but she could see his form in the faint glow of his atomic DNA as he moved through the room.

"You can't hide from me," he said. "I only want to give you peace. You will feel no pain. Do not be afraid."

She was just the female specimen of a foreign species to him. All identity had been lost in a haze of emotions and sensations as Eddie tried to deal with his new awareness and his growing fear

He was almost on her now, walking slowly in her direction only a few feet away. Despite her predicament, Connie was not at a total disadvantage, for she had worked many months in this lab and knew every piece of equipment and chemical element in the place, even in the dark. If she wasn't mistaken, the vat she was standing behind held an acid bath used to clean out tanks of bad batches of nano-tubes, like flushing a Petri dish of bacterium with chlorine. As far as she could tell it had not been dismantled and still held its contents.

Suddenly, she sprinted from her hiding place and ran right in front of the vat. Eddie was only a few feet away, approaching her. They looked at each other.

"Eddie, you're sick. Let me help you," she said.

He let out a hideous, booming laugh and swarmed after her. She turned around and ran to a switch next to the vat. The nano-swarm was halfway across the intervening space, right in front of the nozzles of the acid bath. She had only to press the button to activate it and evaporate him with the acid spray, but she couldn't do it. Something stayed her hand. Maybe it was because she realized what an incredible creation he was, or perhaps some part of her still thought of him as human. Whatever it was, she couldn't destroy him. It would be like burning the Mona Lisa or slaying the last polar bear. She just couldn't do it, despite her overriding fear. Instead, she turned and held out her hand.

"Stop!" she yelled at the top of her voice.

Eddie was almost upon her, but still in front of the acid bath, when he stopped abruptly. Only his face was visible amidst his swarming nanobot body as it gathered up behind him like a storm cloud.

The hair on the back of Connie's neck stood up. She was frozen with terror, but yet she stood bravely in front of him with her hand outstretched.

Something about her vulnerability and frailty, and the way she stood fearless before him, yet so fragile, stopped him. Suddenly, he recognized her. She had a name. She was a friend. Instead of rending her to pieces, he stood still, only a few feet from her, his head swaying in the air like a cobra's, his unformed mass billowing ever larger.

"Wait!" Connie yelled. "I will never tell your secret. It is safe with me. No one will ever know. No one can know. I will protect you. I will be your friend."

Of all the things she could have said, these were the words that touched him the most. Despite his fear of being discovered, his terror of being alone was even greater. He knew he was different, one of a kind, now less human than ever. Yet what he wanted most was to be like them, like these beings that populated the world around him and seemed to glow like diamonds. That was what he had always wanted, to be loved, what he had longed for since he could remember. Now all who had loved him were gone. He was totally alone, but for this one small woman standing resolute and fearless before him. His nano-heart, embodied in the trillions of molecular bots that made up his being, melted. His fear and anger evaporated. The swarm began to organize itself into his body.

Soon he stood before her seeming to have shrunk in size so that he looked like a small seven year old boy, his head bowed in shame.

"Oh, Eddie," she said, rushing forward to embrace him. He met her halfway. She was crying as she hugged him. He felt so real. He looked so helpless. He hugged her back. Was he crying? She wasn't sure.

"I love you," she said.

His body shook.

"I...I love you too," he replied in a small voice.

The End

To Gavin, a gift unexpected, that altered my reality.

Made in the USA
Middletown, DE
24 May 2021